MORE HIGH PRAISE
FOR SUSAN EDWARDS!

WHITE FLAME

"4 1/2 Stars! A Top Pick! A wonderful, romantic read!"
—*Romantic Times*

"Susan Edwards has penned another winner. . . . Her sensual prose and compelling characters are forging a place for her at the forefront of Indian romance."

—*Affaire de Coeur*

"[Ms. Edwards] hooked me with an ingenious plot and held me with heart-stopping tension. Ms. Edwards's books are not just great romance; they are storehouses of knowledge."

—*Rendezvous*

WHITE WOLF

"Ms. Edwards's words flow like vivid watercolors across the pages. Her style is smooth, rhythmic and easy to read."

—*Rendezvous*

"Hop on your plush horse (your couch) and enjoy this romantic western!"

—*Affaire de Coeur*

"A SPLENDID story of majesty, and a very special love you can feel in your heart. 4 1/2 Bells!"

—*Bell, Book, and Candle*

WHITE WIND

"Talented and skillful, this first-rate author has proven her mettle with *White Wind*. Ms. Edwards has created a romantic work of art!"

—*The Literary Times*

PASSION'S PRISONER

"Do not push too far, *pohkeso*." Perhaps "kitten" was not the right word to describe his captive. "Wildcat" seemed more fitting. All fierce spitting and clawing. No tears. No begging. Just defiance. Even in a position in which he could take advantage of her, she refused to panic.

She opened her mouth. Knowing she was about to spit another name at him, Night Shadow narrowed his eyes. "Do not. I have heard enough from you this day." He glared down at her. Though the light was fading fast, he had no trouble seeing the furious glint in her eyes. He was thankful that both her feet were pinned.

"If you do not wish to hear my opinion of you and your actions, then you will release me. And Spotted Deer."

"No."

"You have no honor. You are a coward. A—"

Night Shadow closed his mouth over hers. It was a fast, furious, hard kiss.

WHITE SHADOWS

SUSAN EDWARDS

LEISURE BOOKS NEW YORK CITY

A LEISURE BOOK ®

November 2003

Published by

Dorchester Publishing Co., Inc.
200 Madison Avenue
New York, NY 10016

ISBN 0-8439-5109-5

Visit us on the web at www.dorchesterpub.com.

Family, oftentimes an overlooked treasure in our lives.

*White Shadows is a story about family
so it seems only fitting to dedicate it to family.*

*To my brothers, Dennis and Karl.
We were a rowdy bunch known as the "Swenson" brats.*

*And to my Aunt Nicki, and her daughter, Deb.
Your story of finding each other still touches me deeply.*

WHITE SHADOWS

White Series Genealogy Chart

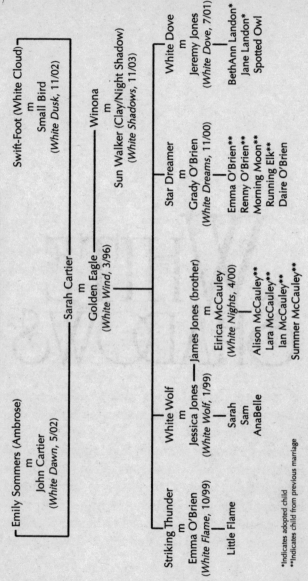

Emily Sommers (Ambrose)
m
John Cartier
(*White Dawn*, 5/02)

Swift-Foot (White Cloud)
m
Small Bird
(*White Dusk*, 11/02)

Sarah Cartier
m
Golden Eagle
(*White Wind*, 3/96)

Winona
m
Sun Walker (Clay/Night Shadow)
(*White Shadows*, 11/03)

Striking Thunder
m
Emma O'Brien
(*White Flame*, 10/99)

Little Flame

White Wolf
m
Jessica Jones
(*White Wolf*, 1/99)

Sarah
Sam
AnaBelle

James Jones (brother)
m
Eirica McCauley
(*White Nights*, 4/00)

Alison McCauley**
Lara McCauley**
Ian McCauley**
Summer McCauley**

Star Dreamer
m
Grady O'Brien
(*White Dreams*, 11/00)

Emma O'Brien**
Renny O'Brien**
Morning Moon**
Running Elk**
Daire O'Brien

White Dove
m
Jeremy Jones
(*White Dove*, 7/01)

BethAnn Landon*
Jane Landon*
Spotted Owl

*Indicates adopted child
**Indicates child from previous marriage

Chapter One

Spring came gently to the expansive prairie. A siren floating over her lover, she caressed fragile green blades emerging through soil moist from recent rainfall. Rippling eagerly in response, miles of immature grass celebrated the birth and renewal of the world.

Fluttering among the tender shoots, meadowlarks greeted the new day with joyful song. At the approach of two young women, one songbird flew upward in a startling flash of yellow and black.

Drops of dew scattered like tiny iridescent jewels when one woman jumped in front of the other, then twirled in a circle. Excitement hummed through Winona. "I am so happy." She clasped her hands over her heart. "Tonight I become wife to Hoka Luta." And wife to an important medicine man, she added silently.

Walking at her side, Spotted Deer yanked hard on Winona's arm to prevent her friend from stepping barefoot on a sharp rock. "Pay attention where you walk or put your moccasins back on."

Winona bit back a smile. Spotted Deer did not share her enthusiasm for early mornings. But she stopped and put her plain, smoked-hide shoes back on. It wouldn't do to cut her foot and not be able to dance and celebrate after her wedding.

As they made their way downhill to the stream Winona saw several women belonging to her Hunkpapa tribe strolling by the river. Scattered across the prairie, several other Sioux tribes were camped. Many had come to witness and celebrate the marriage of the daughter of a respected Sioux chief to a powerful Sioux medicine man.

It was early, yet many were already up, eager, as was she, to start the day. Deep laughter from the left drew her attention. Three men were returning from their baths.

Her gaze sharpened. Behind them she glimpsed Hoka Luta, her soon-to-be mate, emerging from the brush-lined stream. Winona veered slightly to the left. In the early dawn Hoka Luta's bare torso gleamed wetly. It pleased her that he too favored early risings.

Though Hoka Luta had arrived with a dozen warriors at his side, he walked alone. Staring at his profile like the love-struck woman she was, Winona eagerly anticipated starting each day with a solitary morning walk with her husband.

"Is he not the most handsome and bravest warrior?" Her voice softened, turning dreamy with anticipation of the life they soon would share.

Winona lowered her gaze as she and Spotted Deer drew closer, but couldn't stop herself from peering beneath her lashes to catch glimpses of Hoka Luta's muscular golden frame. Her heart fluttered, making her feel like a young girl who'd just discovered the mysterious wonders of the opposite sex.

A secretive smile curved her lips. Maybe she had—or would soon. For as long as she could remember she'd set her mind and heart on finding a mate who'd love her and make her soul sing.

Growing up with parents whose love seemed to grow stronger with each passing year had made Winona determined to find the same. Hoka Luta, whose name meant Red Badger, was everything she'd ever wanted in a man.

Like the badger, Hoka Luta was tenacious, bold, and ferocious. His sheer size made him a force to be reckoned with. Stories of his courage and power had circulated at last year's Sun Dance. Like a badger, Hoka Luta did not back down from a fight. And because his father had once been a powerful medicine man, his enemies feared his spiritual power too.

He was a good leader, and commanded respect much as her own father did. He'd make her a good husband. Winona caught her lower lip to keep from grinning like a besotted bride-to-be. "I cannot believe he chose me," she whispered to herself.

As they drew closer, Hoka Luta veered slightly away. Still, Winona's gaze lingered. One could not call Hoka Luta handsome. His forehead was perhaps too broad. His square jaw jutted forward, and his long, hawkish nose hooked slightly to the left, as if it had been broken many times.

Streaks of blood-red divided his face; two bold slashes from temple to chin. Where badgers had white stripes going from their nose to the back of their heads, Hoka Luta chose red. Even this early in the day, his wore his paint on his face, and his chest bore red and black markings—strange symbols, their meanings known only to him. All too quickly the warrior passed from her sight. Unable to help herself, she turned to watch him.

Spotted Deer jabbed her in the ribs. "Enough. You will have plenty of time to admire him later."

"You are jealous," Winona teased.

"I am tired," Spotted Deer retorted. "Why you insist on rising so early—"

"Admit it," Winona teased.

Spotted Deer rolled her eyes. "Only if you will be silent." She eyed Winona, her expression changing. "You are fortunate. He is *tanwaste*."

"Very handsome," Winona agreed. She slid a look at Spotted Deer and lowered her voice. "And, um, big." She nudged her friend in the ribs, making it clear she wasn't commenting on his sheer bulk.

Spotted Deer started coughing. "What do you know of such things!" Twin splotches of pink colored each cheek.

Now waves of heat burned Winona's throat and face. She lowered her voice. "He was bold last night. He wants me. I felt . . . him."

In his supervised walk with her last night Hoka Luta had made no secret that he desired to mate with her. After presenting her with a black mare, he'd used his blanket to shield the two of them from watching eyes so they could talk privately. The blanket covering their heads and upper bodies and the large bulk of the horse against her back had formed a shield for his roaming hands, and the stolen kiss they'd shared.

Winona's heart raced. Whether it was from excitement or fear, she wasn't sure. She knew how men and women mated. She recalled the time when she and Spotted Deer had come upon Lone Shield mating with a widowed woman in the woods. That embarrassing encounter had ended Spotted Deer's wish for the warrior to court her. After seeing him in all his manly glory, she was far too mortified to face him—much to his amusement.

"Remember when we saw Lone Shield?" Winona asked slyly. She studied her friend's flushed features and relented. "Lone Shield does wish to court you. He has spoken to my father and brother about you."

"No more," Spotted Deer warned.

"You are sister of my heart. You know I speak the truth. He watches you." Winona wanted to see her friend married and happy— she wanted Spotted Deer to experience her own excitement and joy. But her friend refused to even hear what Lone Shield offered.

Spotted Deer tipped her head back. "Lone Shield does not hold my heart."

Though Spotted Deer acted repulsed, Winona knew better. Her friend had long adored the warrior. "You are being stubborn. Just because you saw—"

Spotted Deer quickly changed the subject. "There is much to do before the ceremony. We should return. Your mother will be expecting us."

Winona fell silent. How she wished the peace and quiet of the morning could last forever. While she was thrilled that this was her wedding day, she didn't look forward to the noise and bustle. For days the camp had been in an uproar preparing for the feast to be held that evening.

She sniffed the air. The aroma of cookfires mingled with the acrid scent of roasting coffee beans that White Wind, her older brother's white wife, had introduced them to. A wave of unexpected sadness washed over her.

Tomorrow she would have to say good-bye to her old life. Marriage to Hoka Luta meant she'd have to leave her family—and Spotted Deer—behind. "I will miss you," she whispered to Spotted Deer. Stopping, she hugged herself. "How can I leave my family and friends behind? How can I leave you—my best friend, my sister—behind?"

The realization that the two of them had only this last day together dimmed their excitement, lending a sadness to what should have been the happiest day of Winona's young life.

Normally a man left his tribe to join a

woman's tribe, allowing female relatives to remain together, work together, and raise their families together. But Hoka Luta was a medicine man for his tribe, so Winona had agreed to live with his people.

Winona turned her head to the side, unable to bear the stricken panic in Spotted Deer's face. This woman was more than her best friend. The two girls had been inseparable for as long as she could remember. When illness had claimed Spotted Deer's parents, Winona's parents had welcomed the girl into their home.

"I will miss you," she whispered, nearly breathless from the sick, hollow feeling in her stomach. Only now did she realized just what she was leaving behind. Her mother and father. Golden Eagle and his wife, White Wind, and their four young children. All of a sudden, marriage didn't seem all that appealing.

Spotted Deer's eyes misted over. "Promise you will visit often."

"I promise. And you will come visit me." Winona tried to force a lightness to her voice that she didn't feel. For a long moment the two friends stared at each other.

Blinking back tears, Winona turned her head to stare out at the large herd of horses grazing down the hill. Since Hoka Luta's arrival, the herd had grown even larger for her soon-to-be husband had brought with him more than twenty horses that he'd presented to her brother, Golden Eagle. As her *hakatakus*, her male relative responsible for negotiating their marriage, Golden Eagle was entitled to her bride price.

The two women continued walking downhill toward the fast-flowing stream. "I wish you could travel with me to my new home," Winona said wistfully. She stopped suddenly, her eyes growing as wide as her grin.

"I know that look, Winona. What are you planning? Today is not a day to get us into trouble." Spotted Deer watched her warily.

"Me? Get us into trouble? We are women. We don't get into trouble anymore." Winona burst out laughing at the look of sheer disbelief on Spotted Deer's face. She clasped her hands in front of her. "Mine is a good idea."

Spotted Deer scowled, walked around Winona, and continued down to the stream. "No. Whatever it is you are planning, the answer is no."

Now it was Winona's turn to scowl. She caught up with Spotted Deer. "You have not listened to what I have to say."

Lifting one brow, Spotted Deer shook her head. "Whenever you get that look on your face we get into trouble. So whatever you are thinking, or planning, the answer is no."

Winona grinned. Spotted Deer knew her too well. She tipped her head to one side and said slyly, "Hoka Luta has many handsome warriors in his tribe. Do you not agree?"

Spotted Deer glanced over her shoulder toward the visiting warriors. "Yes. So?"

Striving to keep her voice neutral, Winona hid her smile. "Which warrior has caught your eye?" She turned and walked backward so she could observe her friend's expression.

Spotted Deer relaxed, as though reassured that Winona harbored no harebrained schemes in her mind. She shrugged. "There are two, but it matters not. They will leave with you and Hoka Luta tomorrow."

A slow, satisfied smile curved Winona's lips. "You could come with us."

Stopping abruptly, Spotted Deer shook her head. "No, you are crazy. You will be newly married. I would only be in the way. Besides, that would not be proper!"

Newly married! Winona sighed. She was already happy, but if Spotted Deer made the move with her she'd be truly thrilled. The more Winona thought about it, the more determined she became. When she made up her mind, nothing could sway her.

"I will speak to Hoka Luta. Surely there is someone you could stay with—a family in need of a daughter."

Spotted Deer's eyes lit up. "Do you think he will agree?"

Confident and pleased with her simple solution, Winona nodded. "He will agree." In her mind, the decision had been made. Hoka Luta loved her. He'd put her happiness first.

Pulling Spotted Deer by the arm, Winona changed directions, heading toward the herd of horses. "Just in case, we will ask the spirits for their help."

Spotted Deer pulled back. "Oh, no. We cannot leave camp unescorted."

Impatient, Winona jerked harder. "We will not be gone long. Now come on. Do you want to come with me when I leave tomorrow or not?"

Groaning, Spotted Deer followed. "You know I do. It is just—"

"It is decided. We will make the spirits an offering of sweet grass and sage. They will be pleased, and will grant us our wish." She let go of her friend's arm and took off at a run.

With a long-suffering groan, Spotted Deer ran after Winona and caught up with her. "Do not expect me to climb all the way to the top of the rock with you! Being that high makes me sick."

Feeling incredibly happy and fortunate, Winona slowed, dropped down low, and circled the herd of horses. A quick glance showed that the braves guarding the herd were chatting down by the stream. With a soft whistle, she called her mare.

"Let's go."

Swaying heavily on slender pine branches, ravens cried loudly from their high treetop perches. Below, standing on the limb of a tree split by lightning, a squirrel chattered at a silent enemy crouched behind a thick wall of pines and brush.

Night Shadow ignored the warning chatter and cries. He held himself perfectly still. From his vantage point he had miles of unobstructed view. Around him the trees were so tall and thick, there was little light. But just a short distance in front of them the trees thinned as though someone had drawn a line separating forest from prairie.

Shifting his gaze without moving his head, he picked out dark shadows far away. Buffalo, he thought. Sudden movement drew his attention to the left. A hare sat tall on its powerful hind legs. In the blink of an eye it was gone, a blur of gray among green.

Night Shadow returned his attention to the Sioux camped a short distance away. Like the Cheyenne, the Sioux preferred to make their camp out in the open prairie, where the danger of surprise attack was minimized.

He narrowed his eyes as he studied the Sioux camp. The number of tipis remained the same, yet something had changed. He studied the herd of horses, then smiled grimly. The groom had arrived.

Night Shadow fingered a long scar running down the side of his face. At last. After years of waiting, months of careful planning, and weeks spent watching the Sioux, he would soon have his revenge.

A low rustle in the bushes warned he was no longer alone. "We take her tonight," he said as his companions settled beside him.

Crazy Fox hunkered down on his left. "We are four against so many."

Night Shadow's gaze followed a group of warriors riding out onto the prairie. "The Sioux prepare to celebrate. The wedding will take place today." He narrowed his eyes. "I have waited long for this day."

His plan was a good one. He'd wait until after the marriage ceremony, then, after the new couple was left alone for their first night together, sneak in and kidnap the woman. A woman for a woman. When he got Jenny back, they'd get Winona back.

Night Shadow breathed deeply. Anticipation

flowed through him. For fourteen years he'd suffered. He'd hated and he'd despaired and he'd survived—just for this day.

He flexed his fingers over the hilt of his knife. So close, yet he dared not act too soon. Not until he had Jenny back. Then the bastard who'd taken her would die a slow, torturous death.

Without taking his eyes off the Sioux camp, he stood. "Come. We have much to do before the sun lowers." He took one last look at the Sioux camp, then froze when he spotted a lone rider heading toward him.

Motioning the others down, he watched the rider draw near. Long, shiny black hair flew behind her as she entered the sparsely wooded hillside just below his hiding place. She said something and laughed. The young woman sitting behind her didn't look so happy.

Night Shadow studied the Sioux women. A ray of sunshine pierced the thick canopy of pine leaves, falling on the upturned face of the woman controlling the gleaming mare.

"The spirits smile down upon us," he said under his breath. He recognized the young, carefree features of the Sioux chieftain's eldest daughter. As soon as he'd learned of her upcoming marriage to Hoka Luta, he'd made it a point to learn everything he could about the woman.

Weeks ago he'd shown up at the Sioux camp with his loyal warriors to trade. They'd spent three days with the Sioux, and during that time he'd watched and studied the one called Winona.

He grinned. The Sioux chief was foolish to allow his daughters to ride without escort. Incredulous at this turn of events, he let his gaze follow the women and horse as they rode past. As soon as they were out of sight he stood, his heart thudding with anticipation.

What a stroke of luck this was. Although he'd been interested in taking only Winona, he couldn't pass up the opportunity to take them both.

The spirits watch over you.

He grimaced at the words his mother had often said to him. Once he'd believed in unseen forces, but no more; not in the white man's God his father spoke of, or in the many spirits of his mother's people.

Life was nothing more than a long string of events, some good, some bad. A man had to take control of his own destiny. And right now he planned to take advantage of this turn of events. The horrific events of the past would soon be avenged.

He motioned to the others. The four warriors separated, each merging with the shadows.

Chapter Two

Winona surveyed the world from the flat top of a towering rock of granite. From her lofty height, the congregation of trees below appeared to be worshiping *Wakan Tanka*, the chief God. He was the Creator, the Great Spirit, and it was He who directed other spirits.

Imitating the prayerful stance of the pines below her, Winona moved in a slow, sensuous circle, her arms held down away from her body. Slowly she lifted her fingers, then her wrists, until her arms were held out to her sides. Another careful twirl brought them overhead, the backs of her hands touching, her fingers twining. Happy, free as the birds soaring around her, Winona moved to the music of a new day.

As she stared out at the glorious view it seemed fitting to be alone, celebrating and giving thanks, for this would be one of her last moments as a young maiden. Never again would she dance just for herself and the spirits. This sunrise might be the last she viewed alone.

After tonight she'd dance for her mate. She'd be a part of him, as he'd become a part of her—each needing the other to be complete, like *Wi* and *Hanwi*. Sun and moon. Light and dark.

Stopping, she walked to the edge of the sheer drop. This place that reached high into the sky held special meaning to her people, especially to her family. It was their power place. Her father, his father, and even her own brother had received many visions here. And when she felt at odds with the world, she came here in search of comfort.

She smiled. Sometimes her parents, or her brother and his wife, came to this special place to talk and be alone. A soft giggle escaped her. Talk wasn't all they did, she'd wager.

Winona sighed. How she wished she could share this breathtaking view with Hoka Luta. Clasping her hands, then holding them to cheeks suddenly hot, she sank down onto the rough, rocky ground.

"I will bring my husband to this place," she vowed. "Together we will sit among the spirits."

Content, Winona stared out at the land of

birth. The spirits showed their pleasure in the shades of green that ruled the upland prairie. Bright grass rippled over rolling hills. Slashes of darker green marked shallow valleys where water collected. Farther away, toward the south, the forest grew so thick the dark green appeared black. So much color and life.

Spring.

This was her favorite season, and mornings were her favorite time of the day. Both represented beginnings: fresh, new, and filled with hopes and dreams. This was why she'd insisted her marriage take place now instead of at the end of summer. She sighed happily. Even her name, Winona, which meant firstborn daughter, had given her parents new hope after so many years of not conceiving. So it was fitting to start a new life during a time of rebirth.

Lifting her hair away from her neck, she released the long, silky strands, giving them over to the gentle breeze to tease and stroke. With so much emotion filling her to bursting, she felt as though she were on the brink of something wonderful. Her laugh rang out, drawing an answering call from an eagle soaring far above her.

Life was good.

A wisp of smoke in the distance drew her gaze. She sighed at the reminder that she and

Spotted Deer needed to return. It wasn't hard to imagine her friend pacing below, eager to return before someone learned they'd left camp without permission.

She sighed. There was so much to be done upon her return that selfishly, she gave in to the need for a few more stolen minutes. Stretching out on her belly, Winona stared down at the pines below. A handful of crows flew over the treetops. The long drop from her perch didn't make her nervous. This tall throne was her special place.

Her gaze shifted to a ribbon of water cutting a wide blue swath through the green prairie along one side of her tribe's camp. The tiny tipis perched atop the green swell of land looked as though they'd sprouted from the earth. Smoke curled from many cookfires. Another contented sigh slipped from her lips.

Home.

A pang of regret at the thought of leaving her family settled in her belly. Hoka Luta's tribe wasn't of the same clan as hers. The Teton Sioux were seven nations. She was Hunkpapa, while Hoka Luta belonged to the Sichangus. His was a much larger clan. Only the Oglala had more members.

The cool early-morning breeze brushed bits of dried sage across her arms. Winona glanced over her shoulder, noting the pile of rocks that formed a circle where she'd sprinkled sage and sweet grass from a tanned leather pouch hanging from her waist. Her offering of thanks to the spirits had been swept away by the hand of *Tate*.

Closing her eyes, she rolled to her side, then sat up slowly and turned her back on the magnificent view. Small pebbles ground into her palms, but she didn't care. There was something wild about being perched so high above the world.

The massive rock she sat upon rose like the strong trunk of a tree from the forest floor. One side of the rock was smooth, unclimbable, while the other side was rough and jagged, with enough rocky crevices, boulders, and scraggly, woody brush to offer hand- and footholds.

Directly opposite from where she sat, two large boulders with round, wide bases marked the path down. One rose to shoulder height and was slightly angular; the other was short and squat. Movement on the tall one drew her attention. A small lizard warming itself in the rays of the sun eyed her and flicked its tongue in and out, but didn't move.

Winona sighed. She knew she needed to head back, but the bright rays of *wi* warmed her face, leaving her as drowsy and contented as the liz-

21

ard. She too could sit here in the sun all day.

As she watched the lizard, her sight blurred from the brightness of the sun rising in the east. The air shimmered like the ground on a hot summer day. And then, without warning, a snarling *igmuwatogla* appeared.

Winona froze as she stared into the eyes of the mountain cat. Her heart pounded painfully against her chest, her blood racing through her body. It took all her courage to keep from scooting backward. Death at the hands of the cat, or by falling. Neither appealed.

Her eyes burned until she was forced to blink, and it was then that she realized that only the face of the mountain cat appeared to her. No tawny, powerful body—which meant this was a . . . a vision.

Stunned, Winona held her breath. She'd never experienced a true vision. Not like this. Animals had appeared before her. All living things communicated—whether animal, bird, or insect. Even the land spoke to her people. But this . . . this was different.

Igmuwatogla taught power. What did he want her to learn?

"Why do you appear?" she asked breathlessly, her voice shaky from excitement and fear. But as quickly as the vision came, it faded. Winona blinked again and it was gone. Only the familiar shape of the boulder remained. Even the tiny lizard had vanished.

Jumping to her feet, breathless and charged, she ran to the rock, touched it reverently, then started down. Mindful of the tricky descent, Winona was suddenly eager to get back to camp. She needed to tell her father, and together they'd consult with their shaman—and Hoka Luta. As a medicine man, he'd know what this vision meant.

Power. Hoka Luta he was powerful. Was she to add to his power, or he to hers? Of all the things a vision could have imparted, power was not one she ever expected to receive.

Loose shale rolled down the path, making the descent difficult. Finally she reached a large outcrop of boulders at the base of the stone tower. Winona jumped easily from one to another until her feet touched the soft forest floor once more.

Glancing around for her horse and Spotted Deer, she left the sunshine for the damp chilly forest. The sudden ruckus of a squirrel's scolding to her right drew Winona's attention. She spotted the small animal clinging to the trunk of a pine tree. Flicking its tail back and forth, nose pointed to the ground, twitching madly, the squirrel made his displeasure known.

With her mind still in a daze over the vision

and its possible meanings, she smiled up at the small animal. "Do not scold," she admonished as she approached. "I am leaving." If she could find Spotted Deer.

With hands on her hips she scanned the area. "Spotted Deer, where are you?"

Winona groaned. It was a fine time for Spotted Deer to wander off. Whenever she and Spotted Deer sneaked away to come here, her friend used the time to collect plants and roots for food and medicinal purposes. That always provided the cover for Winona's trips to Gray Rock—not that her mother had ever been fooled.

The snap of a twig made her smile. She turned. "I'm over here," she called excitedly, eager to share her vision yet knowing she had to talk to her father and their *pejuta wicasa*, medicine man, first. Winona hurried past the chattering squirrel. "We need to return quickly. I have news for my father—"

Winona's smile faded when a large warrior stepped out from behind the tree. It took only a quick glance to realize that this was not one of her father's men. Nor did he appear to be one of Hoka Luta's warriors. Worse, he didn't look friendly—she didn't need to see the knife in his hand to tell her that.

Hatred blazed from nearly black eyes, and his

lips were drawn back into a snarl every bit as fierce and as deadly as the mountain cat's. Taking a step back, Winona felt an icy shiver run through her. When the enemy warrior took a step closer, Winona's heart stopped.

Instinct took hold. This was no game of frightening a lone woman. Something about this warrior warned that whatever he was about, he meant business. Winona had no intention of waiting around to determine who he was or why he was there.

Whirling around, she ran.

The ground, wet from recent rains, gave way beneath her leather-clad feet as she ran surefooted through the dense forest. Leaping over fallen logs, running through thick clumps of trees, Winona deliberately chose a path difficult for the pursuing warrior.

Pulling branches down, she released them as she ran past so they slapped at the warrior. All the while she had to fight to keep her feet from slipping out from beneath her.

Shoving a twiggy branch forward, she ducked her head and then released the branch. It whipped back over her head. The low curse behind her would have made her smile if she didn't have to concentrate hard on trying to lose the furious warrior.

Coming to a small clearing, Winona zigged

to the left, heading for more low branches. One good swat at the warrior might give her enough time to gain her freedom. She put on a burst of speed.

One minute her feet were flying across the ground; the next they were swinging in midair. She screeched when she felt an arm tighten around her waist. The forest spun as he swung her around. He tightened his arm, cutting off her breath. Her scream came out a weak croak.

"Hiya! Hiya! Nanpoi yuze sni ye!" He ignored her commands, spoken in Lakota, to take his hands off her. She clawed at his arms and kicked. One foot made contact with the warrior's thigh. Twisting, she formed a claw with the fingers of one hand and snagged a fistful of his hair.

The warrior cursed. Baring his teeth, he used one hand to squeeze her wrist until she released his hair. Despite the pain, Winona became more desperate to gain her freedom. She scratched, pinched, even tried to bite the warrior. One elbow connected solidly with his face. She felt a surge of renewed strength as she continued her assault. She was the daughter of a courageous chief. She wouldn't go down without a fight.

Lifting her knee to her chin, Winona grabbed her utility knife from the sheath wrapped around her upper thigh. At the same time she kicked both feet outward. The momentum of her arched body sent her would-be captor stumbling back. He fell, his arm still firmly holding her around the waist.

The air whooshed out of Winona's lungs at the impact of landing against his hard chest. She gasped. That one moment of weakness was all the warrior needed. In the blink of an eye he flipped her over onto the ground, pinned her arm above her head and forced the tip of her blade into the softened ground. With one knee in the small of her back, his muscular thighs and legs pinning her legs, it took him almost no effort to pull both her arms behind her back.

Though stunned by how fast the warrior had immobilized her, Winona refused to give up. She spat dirt and leaves from her mouth. "You will die," she promised. "My father and brother will kill you for this," she said in Lakota.

Breathing hard, Winona lifted her head and glanced around frantically. Spotted Deer ... where was she? Had the enemy hurt her? Fear crept through her. If anything had happened to her friend, Winona would never forgive herself. Too late she wished that they hadn't left camp.

Winona prayed that Spotted Deer's absence meant that she'd had time to flee. Closing her eyes for just a moment to gather her strength, Winona didn't struggle when she was turned over. Both hands were now pinned overhead, and for the first time Winona got a good look at her enemy.

Hard. Cold. Those were her first impressions. His face could have been carved from stone. And his eyes . . . Winona tried to look away but couldn't. Anger boiled in the dark depths and warned that when unleashed, a storm unlike anything she'd ever experienced would erupt.

His rage made it impossible for her to swallow. Or breathe. The hatred rolling off him choked her as though his hands had closed around her throat. This warrior hated. He thirsted for revenge. She'd seen that same look far too many times on warriors in her own tribe when they lost loved ones in battle.

Winona tore her gaze from his and dragged in a ragged gulp of air. Her eyes focused on the hard, rugged line of his shadowed jaw. A few strands of pale brown hair clung to where his face was rough with the stubble of a beard. His hair was almost a golden brown, soft and silky-looking. Hair much like her nephew's. Hair almost like that of a white man.

Her eyes narrowed as she examined the warrior's face. The dappled sunlight revealed a portion of his features. Winona carefully picked out the signs of mixed blood: the shadow of stubble that would become a full, thick beard if not plucked or kept checked by the blade of a sharp knife, the earth-colored hair, and a deep dimple in his chin. .

"Wasicun!" she spat out, disgusted to have been captured so easily by a white man.

"Get off me," she ordered, this time in English. Between her own father's foresight in learning English from the trappers they traded with, and her brother and his French-English wife, she was fairly fluent in several tongues.

Incensed that she'd allowed herself to be taken by a white man dressed as a warrior, she twisted and bucked to gain her freedom. But her captor was larger, heavier, and stronger. "You will die!" she said, reverting back to Lakota.

Furious dark eyes glittered down at her. *"Ovanohoo'estse!"*

Winona froze. She recognized the soft, melodic language, though she did not understand it. This man was *Sahiyela*—Cheyenne. He might carry white blood in his veins, but he was Indian where it counted—in his heart and soul. And cold, dark hatred burned in his gaze. Fear slid through her, and she shivered when he broke eye contact to pull a length of rope from around his waist.

Afraid as never before, Winona renewed her struggles. Her senses sharpened. The crisp morning air seared her heaving lungs, the silence of the forest rang loud in her ears, and the acrid scent of fear mixed with another scent, one she didn't recognize, but knew belonged to this man. The churning in her stomach crawled and clawed at the back of her throat.

Despite her struggles, the Cheyenne warrior made quick work of binding her hands in front of her. With her heart racing and pounding against her ribs, Winona glared into the eyes of the enemy. Drawing in a ragged breath, she tried to look away but couldn't.

There was something in those hard, emotionless eyes. Something that lived deep within his soul, something that frightened her more than anything he could say or do. It wasn't just hatred or cruelty. It was more. Much, much more. This man had no light in his soul. In his eyes she saw only darkness. Bitterness. Despair.

The Cheyenne warrior stood and yanked her to her feet. In his hand he held tight to the short length of rope he'd left dangling when he'd bound her wrists.

"Noheto!"

Winona stumbled at the obvious command. What was going on? The Cheyenne were allies of the Sioux, not enemies. "Wait," she cried, digging in her heels. She had to hold on to the hope that Spotted Deer had managed to escape with the horse.

Help would arrive and this harsh man would pay for his actions—with his life. She just had to stall. Normally she dreaded her father's lectures on her foolish, impetuous ways, but right then she'd have given much to be soundly chastised by her father.

Impatiently the warrior whipped around, revealing his profile. A stream of light fell onto his unpainted face, highlighting a long crescent scar that curved from his temple, past his ear, and along part of his jaw. Shocked, she stared. She recognized this man. He'd been a visitor to her village several weeks ago. He and several other Cheyenne warriors had stopped to trade with the Sioux.

In dawning horror, she recalled serving meals to him and three others. The Cheyenne warrior lifted a brow. He knew she recognized him, but he didn't say anything—just turned his back on her and yanked hard on the rope binding her wrists.

The fact that he turned his back on her showed he considered her no threat. Frantically Winona glanced around for a weapon but saw nothing of use—especially as her hands were bound. Stumbling into the cool shadows, she blinked. Then she blinked again at the sight of her horse grazing unconcerned several feet from her.

"No," she whispered, falling to her knees. If her horse was still here . . .

Her legs shook as she searched for, and found, Spotted Deer. She was bound to the trunk of a tree a short distance from the horse. Gagged, her face pale, Spotted Deer blinked tears from her eyes. Behind her, sitting on his heels, sharpening a twig with his knife, a second warrior looked bored.

Tears burned behind Winona's eyes. "This is my fault," she whispered hoarsely in Lakota. Glancing around wildly, Winona knew she had to do something to save them. She lunged forward and kicked her captor behind his right knee, then moved swiftly when he stumbled forward. With a hard yank she pulled free and ran for her horse.

Curses and amused laughter followed her flight for freedom. She didn't need to glance over her shoulder to know her pursuer was close. She felt him—felt his heat and his fury. She heard the low rumble of his voice. There was nothing soft or soothing about that voice. Or the words spoken. When he caught her, she knew she'd pay.

The scrape of his fingers on her shoulder made her cry out. She leaned to the right, eluding capture, and eyed her horse with desperation. She had no hope of outrunning the warrior. He'd overpower her in seconds. Frustrated that she wouldn't have time to mount the animal and ride for help, she figured she'd do what she could.

When she came within a foot of her mare, she threw her arms high and snapped the loose rope binding her hands toward the now-startled horse. The mare danced away, then stopped, unsure of her mistress's behavior.

"Go," Winona screamed, waving her arms.

When a hard hand clamped down on her shoulder, she screamed and twisted, moving closer to the wild-eyed animal. For the second time that morning she felt an arm snake around her waist. Winona refused to go quietly. She continued to scream at the top of her lungs and wave her hands. Each time the end of the rope brushed the mare, the animal backed away with a fearful snort.

With one last desperate attempt to send her horse fleeing, Winona kicked out with her feet. One foot struck the mare's hindquarters. The horse, already skittish from Winona's screams and struggles, reared up, front hooves pawing the air.

"*Tigli! Tigli!*" she commanded the horse. Another kick sent leaves and bits of loose dirt flying toward the animal's face.

Behind her, the Cheyenne warrior tried to

grab her hands. Out of the corner of her eye Winona saw the second warrior racing toward the horse.

"No!" Desperate, she leaned her head down and bit the warrior on his upper arm. He yelped. The slack in his grip was all she needed to twist free. Lunging at the horse, knowing she couldn't mount fast enough, she slapped the animal.

"Go! Go!"

The mare whirled around and shot forward, racing through the trees, hooves thundering long after the animal faded from sight.

A loud curse in her ear made Winona smile. This time when the Cheyenne warrior snagged her she didn't struggle. She'd done what she could. Turning, she faced her enemy with her chin jutting forward, her eyes twin slits of fury.

"I am Winona, daughter of Chief Hawk Eyes, sister of Golden Eagle. Prepare to die."

Seeing Eyes felt the first icy finger of dread slide down her spine. Darkness crept like a rolling bank of fog across her vision. *Not again,* she thought. *Not again.* It had been years since she'd experienced the frightening and paralyzing effect of a vision.

She fought the sensations, opened her eyes wide, and tried to focus on the activities going

34

on around her, but reality faded. The darkness enveloped her; her heart raced and her chest tightened as though a giant invisible fist were squeezing the air from her lungs.

So cold.

Something was wrong.

Terribly wrong.

The sun. Where had it gone? She needed warmth; her head screamed for the darkness to lift. She no longer existed. Or felt. Or was. Her spirit floated through the darkness, became one with the darkness.

Down below she saw a child standing high on a cliff with arms outstretched. Sky-blue hair flowed around her body and tiny dots of light danced and became her shadow. As the girl-child danced, the light mingled with the darkness and swirled until everything appeared blue, black, and white.

Seeing Eyes smiled as she floated around the child. The child shimmered and glowed before slowly losing shape. Once more the scene spun until Seeing Eyes felt slightly sick and dizzy. To her horror, the tiny white dots turned bloodred. She held her hands up to ward away the vision. But she couldn't. She was a part of it. In her head she heard screams.

Blood.

Death.

It choked her. There was so much of it. Too much. And the child? Where was the child? Frantically Seeing Eyes reached out, not with her physical body but with her spiritual self. She had to find the child.

Without warning, the sensation of death changed. The red remained, a dark glow, but now it glittered in the sun, the sparks of color nearly blinding her. The frightening roar in her ears became giggles. Soft, sweet laughter. The child had returned.

She relaxed and reached out to the child. The child reached out a hand, then abruptly turned and ran. Laughter turned to screams.

"Stop," Seeing Eyes called out.

With a suddenness typical of her visions, it was gone. So was the child, but not the echoing screams. Seeing Eyes opened her eyes and rubbed her arms in a vain attempt to warm herself. No matter how fast she rubbed, she felt chilled to the bone. Her heart hammered as her gaze slid over her people. Why had the visions returned? Who was in danger?

Scanning the camp, she found nothing wrong or out of place. Just the opposite. Excitement over her daughter's marriage to Hoka Luta lent a festive gaiety to the camp. Women were either cooking or working on gifts to present to the soon-to-be-joined couple. Young children ran every which way, many holding food from one of numerous cook pots.

Seeing Eyes stood. A pouch of dried cherries fell unheeded to the ground. Her family. She had to be sure they were safe. She spotted her son, Golden Eagle, kneeling beside his tipi. In his hands he held a knife. Squatting in front of him, his two young sons, Striking Thunder and White Wolf, chattered as they watched their father fashion a small bow.

In front of the tipi, White Wind nursed White Dove, their youngest child. Star Dreamer, White Wolf's twin sister, stepped out of the tipi. Instead of running to play with other girls her age, the youngster stared at her grandmother.

Seeing Eyes felt her heart tug. At the age of seven, her granddaughter already showed signs of having inherited from her a gift that often seemed more of a curse. Two hands on her shoulders startled her. Seeing Eyes spun around and stared up into the beloved features of her husband.

"What is wrong?"

"It is nothing," she began.

"You are not truthful, wife."

"This is a day of celebration, not—"

Hawk Eyes cradled her face in his hands and forced her to meet his gaze. "The visions have returned."

Everything in her cried out for her to deny his words, but he knew her well. "Yes, husband."

As she'd done, he scanned his tribe. Coming up the rolling hill from the stream, a trio of unmarried women the same age as their daughter laughed and giggled as they eyed the visiting warriors.

Realization hit them both in the same moment.

"Our daughters," she whispered. Winona should have been back from bathing a long time ago. It had been barely light when she and Spotted Deer had left the tipi. The sun had now risen fully.

She turned to stare out at the hills a short distance away. The flowing stream near their camp led to the base of those hills. The rolling prairie broke away to climb steeply, far above the prairie floor. Her gaze found and rested on the tip of massive gray flat-topped rock. It was a favored spot for warriors to seek vision quests, for praying, and for giving thanks. It was also Winona's favorite place to go when she needed or wanted to be alone.

"She would not leave camp without asking permission," Hawk Eyes said. But the frown between his eyes belied his words. They both knew Winona had on many occasions done just that.

Icy fear clutched her heart. "Something has happened."

Hawk Eyes put his arms around his wife. "She is most likely down at the river."

"No, she is not." Seeing Eyes didn't need anyone to check. Movement out on the prairie held her gaze. A horse rode toward them.

Hawk Eyes nodded. "There is nothing to fear. She has returned."

Seeing Eyes shivered and shook her head. "No. Only the horse." She wasn't sure how she knew; she just did. Hugging herself, Seeing Eyes stared up into hills so dense with pines that they looked black. The *Paha Sapa*. The Black Hills. Her daughters were there. Somewhere. She clutched at her dress and twisted the softened hide with nervous fingers.

Hawk Eyes gave a shout. Seeing Eyes was grateful that he didn't wait for the horse to confirm what she knew in her heart.

"I will find her. She probably fell asleep and something startled her horse into fleeing."

Meeting her husband's worried gaze, Seeing Eyes prayed it was so. But they both knew the appearance of her visions meant that something was wrong. She watched her husband handpick a handful of warriors, including Hoka Luta.

Watching the warriors ride out across the

prairie, Seeing Eyes had never felt so helpless. Or alone.

A small hand slipped inside hers. Glancing down, Seeing Eyes stared into the dark, worried eyes of her granddaughter. No words were needed between them. Their eyes said it all. Together, with fear in their hearts, they watched the group of warriors ride away.

Chapter Three

Night Shadow curled his upper lip, disgusted about losing control of his captive. How could he have let her get loose? She'd spooked her horse and the animal wouldn't stop until it reached home, alerting her father.

Of all the possible scenarios that he'd taken into consideration, this hadn't been one of them. Furious, he glared down at Winona. The moment he'd heard of the impending marriage, he'd spent the winter planning for this moment. And then he'd gone and tossed his perfect plan over his shoulder, ending up in a situation he'd lost control over.

Still, Night Shadow couldn't help but admire Winona's quick and clearheaded thinking. She'd shown courage in defying him.

She sent him a satisfied smirk, which only

heated his fury. "You will die," she repeated in English.

Night Shadow reined in his emotions and forced the muscles on his face to go slack with indifference. He stroked the scar on his face . . . a daily reminder of all that he'd lost. The scars he carried, both inside and out, had come from his will to live. So did his deep-seated hatred and need for revenge. Soon he'd avenge the past and set his future free. If he died trying? It couldn't be worse than living in a shell with no heart, no soul.

"I have faced death before," he said in fluent English.

Winona lifted a brow. "You speak the white man's tongue." Her lips twisted with scorn. "You have two faces but I see only the *wasicun*. Like the spirit of *mica*, the coyote, you are a coward. You take innocent women; there is no honor in your heart."

Her anger kept him from feeling guilty. Jenny was all that mattered. "I *have* no heart." Night Shadow shoved Winona toward the tree where the other woman, Spotted Deer, watched with wide eyes. He knew little about her, and hadn't even thought to include her in his plans. At least in this the stakes were raised in his favor.

"Pray to your spirits that my demands are met, or it will be your life and that of your sister that are forsaken."

Winona swung her head around. "My sis—" She snapped her jaw tight. If this warrior learned that Spotted Deer was not her sister, not the daughter of Hawk Eyes, he might kill her here and now. She sent her friend a look of warning before tipping her chin at her captor.

"Our father is a great chief, and Golden Eagle, our brother, will show no mercy to those who dare harm us. They will come for us, as will Hoka Luta."

Night Shadow grabbed a handful of long, silky-black hair and wrapped the strands around his fist, yanking hard. "Say nothing more or I will cut out your tongue."

Night Shadow shoved Winona away in disgust. His fight wasn't with either woman, but just the sound of his enemy's name spoken aloud was enough to send his blood roaring through his body. As he had for so many years, he banked his emotions and brought back under control the hatred that had once saved him from the icy clutches of death.

He'd lived for revenge. Soon he'd face his old enemy and have the satisfaction of watching him die a slow, painful death.

With eyes glittering with what could have been tears of sorrow or fury, Winona stopped when they reached the others. She visibly squared her shoulders. "Let us go. Give us back our lives and I will give you this chance to leave and never come back."

Incredulous that this woman didn't seem to fear him or realize the danger she was in, Night Shadow resisted the urge to battle with her verbally. "You are either very brave or very foolish," he said softly, meaning it. She had no idea how far he'd go to find Jenny. Only then could he kill his enemy and taste sweet victory.

With a none-too-gentle hand, he shoved Winona toward Crazy Fox, who caught and held her firmly by the upper arm. Night Shadow retraced his steps and retrieved her knife. Turning, he saw both women standing shoulder-to-shoulder. He nodded to Crazy Fox. "*Noheto!* Let's go."

Night Shadow returned to the group, slung Winona over his shoulder, and took off at a hard jog, careful not to break branches or kick stones loose from the dirt. He didn't have time to cover all his tracks, but he wouldn't make it easier than necessary for the enemy to track him.

No more than a minute later, he found himself cursing beneath his breath. He'd thought he'd learned all he could about the chieftain's daughter. She'd seemed meek, obedient, and quiet during his visit to her tribe. Instead she was a she-wolf. Most women would be too frightened to fight and struggle. Not this woman.

Her feet kicked wildly and her balled fists pounded his back. He winced when she raked her nails across his back and pinched his flesh. Gritting his teeth, he ducked beneath a low branch. Night Shadow nearly lost both his balance and the woman when she reared upward. *"Eaaa!"* Without slowing, he ran between two trees, then jumped over a log, deliberately coming down hard.

Winona shrieked, but instead of settling down she renewed her struggles. "Wait," she said, panting. "Just . . . wait." She jabbed her elbows into his back, then pounded him with her bound fists. "I . . . will kill . . . you . . . myself."

Night Shadow ignored her and made another leap over a log. He flew through the air and came down squarely on both feet, but before he could spring back into a run his captive was yanked from his grasp.

He whirled around as something slammed into his belly and sent him sprawling. He landed flat on his back. Stunned, breathless, Night Shadow gasped for air. Rolling to the side, then leaning on one elbow, he gasped at the sharp, stabbing pain in his ribs. *Great.* Bruised or broken ribs. He sucked in a breath of air slowly as he tried to focus on what was happening around him.

45

Palming his knife, he jumped to his feet in a low, tight crouch as he sought the enemy who'd snatched his prize. He furrowed his brows. He didn't see anyone, not even the woman. "Damn," he said, air hissing through his teeth at the pain burning with each breath. He started to stand, but when something brushed against his head he ducked.

Glancing up, he blinked with surprise when he saw his captive hanging from the limb of a dead tree. She swung her foot at him again, and again she missed. Reaching up with one hand, Night Shadow tried to grab her ankle.

She evaded him. "You snake. You low, vile snake. You will die." She continued to curse him.

Fury built when Night Shadow realized that Winona had somehow managed to grab the limb with her bound hands when he'd jumped. The blow to his back had been her swift kick. Why didn't this ploy of hers surprise him? Right then he knew nothing was going to go as planned. He should have stuck to his original plan.

Beneath his hand he felt the vibrations of an approaching runner. "Stop," he called out to Crazy Fox reverting to English without a second thought. But his warning was too late. His friend, hearing the commotion, rounded the stand of trees that Night Shadow had cut through at a full run. As soon as Crazy Fox saw Winona dangling from the branch he tried to stop, but he too lost his balance when Winona's swinging foot made contact with his jaw.

With a loud grunt, Crazy Fox fell down. A softer groan came from Spotted Deer, who bounced off the Cheyenne's shoulder and rolled to a stop a few feet away. She yanked the gag from her mouth and screamed.

Her screams mixed with Winona's and sent crows flying from the treetops.

"Shit!" Another expletive that his trapper father had used on a daily basis slipped from the past, into the present, and right out his mouth. The white man's curse's fit the moment better than any Cheyenne word, so he cursed again as he reached up and snagged one swinging ankle.

She screeched. He grabbed hold of her second foot, then yanked hard. The sound of a sharp crack drew from him yet another round of curses. Instinctively he reached out and caught the falling woman and rolled so that the thick branch hit him squarely across the shoulders instead of falling onto the back of her head.

Winona yelped. He clamped his jaw tight against the pain. So much for an easy capture. Where were the tears? The paralyzing fear? The instant obedience?

Night Shadow stared down into Winona's wide gaze. Furious with her stunt, he opened his mouth to threaten dire harm should she try anything else. Nothing came out of his mouth. Her eyes mesmerized him, held him captive. Everything had happened so fast that he'd forgotten how beautiful Winona was.

Her smooth skin was exquisite, warm in tone as freshly gathered honey. Delicate bones, a short, gently sloping nose, and a smooth forehead gave her a fragile perfection.

But of all her features it was her eyes that held him spellbound. Wide, thickly lashed, and enticingly angled, Winona's eyes were also the eyes of a wild mountain cat. Not brown, not yellow, but a tawny combination.

He grunted. To go with those eyes, she had the claws of a cat, and the cunning of the majestic animal. For just one breath in time, they stared at each other. Silence surrounded them. She looked as stunned as he. But not for long.

"Winona!" Spotted Deer's frantic cry broke the spell.

Winona sprang to life with a growl and tried to rake her nails down his face. He grabbed her wrists. Her furious curses were added to his. With Crazy Fox's yelps as he struggled to subdue Spotted Deer, it sounded as though war had broken out in the peaceful forest.

Feeling the tensing of the woman's thigh beneath his, Night Shadow shifted his legs and pinned her so she couldn't do any more damage to his body. He winced. *Damn.* His chest still hurt and his shoulders ached from being struck by the falling branch.

"Let us go," Winona panted, glaring up at him.

"It will do you no good to fight," he warned as he grabbed her wrists and held them above her head. A ray of sunlight washed over them. She lifted her head and tried to bit his arm.

"You she-cat. Settle!" How could he ever have thought this woman to be meek and easy to control? He'd assumed that, like most maidens, she knew her place, and would be passive and even boring, as were most of the women whom he encountered. But no. Each of her delicate features expressed emotion, none more than those golden eyes that spat fury.

With effort he kept control of his emotions. He had no grudge against her—just the man she planned to marry. He had no desire to hurt her or use excessive force—unless he had no other choice.

Behind him, Night Shadow heard his friend's low, furious voice as he ordered the other woman to be still. His mind cleared immediately. Rolling, he stood, pulled the woman up, and held his knife to her throat as a warning to be still.

Noticing the broken leaves and branches, freshly scored lines in the dirt, and crushed plant life, he swore again. Then he tipped his head back. The raw wood and ragged bit of pale bark where the branch had broken off were signs no warrior—or young brave—would miss—not that he'd be able to cover up all of the other signs of struggle.

"For a great warrior who earned the name of Night Shadow, my brother makes much noise." Dream Walker sounded amused as he and Sharp Nose rode into view. Each led a horse.

Relieved to see the horses, Night Shadow ignored the glint of laughter lurking deep in Dream Walker's eyes. With his patience just about gone, Night Shadow tightened his grip on Winona's upper arm and stalked over to Crazy Fox and his wide-eyed captive. Grabbing the girl, he held his knife to her throat.

"Another word and I will kill her." He spoke slowly, in English, to be sure Winona understood him, but he didn't dare glance at Dream Walker or the others, who knew him well. After what had happened to his family they knew Night Shadow would never kill any woman or child. But his captives didn't know that. "Understand?"

Subdued, Winona nodded. Stalking off, Night Shadow removed a square of leather from his pouch and used the woman's knife to pin his demands to a thick tree trunk. Only one person would understand.

Slowly Night Shadow took out an intricately carved leather sheath from the same pouch and stared at it. A wave of regret pushed through the anger and hate that were as natural to him as breathing.

"Pa," he whispered, tracing the curves, noting the worn darkness of the leather. He brought it to his nose and inhaled the faint scent of tobacco that clung to the hard leather after all these years.

Everything around him faded when he pulled the blade from its sheath. Unlike the woman's utility knife, the blade on this knife shone brightly but for one dark stain near the hilt. A ray of light sparked off the smooth surface, nearly blinding him. Holding it up, he gripped the handle, noting the weight, the curved fit to his hand.

After a moment he shoved it back into the sheath, then hung it from the protruding handle of the woman's knife. Slowly he stepped back. It was done. Everything was ready. He'd either succeed in finding Jenny and killing the enemy or die trying. Night Shadow stared at the message with his jaw clenched so hard it sent waves of pain clear up to his temples.

There was only one man who knew where Jenny was. Ultimately, he'd pay with his life.

Returning to the others, he mounted his horse with Winona before him. "Choose, woman," he said to her. "Give me no trouble and you ride sitting before me. Struggle, and I will bind your hands to your feet beneath the horse, and you will ride like a sack of flour."

Winona turned her back to him. Wrapping a hand around her, he sent his horse surging forward.

The horses and riders left the cool darkness of the forest for the gentle warmth of a secluded meadow. Surrounded by trees on three sides and rough mounds of rock on the other, the area provided a quiet haven for white-tailed deer, song-birds, and other creatures. Above her head, Winona eyed the soaring path of a solitary golden eagle.

Her captor led the way, following the line of trees. The horses snorted and snatched mouthfuls of soft grass but kept moving. Woven throughout the carpet of grass tiny bursts of spring color gave the scene the appearance and feel of peace and calmness.

Calm!

Any other time, this small bit of land would have held Winona enthralled, lured her into spinning around and around until she collapsed onto her back amid the sweetly scented blooms. But now anger and fear dulled her natural appreciation for her surroundings. Worse, guilt made the beauty surrounding her painful.

It had been her need to be alone, to stand atop the world, that had turned her and Spotted Deer into captives. Her guilt for doing this to her best friend sat like a boulder in her belly. Every time she glanced at Spotted Deer, looked into her friend's wide, scared eyes, Winona felt sick.

Grabbing a fistful of flowing black mane in her hands, she felt the arm around her waist tighten. "Do not try anything foolish," her captor warned, his voice devoid of emotion, as though kidnapping women were an everyday occurrence.

"I do not have much to lose," Winona retorted. It would be so easy to yank hard on the mane and send the horse into a rear. Yet as her fingers flexed, she knew she wouldn't do anything so rash.

Not only would she risk her own neck should the horse bolt, but she might lose all chance at gaining freedom should her captor truss her up like an animal brought in from a hunt. She chose not to believe his threat to kill Spotted Deer, but wisely decided not to put her instincts to the test.

Instead she stared down at the muscular arm banding her middle. A long, faded scar as wide as her finger ran from wrist to elbow. For just a moment she wondered about this warrior. Who was he? Why was he risking his life? She shook her head and focused on the rocky ground. They'd left the pretty meadow behind. "You can relax. I am not so foolish as to risk my own neck."

Her captor gave a bark of disbelief. "From what I have seen so far, that is precisely something you would risk."

Frowning, Winona contemplated not the Cheyenne's words, but his speech. The more he spoke, the better his English. No, not better, she realized, but more natural, as though most of his life he'd spoken the white man's tongue.

"Who are you? Where are you taking us, and why?" Winona wanted to know, yet feared the answer.

She got no reply, but the warrior loosened his hold slightly as he turned his mount to follow a downward slope. A quick glance over her shoulder confirmed that Spotted Deer was right behind her. The other two warriors brought up the rear. She met Spotted Deer's gaze.

Hold on. Be brave. She tried to give comfort and courage but had to wonder if it wasn't for herself as well. The silence continued but for the sound of horses picking their way over the rocky ground.

"Afraid to answer?" She tipped her head back. Better to know the enemy, know his plans and motives.

Though he didn't look at her, Winona saw the tightening of his jaw—and noticed another scar on the underside of his chin. By the time she'd blinked her eyes, she'd spotted several other scars. Though he bore many scars, she sensed it was the ones inside that had done the most damage. She turned and faced forward again, troubled by her thoughts. It was nothing to do with her if he was dead inside, as he claimed. So he had no heart. No soul.

A man with no heart or soul also had no conscience. What did that mean for her and Spotted Deer? She didn't know, and was afraid she'd soon find out.

Along the path, blackened trees and stumps gave testimony to a fire. Renewal of the land was evidenced by clumps of greenery emerging from the charred ground. As the horse picked his way carefully down the hillside Winona tried to put room between her and the man riding behind her. But he tightened his hold, forcing her to ride with her back firmly against his front.

As the sun moved overhead, she grew tired but refused to nod off. Instead she kept a careful watch on their progress, noted the sun's position and any landmarks they passed. While she had confidence in her father's ability to track them, she had to admit that these warriors knew what they were doing. She'd hoped that the leader would make a mistake that would make it easy for her people to find them, but so far he'd proven his skill at moving across the land with little trace.

Her spirits sank. When her captor had first run through the trees with her slung over his back, she'd held out more hope. The white warrior had not taken the time to conceal his tracks, and she had been able to snatch at leaves and twigs and leave a trail so obvious a brave as young as her nephew could follow it.

But ever since they'd mounted to continue on horseback, the warriors traveled slowly and carefully across the land as though unconcerned that they were being followed. Each stream they rode through, each path, had obviously been chosen carefully. This more than words told her that her kidnapping was well planned and not random.

The fact that he and the other two warriors

had been in her camp weeks ago proved this. Despair slid over Winona. Recalling her captor's fury at the mention of her husband-to-be, she could only assume that the two warriors were enemies and that she was being used as a method of revenge. But for what?

Once the trail leveled out, Winona sat forward, putting space between her and her captor. This time her act of rebellion was met by indifference, and after a while her back and shoulders ached from the stiff position. Stubbornness kept her upright, and by the time her captor stopped at the edge of a gushing stream, she could have wept with relief.

"We stop only for a short break." Without helping her down, the Cheyenne warrior dismounted.

He paused below her. "Do not try anything foolish," he warned.

Head and shoulders straight, Winona refused to speak. Instead she narrowed her eyes and watched as he walked away. Her fingers flexed in the horse's mane.

"Do not bother," the warrior called out without even turning his head. "He won't respond to any command but mine." He swung his head around and pierced her with his dark gaze. "We won't stop again until after nightfall."

Did she believe him? Dared she try to escape?

She glanced at Spotted Deer, who stood on the ground. She looked frightened. With a sigh, Winona swung her leg up and over the broad back of the gleaming horse and dropped down to the ground to join Spotted Deer.

After a brief hug, Spotted Deer stepped back. "You should have tried to run," her friend whispered, sending fearful glances at the warriors deep in conversation. "It is not too late. Run. Get free."

"No," Winona said fiercely. "I will not leave you." She swallowed hard at the ball of guilt lodged in her throat. For the first time since their capture tears threatened to overwhelm her. Not only was this her fault, but she'd made it incredibly easy for these warriors to take them captive.

She reached out and took Spotted Deer's hands with her own. "I am so sorry, my sister. This is my fault."

Spotted Deer's hard grip on her arm made her wince. "No. It just happened."

Winona closed her eyes and nearly wept at Spotted Deer's assumption. But she didn't say anything—she didn't want to frighten Spotted Deer further. A sharp tug on her arm brought her attention back to Spotted Deer.

"Promise that if you get the chance, you will

run." Spotted Deer's voice wavered, and her grip on Winona's arm left marks.

Unwilling to make a promise she could never keep, Winona pulled her friend toward the thicket—and privacy. Though none of the warriors were watching, she knew the leader, the one who'd kidnapped her, was fully aware of their actions. She scowled.

"He acts too sure of himself," she muttered. It would serve him right if they kept going or found a place to hide, but realistically Winona knew this wasn't the moment to do either. She'd just have to bide her time. And the time would come, she vowed. She'd gotten them into this mess; she'd get them out of it.

Each woman kept an eye on the conversing warriors while the other took advantage of the stop and relieved herself. When they were finished, Winona led them back to the edge of the thicket. Rebellion kept her from returning to their captors like a well-trained dog.

Three of the warriors wore their long hair in twin braids that reached midback. The leader, the one she'd been forced to ride with, wore his hair short and free, the soft strands brushing the tops of his broad shoulders.

With breechclouts swaying in the brisk breeze, leggings accenting long, strong legs, and tight buckskin shirts that outlined bodies honed to perfection, any maiden—attached or unattached—would cast her admiring gaze over these men.

Curving her lips into another scowl, Winona tipped her chin. But not her. Hoka Luta was the only warrior for her. She ignored the small voice that reminded her that she had noticed these warriors weeks ago, as had every maiden.

But her mind and heart had been so eagerly awaiting Hoka Luta's arrival that she'd paid them little attention. The man she planned to marry was brave and honorable. He didn't terrorize innocent women.

Winona glared at the leader. He was *tatunkce*. Dung. He would pay dearly for his crime, by her own hand, when the opportunity arose. Without warning, her captor turned his head. His gaze locked with hers as if he'd felt her eyes upon him. She tried to glance away as if he meant no more to her than an annoying *tehmunga*. But to her discomfort, he held her gaze with nothing more than his own.

Winona's mouth went dry and she couldn't look away.

Not because she was frightened of him. He'd soon learn she had a bite. And he didn't hold her gaze because he was handsome. With his scarred face, he wasn't, though he was undeniably better-looking than Hoka Luta.

But while Hoka Luta was impressive, with his sheer size and commanding presence, this warrior possessed something else. Something she couldn't name. It wasn't just his body—not even under these circumstances could she find complaint with his fine form. It wasn't his face—the scar itself had destroyed the perfection he must have carried in his youth. There was something else, something intangible, and whatever it was, it encompassed the man. The whole man.

The fact that she could even notice or acknowledge him in this fashion upset her almost more than the circumstances she found herself in.

"What are we going to do?" Spotted Deer whispered, breaking into her silent contemplations.

Winona drew in a deep breath. She was *not* admiring the enemy! She absolutely was not! She was simply studying him, searching for weakness. To prove that he held no control over her, Winona held his gaze and answered, "We wait until dark. Don't sleep. When my father and Hoka Luta come, we must be ready."

Finally, and to her secret relief, the Cheyenne warrior turned his head back to the rest of the warriors, releasing her from his spell with an abruptness that left her insides churned up.

"That is a good plan. They will attack when darkness falls." Spotted Deer's voice trembled.

Another wave of guilt curled and twisted through her insides. She put her arm around Spotted Deer. "Do not worry. They will come."

Winona tried to believe her own comforting words, but they brought her no relief, for she knew just how difficult it would be for her father to follow. That he would pick up their tracks she had no doubt. But would he be fast enough to catch up with them? Nature would easily erase signs of their passage—unless she could leave some sort of sign. While relieving herself, she'd disturbed as much of the underbrush as she could.

With that in mind, she broke off a few more branches and leaves. A sharp command snapped her head up. Reaching out, she took Spotted Deer by the hand. "All will be right. You will see."

Spotted Deer hung back. "Promise, Winona. Promise to escape if you get the chance."

Winona opened her mouth to tell Spotted Deer no, but changed her mind. If a small untruth gave comfort to her friend, then she would offer what comfort was at her command.

"I promise." To herself she added, *to get us out of this mess.*

"*Nenaestse!*"

At the stern command, Winona turned her gaze back to the Cheyenne warriors. Two were already mounted. To her surprise they rode off, taking no particular care not to leave a trail. Her mouth went dry.

"We'd better hurry," Spotted Deer whispered.

Lifting her brow, Winona glared at the leader. Tempting though it was to make him come get her, she allowed Spotted Deer to pull her forward. Retaliation, had it been just herself to worry about, was one thing. But she'd done enough to her friend already.

The two women separated. With worried eyes, Winona watched as Spotted Deer was hauled up in front of a different warrior. Standing beside the black horse, Winona waited for her captor to mount and pull her up in front of him.

To her surprise, he grabbed her wrists and worked the rope free. Immediately Winona's mind began to work. With her hands free, there was much she could do: grab a rock, a tree limb, maybe even snatch the knife from her captor's sheath.

"You will do nothing," the Cheyenne warrior said.

Winona narrowed her eyes and tilted her

chin. "You are a fool. I will find a way to escape."

"I think not." He jerked his head toward the other warrior. After a terse command, the warrior rode off with Spotted Deer.

With his dark eyes holding hers, the Cheyenne warrior warned, "Run, or harm me in any way, and you will not see your sister again."

Eyes wide, heart pounding, she tried to run after Spotted Deer, but her captor had a firm grip on her upper arm. Winona whirled about. "Do not do this. I give my word to do as you wish. Do not separate us. My . . . sister—she is frightened." Winona had almost forgotten that he thought them sisters. She had to be careful, for if he learned the truth he might not hesitate to harm Spotted Deer. He clearly thought her valuable because of her relationship to Winona.

The Cheyenne warrior lifted a brow. "And you are not frightened?"

Winona called upon every ounce of her courage. "Hoka Luta is the son of a powerful medicine man. It is you who should be afraid."

A bitter bark of laughter made her wince. Deep shadows dulled the warrior's eyes. "You have much to learn, wild one," he said. "Sometimes the one you should fear is the very one you trust. Let us hope you never have to learn that lesson."

With that he drew his knife out from the sheath he wore around his shin. Winona's eyes widened when he grabbed her dress and sliced a piece from the hem. Without taking his eyes off her, he cut his arm and used the hide to soak up the blood.

Horror dawned as Winona watched him stab an arrow through the middle of the jaggedly cut hide and shoot it into a nearby tree trunk—one near the place where she and Spotted Deer had rested.

In disbelief Winona realized that he wasn't trying to hide his tracks but was instead luring her father and Hoka Luta in the direction he desired. "What game do you play?" she whispered.

"This is no game," the warrior said, his voice devoid of emotion.

He lifted her up onto the horse and mounted behind her. With a triumphant yell, the only real emotion she'd heard in his voice so far, the Cheyenne warrior with no soul sent the horse surging forward—in the opposite direction that Spotted Deer and her captor had gone.

Chapter Four

Hawk Eyes studied the rotting layer of leaves, scraped from the ground in telling piles. His heart pounded as he sifted through the disturbed plant life. He scraped his finger through the top, dry layer of dirt to the darker, richer, moist soil below. Waves of heat fused with cold chills. The enemy had many hours on him.

"They are alive," Golden Eagle said from where he examined a similar site of recent struggle. He walked over to his father and bent down to pick up the broken tree limb.

"Yes," Hawk Eyes said. He lifted his gaze upward to the torn flesh of the tree above their heads. His daughters were alive, and kicking and fighting. Though he feared for them, he was proud of their courage. He closed his eyes and let his shoulders slump.

For days Winona had been asking him to take her to Gray Rock. She loved that place and had never shown any fear of heights, not even when she'd been just a toddler. He smiled softly at the memory of carrying her up there at only two winters, and the look of wonder on her face when she saw a world more vast than any one person could comprehend.

From that moment on he'd taken her there often. He suspected she went there a lot more than just the few times he'd heard of her sneaking out of camp. He bowed his head. As she had done this morning.

Golden Eagle's hands rested on his hips. He looked worried. And angry. "My sister is a fool. Why did she not seek one of us out to take her, and why did Spotted Deer not try to stop her?" He held up one hand. "I know. No one can stop Winona when she makes up her mind."

Hawk Eyes understood that his son was worried. Turning in a slow circle, he himself felt sick. Had he put his daughter and her needs first yesterday, this would not have happened. Instead he'd been more concerned with getting ready for visitors and planning her marriage to Hoka Luta.

"I put her off three times over the last three days. How many times did she ask you?"

Golden Eagle bowed his head. "We are the

fools." Father and son stared at each other. Guilt from one set of eyes mirrored the same wrenching emotion of the other. Hawk Eyes walked away.

"Search the area," he called out to the waiting warriors. The warriors fanned out, each keeping low to the ground—for safety, and to better find signs of their enemy.

Pacing a few feet from where Golden Eagle continued to search, Hoka Luta tossed a rock he'd been examining. It hit the root of a tree, bounced, then plopped onto a bed of pine needles and earth. "No one takes what belongs to Hoka Luta and lives. I will kill whoever took her."

Hawk Eyes narrowed his eyes at the man his daughter had chosen for her mate. "He is mine." For a brief moment he held the younger warrior's gaze, until Hoka Luta stalked away.

Grimly Hawk Eyes turned on his heel. He understood the younger man's intense desire to exact revenge. He felt the same. But he was Winona's father and also Spotted Deer's. When his adopted daughter had been small, he and Seeing Eyes had become the girl's second set of parents, a common practice among his people to keep parents from spoiling their children. When Spotted Deer's parents died, she'd truly become his daughter.

Today he'd lost not one daughter but two. The father within demanded that they hurry and find the girls. From deep inside he called upon the seasoned warrior who, through training, was able to put emotion aside and balance need with caution. Fear led to carelessness. Yet nothing could ease the nearly crippling fear racing through him.

In the past his people had been victim to the cruelties of the white men who took unprotected girls and women for sport. Some were never found; others were found beaten and badly treated. Still others managed to take their own lives rather than submit to the horrors of rape. Everything within the man who was a father screamed against this terrible, unspeakable end.

"No," he whispered harshly. He would not fail his daughters—or his wife and his promise to bring them back.

The sound of vicious cursing made him swing around. Hoka Luta stood a short distance away. Other warriors gathered about. Hawk Eyes tore through the waist-high brush, his heart beating so fast he feared it would explode. What had they found?

"What is it?" he asked, his voice deep and raw with fear. His warriors quickly parted for their chief. Hawk Eyes swept his gaze over the forest floor. No bodies. Noting that his warriors were staring at the tree, he nudged aside two of Hoka Luta's warriors who were blocking his view.

He stopped when he saw a square of hide pinned to the tree by a knife. Hawk Eyes recognized the knife as the one he'd given Winona two summers ago. Reaching out, Golden Eagle pulled the blade from the tree and handed the leather hide to his father.

With hands that shook, Hawk Eyes studied the message. He felt no shame at the shaking in his hands. His daughters had been taken. Their lives were in danger. He might be a great warrior and leader, but he was also a father. Right now the father feared for both the daughter of his blood and the daughter of his heart.

Golden Eagle stood close, studying the message. "I do not understand," he said, frowning. He slapped his sister's knife against the palm of his hand.

Hawk Eyes forced his eyes to focus on the painted scene. In the upper left-hand corner a stick figure with the head of a bear stood with a knife poised over the body of another. Several fallen bodies had been painted to the right. "Death," he whispered. "This speaks of death."

A hush fell over the band of warriors. Golden Eagle traced what looked to be bear prints from the first scene to the second, which depicted a young girl. Tears flowed from her face and led down to the bottom right-hand corner, where a man stood with arms outstretched.

"This makes no sense," Golden Eagle said.

Hawk Eyes balled one hand into a fist. "The enemy left this for us to find. It has meaning. It is the reason my daughters were taken." That much was obvious to him, but the message did not make sense. He shifted his gaze to the knife Hoka Luta held. He held out his hand and took it from the quiet warrior.

Holding up the finely tooled leather sheath, Hawk Eyes studied it. The leather was dark, worn, and shiny from wear. He pulled the knife out. Whoever had owned this knife had prized it, for the blade was well cared for. He ran the pad of one finger over the cutting edge and drew blood. Sharp as well.

"This is a white man's knife," he bit out. Fury beat against his temples.

He slid his hand over the smooth white handle of the blade, then held it up for all to see. Sunlight sparkled off the shiny blade. This knife had been made by a master craftsman. Most warriors carried knives made by the white man. They were sharper and lasted much longer than knives made of sharpened stone. But few of his people got their hands on blades of this quality.

Frowning, he studied the knife. "Why would anyone leave a valuable tool such as this behind? What game does the enemy play?" He glanced at Hoka Luta, who'd so far been silent.

Hoka Luta stepped forward. He pointed to the painted scenes and spoke with anger. "This looks as though the daughter of Hawk Eyes seeks another. Has she run to join with someone else?"

A hush came over the group. Warriors who were discussing the events looked at Hoka Luta, disbelief in their eyes.

Golden Eagle whipped his head around. "What are you saying?" he asked, his voice low and deadly.

Hoka Luta punched a finger at the leather. "Does the woman I should have married this day shed tears for another?" He flicked the back of his middle finger at the man in the bottom corner. "You said she left on her own this morning. Perhaps all this is a ploy." He held out his hand to encompass the scenes of struggle.

For just a moment Hawk Eyes felt doubt. Then he shook his head. "My daughter chose you. She does not yearn for another." Of that Hawk Eyes was certain. Winona had made her choice in her mate, and had she changed her mind she'd have come to him. Besides, that wouldn't have explained Spotted Deer's disappearance.

Hoka Luta reached out and took the knife from Hawk Eyes. "Then the man who dared to take my woman will die," he shouted. He held the knife high. Hoka Luta's knuckles turned white from gripping the large knife handle so tightly.

Hawk Eyes turned to his warriors. "Find the trail of our enemy. We have spent enough time here." Warriors around him spread out once again while he rolled the message into a tube and tucked it beneath the leather thong around his waist. He held out his hand for the knife.

Hoka Luta lifted his chin. "This belongs to the enemy who dared to take my woman. I shall use it to kill this man."

"She is still my daughter, and the fate of the enemy is mine."

After a terse moment, Hoka Luta handed over the knife.

The three warriors joined in the search for the trail that would lead them to Winona and Spotted Deer. With the enemy on foot, they would be able to catch up quickly.

"Here," a warrior called out. Once more the warriors gathered. Staring down at four sets of hoofprints, Hawk Eyes buried the father in him deep inside and called upon his warrior's training. The number of enemies was now four, and no longer were they on foot. Did they ride to meet up with many others?

Hawk Eyes signaled two of his warriors and ordered them to return to camp and gather more men. By following the trail left by Hawk Eyes and the warriors they'd catch up quickly.

With a heavy heart, Hawk Eyes mounted his horse and vowed not to return home without his daughters.

Tall pines stood shoulder-to-shoulder, like soldiers standing guard in the light. Branches interlocked to form an impenetrable barrier, keeping out all but the smallest of creatures. Above, rays of moonlight tried to pierce the canopy formed by the thick stands of trees, but darkness ruled in the deep shadows of the forest.

Sitting on a bed of pine needles at the edge of a small triangle of trees, Winona scrunched her eyes in a vain attempt to see her captor in the darkness.

"Why have you kidnapped me?"

"It is not your concern." The harsh, low answer came from somewhere in front of her.

Winona narrowed her gaze, more against the answer than in a vain attempt to see her enemy. All during the long day of hard riding, the Cheyenne warrior had kept silent except for barking out orders during their brief stops to rest the horse. She'd had enough.

She tossed a fistful of pine needles away from her and said, "You made it my concern when you took me and Spotted Deer away from our family. I deserve to know why. And what you plan to do with us," she added.

That was the worst part. She'd never experienced this fear of not knowing.

"I suggest you rest," her captor told her.

"You expect me to rest? How do I know you will not . . . harm me while I rest?"

Her answer was met with a heavy sigh. "As long as my demands are met, you will not be harmed."

Not reassured in the slightest, Winona plucked at the deerskin fringe brushing against her shins. His answer raised more concerns.

"What demands? The Sioux have no quarrel with the Cheyenne."

A twig snapped somewhere in front of her. Though she couldn't see clearly, she knew he'd moved slightly to the right and that he was still in front of her. "Enough questions."

"I am supposed to believe you?" Tired, restless, and worried, Winona knew she shouldn't push, but it was because of how she felt that she couldn't just shut up and let the enemy intimidate her.

Another twig snapped, followed by a soft rustle, as though the broken bits had been tossed. "Believe what you want. I said all I plan to say."

Fingering a twig herself, Winona resisted the temptation to toss it at her captor.

After a few moments she asked, "Then at least tell me your name. What do I call you?"

No answer, which didn't surprise her. That was fine with her. If he refused to give her a name, she'd just find her own name for him. Running her fingers along her jaw, she thought.

"*Sunka*," she said, aloud as though talking to herself.

"What?"

Winona, grateful for the dark cloak of night that hid her expression from his, grinned at the shocked disbelief in his voice. She shrugged. "Do you not understand Lakota?"

When he didn't reply, she answered, "*Sunka* is Lakota for dog. If I must address you, or call out to you while we rest, then that is the name I will use."

A low growl was her captor's only response.

She leaned forward. "If you do not like that name, I could use *zuzeca*." This time she didn't give the Cheyenne warrior a chance to speak. "Yes, that name is also fitting."

Winona took immense pleasure in the heavy silence. She wasn't sure what had come over her. Her own daring surprised her.

* * *

Night Shadow glared into the shadows. What game was this woman playing? His lips tightened; his temples throbbed with pain. Woman? The daughter of Hawk Eyes couldn't be much older than Jenny would be.

But she was old enough to marry. Thinking of whom she'd been about to marry sent throbbing pain shooting down along the scar. It settled in his tightly clenched jaw and ached like a badly torn muscle.

Across from him, almost forgotten, Winona spoke. "It means ssssnake." She'd lowered her voice, slurring the S sound so it sounded as though she were hissing the word.

Night Shadow glared at her. He heard the smug satisfaction in her voice.

"How about—"

"Enough," he ground out.

A twig snapped. "Then give me a name," she demanded.

Night Shadow rubbed his temple and resisted the urge to jump to his feet and gag his troublesome captive. But in order to gag her he'd have to tie her, and he had no desire to hurt her or leave marks upon her body. Thus far he'd garnered her compliance by separating her from her sister. He tried to keep in mind that she truly was an innocent pawn in the game of revenge he'd set in motion.

"I will give you a name if you stop with the questions." Night Shadow waited. He heard her shift position, then sigh.

"For tonight," she agreed.

Night Shadow figured that was reasonable. Why couldn't she have been a submissive, frightened captive? Instead she seemed bent on making each day with him difficult. He stretched out his legs. No matter. His life for the last fourteen years had been hell on earth. What was another few months?

Finding Jenny was all that he cared about.

"Are you asleep? Give me your name."

The demand snapped him from the dark pit of despair that threatened to swallow him.

"Clay," he said, his voice deeper than normal as he struggled to maintain control over his emotions.

"Clay?" Scorn laced her question. "That is not the name of a Cheyenne warrior."

Night Shadow scowled. Did she think him fool enough to give her his Cheyenne name? His fight with Henry Black Bear was his and his alone. He would do nothing to endanger his Cheyenne family. If Winona's father learned who he truly was, he would retaliate against the innocent Cheyenne.

Crossing his arms across his chest he leaned his head back. "You asked for a name. I gave you the name my father gave me."

"Your white father?"

Night Shadow ignored the derision in her voice. Instead of allowing himself to be drawn into a battle of words, he closed his eyes. "No more talk. We ride soon."

The night hid the pain he knew would be reflected in his eyes and etched in deep lines around his mouth. Darkness crept through him, swallowing and invading, smothering his soul and spirit.

The sound of his name spoken aloud for the first time since that tragic day left him shaken. Why had he given her a name long dead to him? He'd planned to give her a false name, but the name Clay had left his lips.

Nightmarish images of a day he longed to forget flew at him like arrows from the enemy: each one found its mark in his heart, until he felt as though he were once again dying.

But he could not forget—dared not forget—not even for a short while. The past had given birth to Night Shadow, a warrior with a thirst for revenge so strong it became the reason he survived, and gave him the courage to live.

His fingers gripped his wrists as he stared into the darkness, seeing nothing but more pain and more black nights ahead. Yet, at the end of that dark tunnel, he still held out hope that he'd find Jenny—his reason for living.

Chapter Five

The next stop during the long night of riding was at the top of a rocky hill with only a few trees for shelter. Across from her, Winona saw that Clay's breathing had slowed and the rise and fall of his chest deepened as he slept. Tipping her head, she stared up at the dark sky. How she envied the warrior his ability to just shut down and sleep, even if only for a short time.

Somewhere below her, deep in the forest, the screech of an owl echoed, drowning out the cadence of insects in the bushes. Rustling in the growth to her left was followed by a series of high-pitched squeaks. Peering through the darkness, she couldn't see anything.

Sighing, she closed her eyes and ordered herself to stop thinking and to sleep. She needed her rest in order to stay alert. But as before, sleep eluded her. Her mind was too crowded with thoughts and emotions and refused to shut down.

Giving up, knowing she couldn't force her body to sleep, she stared into the darkness. She thought about escaping, but only briefly. Clay would wake immediately. Like most warriors he'd learned to sleep on demand, yet remain aware. Besides, even if she did manage to escape, it wouldn't solve the problem of finding Spotted Deer.

Frustration gave way to annoyance. It galled her that he'd so effectively bound her to him without rope. Just the threat of never seeing Spotted Deer had been enough to secure her compliance. He'd been clever; she'd give him that!

Scowling in Clay's direction, she was seized by a sudden urge to toss a stone at him. It wasn't fair that he could sleep without a care when her life had been tossed upside down.

Frustrated with her situation and her lack of sleep, she scraped the toe of her moccasin across the ground and dislodged several chunks of dirt. Reaching forward, she picked one up and crushed it in her fist.

Bored, Winona let the dirt fall from her hand, then brushed her palm over her dress. At each stop she disturbed the land as much as she could. She smiled in grim satisfaction. Clay knew what she was doing, but unless he wanted to bind her hands and feet there was little he could do.

She sighed. She'd already left her mark in this spot. Now what? She wasn't used to just sitting. The days were filled with chores, and each night she fell asleep satisfied with her daily accomplishments.

Clay had taken that from her as well. Turning her gaze upward, Winona tried to find solace in the night sky. For the first time since darkness had swallowed the world, the panic welling deep inside her calmed.

With the night sky hidden from her while they traveled through the darkened woods, she'd felt trapped. Closed in. Out on the open prairie, where her people set their camps, the sky was always there for her. Even inside the tipi all she had to do was pull up the lining or stick her head out the flap.

She closed her eyes as she remembered the first time she'd slept inside a white man's house. It was like the woods, closed in and dark but for candles or lanterns. She didn't like it. Not at all. Leaning back against the tree trunk, Winona drew her knees to her chest and rested her cheek on her folded arm as she stared up into the sky, seeking familiar and comforting patterns in the stars.

Pale blue skies replaced black. Night chirps became giggles. Fourteen harsh years melted away. Night Shadow, hardened warrior, became Clay Coburn, a boy of sixteen, eager to leave the wilds of nowhere come spring and travel to the city before setting out to see the world.

"Clay! Play with me."

Clay sorted through the traps and wiped the sweat from his brow.

"I'm busy, Jenny. Go bother Catherine."

Jenny's tiny rosebud lips formed a pout, then trembled with hurt. She hugged a threadbare rag doll to her narrow chest.

"Ma and Catherine are busy. Play with me. Please?"

Clay grimaced. His baby sister knew just how to get her way. A few tears, a trembling lip, and a soft, bewitching voice wrapped him around her tiny pink finger. He tried to put her off one last time.

"I have a lot to do before we leave."

Eyes that were neither green nor brown filled with tears.

"Please." Jenny drew the word out.

Clay tossed the trap he was repairing into a pile of others, all ready to be sold. Handling his father's traps, knowing the two of them would never trap

84

together again, was suddenly too much. He grabbed on to the excuse to stop the painful chore for even a few minutes.

He sent Jenny a mock growl.

"What shall we play?" He lifted both hands high, crooking his fingers as though they were long, sharp claws.

Squealing with glee, Jenny turned and ran between two trees.

"Bear, bear," she shrieked.

In one long-legged jump, Clay snagged Jenny around the waist and tossed her high. "I've got you."

He allowed her to wiggle free. When she ran into the woods surrounding their tipi, he gave chase. Playing chase was her favorite game.

But only he could be the bear.

"The bear's after me," she yelled. Her laughter made him giggle and took away the overwhelming grief of losing his father. If his father had been there, he'd have stopped whatever he was doing to play with his youngest daughter. Even Pa hadn't been able to resist Jenny's pleas.

Jenny's giggles filled his dreams. He smiled in his sleep—until the first report of a shotgun tore the smile from his face.

Laughter turned to screams.

And Jenny . . .

"No, Jenny! No! Come back!"

Then came blinding pain and more screaming. And blood. He whimpered.

Too much blood.

Too much death.

Everyone was dead.

And Jenny? Where was she?

He struggled against the gripping horrors of his past. "Jenny!" His shout turned to a plea. "Where are you, Jenny?"

"Clay?"

Night Shadow fought the darkness that held him like a spider's web. A voice lured him out of the darkness. "Jenny?"

"Clay, wake up!"

"Jenny!" Night Shadow opened his eyes. She was here. She'd answered. His body, drenched in sweat, tensed as he glanced around wildly.

"Clay? Are you all right?"

Night Shadow blinked, focused, then stared in confusion into Winona's wide, dark gaze. A dream. Another dream. He dropped his head into his hands. "Jenny," he whispered again. "I'll find you. I promise."

"Who is Jenny, Clay?"

He couldn't answer. He felt awkward, humiliated that he'd revealed so much while he slept.

"Clay. You dreamed."

Winona's soft voice wrapped around him, offering comfort that he'd long been without. A gray mist coated the air. Across from him, Wi-

nona watched. She didn't move, didn't say anything else, just watched, which unnerved him
more than if he'd woken to find her standing
over him with a knife poised at his heart.

"Not a dream," he bit out. "Hell. My own
personal hell." He jumped to his feet and strode
past Winona. He couldn't bear the pity in her
eyes; nor did he want the comfort her warm
gaze offered—it mattered not that he could not
see it in the darkness. He knew it was there and
it drove him away.

Only one person could release him from his
tortured night dreams: Jenny. His baby sister.
Only by finding her could he be granted peace.

Staring at the land spread out before him,
Night Shadow struggled to regain control.
Night Shadow the warrior wouldn't have cared
if the woman had seen or heard his tormented
cries, but right then he was Clay, a man tortured by the past and vulnerable to a pair of
soft, wide eyes that had witnessed his suffering.

He clenched his hands. He had to remain
strong, tough. Focused. Allowing any softening
within—or toward his captive—would only
jeopardize his hopes of finding Jenny. Nothing
mattered but Jenny. He'd give his own life to
find her and know she was safe and happy.

Clay concentrated on slowing his heart by
taking slow, deep breaths, releasing them just

as slowly. Controlled. In. Out. After a few minutes the tremors racking his body faded. Opening his eyes, he stared out at the blanket of fog creeping across the land below him.

Though calmer, he made himself stand still. Control. His blood no longer raced through his veins, but thoughts scurried, darted, flew through his mind. He hated the night. Fears ruled his mind, and despair made him feel as though he'd fallen into a deep, dark pit. And during each night the dark tunnel of his life seemed endless.

Breathe. Breathe. Breathe. Focus. Take control.

Each dawn Clay the man, the brother, fought his demons and struggled to regain control. He closed his eyes once more. During the daylight the warrior in him took control with no effort. Night Shadow felt nothing, showed nothing, feared nothing. Night Shadow existed. Clay did not.

But each night and morning it was Clay who stared up at the stars and waited for the dawn, Clay who suffered the horrible nightmares. Clay, not Night Shadow, felt fear each night, and dealt with gut-burning guilt, and it was Clay who cried deep inside where no one could see or hear him.

After several silent minutes, Night Shadow whirled around. *"He'e! Noheto!"* The low, harsh command broke the stillness of the early morning. Speaking the language of his mother's people served to remind him of who he'd become and what was at stake.

Winona stretched while Clay readied the horse. Above their heads the sky remained dark; dawn was hours away. She rubbed the stiffness from the back of her neck. To her surprise she'd slept until woken by Clay's shouts during the night.

She'd been confused, and it had taken her a minute to realize that she wasn't sleeping on her warm pile of furs with the soft, reassuring sounds of her parents sleeping across the tipi from her. As effective as a dousing of cold water, the realization had caused her to throw the mantle of sleep from her.

At first she'd thought her captor had ordered her to get up. But when his shouts turned to whimpers, she'd realized he was caught up in some horrible nightmare. Her first thought had been, *Good. Serves him right to have the night spirits attack his sleep.*

But the despair and the depths of pain in his husky voice had tugged at something inside her. No one deserved that kind of torment.

Winona moaned softly to herself. What was happening to her? Bad enough that she hadn't dared escape or harm Clay. But then to feel sorry for him? That was where her true shame lay. For a few minutes she'd actually been concerned about Clay, vulnerable to his rapid breathing and tortured cries.

Guilt slid through her. How could she feel sorry for this man when Spotted Deer was scared and all alone? Not that she wasn't a bit scared herself. It was just that, of the two them, Winona was the instigator, the leader, the one who seldom felt fear.

Sighing, she shoved her hair out of her eyes and ran her fingers through the tangled strands. "I promise to make this up to you," she whispered.

Promise you will run.

Winona had promised.

Worse, she'd made that promise knowing full well that she'd never keep it. And she hadn't. She'd had not one but two chances to gain her freedom. While he slept Clay might have woken had she tried to escape. But during his nightmare he wouldn't have been aware of her, or her actions. She could have escaped.

But her freedom at the cost of Spotted Deer's was out of the question. Until she was reunited with her friend, she'd stick to Clay like mud to rocks.

Hearing the horse snuffling, she turned to face her captor. He stood an arm's length from her. In the moonlight he looked every bit as controlled and harsh as the man who'd captured her. Gone was the hurt, vulnerable man.

Jenny.

Who was she? She stared at the long scar running down one side of his face. For the first time since her capture, Winona felt truly afraid. Something terrible had happened to him in the past, and to someone he'd obviously loved. Winona bit the inside of her cheeks. Clay risked not only his own life, but his actions against the Sioux risked peace between the Sioux and Cheyenne. And that brought her right back to needing to know why Clay had kidnapped her, for she felt sure that her family could not have done anything to anger or hurt this man.

A harsh shout from Clay reminded her that she was prisoner to a man who was bent on revenge. She was the means. He'd promised not to harm her as long as his demands were met. What were those demands?

When he mounted she reached up and grabbed his hand and mounted behind him. Resting her cheek against his shirt-covered back, Winona wished she knew what was happening.

Clay rode almost nonstop for three more days, pausing only for short periods of rest. Winona wanted to scream. She was cranky, tired, and dirty. And sick of riding. And sick of not knowing what was going on.

"When are we stopping?" she asked. She didn't expect an answer.

He surprised her by stopping at the edge of the lake they'd been following. When he dismounted and walked away, Winona gratefully slid down.

"How long this time?" Winona asked. Usually they stopped only to rest the horse. Clay didn't give her a chance to ask questions. He normally just handed her the water skin and a piece of hard pemmican, then walked off to be alone.

Night Shadow glanced around. "For the night. The horse needs rest."

"So do I," she muttered, irked that her needs meant nothing.

While her captor busied himself, Winona took advantage of the small blue lake to bathe. Shielded by bushes, she removed her dress and walked into the water. The water lapped gently around her; its cold bite stung her skin but also refreshed and cleared the fog from her mind.

Her teeth chattered as she rubbed handfuls of gritty soil from the bottom of the lake over her skin. Her fingers turned blue and she could no longer feel her feet, but after days of nonstop riding, nothing was going to keep her from cleaning the dust and sweat from her hair and body.

And after her bath she planned to soak up the warmth of the afternoon and do what she did every day: watch her captor and learn his weaknesses. When the time came to escape with Spotted Deer she'd be ready.

After scrubbing her hair with the root of *hupestola*, she waded deeper into the lake to rinse her hair, keeping her back to the man beyond the brush shielding her. By the time she finished, dried herself off, and re-dressed in her dusty clothing, she was shivering so hard she could barely walk.

Hugging herself, rubbing her hands up and down her arms, Winona headed for a rotting log bathed in the late-afternoon sunlight. She sat, shook her wet hair out behind her, and glanced around. This side of the stream was heavily wooded. Across the lake there were fewer trees. A peaceful meadow lined the bank. From where she sat she could pick out the tiny splashes of color and see birds darting through the air as they caught flying insects.

She sighed. The beauty, the normalcy of the scene, unsettled rather than soothed. As did the obvious fact that her captor felt safe enough to stop so early in the day. She sat in the open and he seemed not to care. Did this mean there was no one on their trail?

Winona wasn't sure how she felt about that. Yes, she wanted her father to ride in and rescue her. Yes, her captor would pay—with his life. But what would happen to Spotted Deer should her father catch up with her captor before he rejoined the other warriors and Spotted Deer?

Another chill racked her body. This one came not from being physically cold, but from deep inside. This was her fault. Her impetuous actions had put not only Spotted Deer in danger, but each warrior who rode with her father. She had no idea if Clay had more warriors waiting wherever he was taking her.

Winona stared at the pale yellow fingers streaking across the sky. Daylight was fading fast. Night would descend quickly. Where was Spotted Deer? Was she afraid? Hungry? Cold? Worry churned her stomach. She sniffed, then swung her head around. She smelled burning wood.

Clay had started a fire. She frowned. Why would he chance a fire with her father and warriors following? Winona didn't doubt her father was following. He'd never give up. So what was her Cheyenne captor up to? Was this some sort of trap?

A quick glance around showed a normal late

afternoon in the hills. As far as she could tell, she and her captor were the only ones in the area. Studying the leaves of a nearby bush, she noted the presence of *Tate*, the wind spirit. He blew against her, away from camp, taking the smoke and scent of fire away from the direction they'd traveled from.

Either Clay was foolish or complacent. She rubbed her forehead. Something told her he wasn't either. The way he'd taken her and Spotted Deer, the way the four warriors had separated, told her that he knew what he was doing. She tipped her head up and sniffed the air.

He was cooking. Fish. Winona closed her eyes. If Clay felt safe enough to cook their meal, it definitely meant her father wasn't close enough to smell the cooking food or see smoke from the fire.

"Come to the fire."

Winona started at the low command. She turned slightly so she could see Clay. He stood close enough for her to see the moisture clinging to the fine dusting of dark hair covering his thighs. He'd discarded his leggings and buckskin shirt, and the sight of him left Winona drymouthed.

Most Indian men lacked a thick coating of hair on their bodies. This outward proof of his white heritage should have repulsed her, made her think less of him as a man, but it didn't. Instead the hair on his legs and arms intrigued her. Her gaze lifted slightly to the bit on his chest.

Staring at his honed, muscular body sharpened her senses, made her remember how it felt to sit in the cradle of his arms with his front pressed to her back, and the feel of his arms firmly around her waist. Even the backs of her legs had rested and swung and bounced against his. She felt her cheeks redden.

There were other body parts that seemed to bounce and rub together. The thought of those places made her face flame and ignited a strange feeling in her middle that radiated outward. Heat chased the cold bumps from her skin and made her toes and fingers tingle. He was most definitely handsome in a way that Hoka Luta was not.

Horror and guilt spread through her, making her tremble. How could she find him attractive? Handsome? He was the enemy. He was using her, and causing her pain and misery as she fretted daily over the welfare of her friend and worried over her mother and family and what they had to be feeling. Then there were her own feelings of guilt. Had she not insisted on riding unescorted, none of this would have happened.

Guilt plunged the lump in her throat down

into her belly. Swallowing hard, she forced her gaze upward. *Forget his body. Look into his eyes. See the coldness of a man who uses women as pawns.* But her gaze refused to move past his taut, brown, hard-as-stone belly, his equally hard chest.

Winona laced her fingers together and took several deep breaths, striving for control and indifference. Forcing herself to turn, she presented Clay with her back. She had no need to stare upon his body. None at all.

Then why is your mouth so dry, and your heart racing?

Winona preferred to attribute that devious question to the traitorous spirit *Iktomi*, a spider-like man known for pranks and practical jokes. *Iktomi* was a trickster with power to work magic over anything or anyone.

After all, the Cheyenne warrior was no different from any other warrior, and no other warrior had ever made her feel this way. Not even Hoka Luta, which meant this was not real but a prank.

Closing her eyes, Winona called Hoka Luta's tall, strong image to mind. Hoka Luta was braver. Stronger, yet—

"Did you not understand what I said?" Night Shadow's quiet, controlled voice startled Winona.

She opened her eyes and scowled as Hoka Luta's image fled as silent as a hawk carried away by the wind. From the corner of her eye Winona saw Clay move to stand beside her. The edge of his breechclout swayed open, revealing the junction where one thigh joined his torso. She flushed.

To hide her embarrassment, she sharpened her voice. "I have no need of your fire, *waglula*." Though he'd given her his name, she didn't use it. When she did, she found herself remembering how vulnerable he'd seemed during his nightmare. So now she called him a different name each time she addressed him, finding immense satisfaction in insulting him—all without his knowledge. It also reminded her that she was a captive, and he her enemy. And right now, he was *worm*.

He folded his arms across his chest. "It matters not what you call me. You will join me at the fire. You are cold. I have no desire for you to become ill. The battle I wage is between me and my enemy."

Swinging her damp hair hard enough to send droplets of water flying his way, Winona lifted a brow. "If this battle is between you and another, then why am I here?" She speared him with a haughty glare.

He remained silent, his eyes silently commanding her to do as he'd ordered.

"You are *kokayehanla*. *Sahiyela kokayehanla*." She saw that he recognized the Lakota word for Cheyenne. She smirked. He didn't know that *kokayehanla* meant chicken.

Night Shadow clenched his jaw. "Yes. I am *Sahiyela*. *Cheyenne*. *Tsetsehesestaestse* in my tongue, but what you call me is not important. You will come back to camp. Now." He strode away.

Winona wished she dared to run after him, jump on his back, claw his hair out. Better yet, she mused, her gaze falling on large round rock. But she'd do neither, even though it burned that the *wasicu* acted as though she posed no threat. She gave a self-deprecating laugh. The *white man*—from now on she'd think of him as white, not Cheyenne—was shrewd. Clever.

He'd found the one and only way to secure her compliance. He knew, as she knew, that she'd attempt nothing if it meant putting Spotted Deer in danger. She narrowed her eyes. But that didn't mean she had to be weak and mindless.

"*Nenaestse!*"

Ignoring whatever he'd commanded, Winona reached down and plucked a tender blade of grass from the bank of the lake, then nibbled on it as though she had not a care in the world. Though she expected it, she still tensed at the sound of her captor's voice behind her. She never seemed to hear his approach, which also irked her.

"I will not ask again."

Winona shrugged. "Then don't. I prefer to be alone in the cold than to share a fire with a *gnaska*." At his raised brow, she made the sound of a frog.

"Be careful, *pohkeso*." He took one step forward, his hands resting lightly on his hips.

"Or you will harm Spotted Deer?" She meet his angry gaze with a defiant one.

Clay rubbed the back of his neck. "I am no monster. I have not harmed you or your sister. You have not suffered."

Winona stood. Tipping her head back, she glared up into his face. Using one finger, she stabbed him in the center of his chest.

"I suffer." Stab.

"I suffer being away from my family." Stab, stab.

"I suffer knowing my family is worried. My mother is suffering, my father. My people. Do not tell me I do not suffer." Before she could punctuate her outburst with another stab, Clay grabbed her hand.

He looked furious, his eyes nearly black with

anger. "My enemy cared not who suffered at his hand. Blame him." With no warning, his arm snagged her around the waist and he lifted her off her feet, holding her around the waist with one arm as he headed toward the fire.

"Put me down. I will return to camp when I am ready." Winona kicked out with her feet and swung her arms. But her captor tightened his hold around her ribs. She slid down a few inches, his arm slid up beneath her breasts, and her dress rose to the top of her thighs.

With only the thought of freeing herself so she could hide her flesh, she stuck her foot out to stop him. Instead her leg caught between his, and suddenly they were falling.

Chapter Six

Winona found herself pinned beneath Clay. Again. Or sort of beneath him. He lay more on his side, his scarcely clad body angled over hers, his arms wrapped behind her to soften the fall.

His right knee lay bent beneath her buttocks, her left knee caught between Clay's thighs and her right dangled over his hips. Shifting, Clay brought his left over hers so she was trapped beneath him and sandwiched between his thighs. He leaned over her.

Winona licked her lips. She started to lift her arms, which were over her head, resting on the cool, soft mat of her hair. She changed her mind. There was no place to put her hands, except on Clay.

Time seemed to stand still as they stared at

each other. Above them, the last of the sun's rays faded, leaving the sky deep purple—not black, not blue. It was a color for reflecting on the day and preparing for the evening.

Caught in Clay's dark gaze, Winona chewed her lower lip. The mood from defiant and demanding had fled. This new silence between them unnerved her. She felt strange. And hot. Especially where they touched intimately.

Clay said nothing. He just gazed down at her, his eyes warm with an emotion she'd not seen there before. She felt vulnerable yet aware as never before.

Air slid over her body, twisting around her legs, dipping beneath her skirt, which she only now realized had slid up her thighs, helped by Clay's left knee. "G-get up," she said under her breath.

Clay's eyes never left hers. "Why?"

"I-I'm cold."

His brows lifted. "You were in no hurry to come to the fire. Perhaps I should warm you." He shifted over her and planted his forearms on each side of her head.

"Not that cold! Get off me." Winona shoved at him but Clay was immovable.

He turned his head and stared at their tangled bodies. Embarrassed, Winona tried to pull her legs free, but his thighs tightened. The brush of thick, curly hair rubbing against her upper thigh made her gasp.

"C-Clay!"

Slowly Clay swung his head to face her. "Yes?" He ignored her attempts to dislodge him.

"What are you doing?" Her voice came out high and thin.

"What do you think I'm doing?" Once again he shifted his body.

Winona caught her breath. The movement was enough to lift her left leg a few inches higher and cause the skirt of her dress to fall further. And judging by the amount of air brushing against her most private place, she was completely revealed.

He started to turn his head. This time Winona grabbed his head and kept him from looking. "You . . . you *zuzeca*!"

Clay tut-tutted. "Heard that one before. Running out of names?" He bent his left knee even more.

Winona gasped. That small movement was enough for him to be smack against her, his knee, her mound. The hair on his knee mingled with her woman's hair.

Flushing from embarrassment, Winona moaned, "Get off me. It is getting cold a-and I am hungry. You have f-food."

"I am hungry as well. But not for food." He lowered his head slightly.

Winona pushed at his head to keep him from coming any closer. Her gaze flickered from his eyes to his mouth. His lips parted. She closed her eyes, afraid. He was going to kiss her! What torment was this? Did he plan to take advantage of her? Rape her?

Scream, fight, she told herself. Instead she held her breath and waited.

Shove him, use your fist, the heel of your hand. Break his nose.

All her father's instructions for defense came to her. She lifted her hand, but instead of striking she traced the outline of his mouth with her fingers.

Full, soft, and parted. A very nice mouth when his lips weren't compressed with anger. Realizing that something was happening, something that could be more of a threat to her heart than her body, she slid her hands down to his shoulders.

"Please, Clay. I will come."

For just a moment Clay looked startled. Then he laughed, the first genuine laugh she'd heard from him. "Now that would be interesting," he said, grinning.

He was making fun of her and she had no idea why. She punched him in the shoulder. "You have to get off me first."

"No, I think it would be much more fun if we came together." Again he looked amused.

Winona frowned. Something had changed between them. The longer they touched, bantered, and stared at each other, the more she felt as though she were sinking deeper into the unknown.

"*Sunka*," she muttered, calling him a dog. Maybe if she made him angry again he'd get off her. He was too hot and the air too cold against parts of her. The mixture of sensations heightened her awareness of where they touched—and where they didn't.

She couldn't think with all the heat coursing through her body and the peculiar sensations settling deep into her belly, only to radiate outward and make her ache and throb in a place that had never felt the touch of another.

"Name calling is not very nice." He was still chuckling.

"Nor is forcing yourself on me," she shot back.

Clay looked amused. "I have not touched you—yet." He licked his lips. "But you touched me."

Embarrassed by the truth of his words and angry at her own weakness, Winona decided it was time to end the game—before something more happened. No, she corrected herself.

Nothing happened. He was just trying to prove he was bigger and stronger. And in control.

Well, she'd had enough. "You had your fun. Now let me up." To show she meant business she lifted her right foot and brought her knee toward her, then planted the sole of her foot against his hip to shove him aside.

Winona froze in horror.

Clay's laughter died just as fast.

Clay had shifted his body back at the same time. Now her foot lay smack against his manhood. His very hard manhood.

Clay sucked in a breath but his lungs refused to work, so he ended up choking instead. Winona's foot was pressing against the very part of him that longed for her touch.

She looked horrified. He felt . . . hard. The pressure of her foot, the slight twitching, had finished what their close positions and sexual bantering had started. Now it was his turn to swallow hard. Of all the . . .

Winona's eyes flashed: a brief warning. Moving quickly, he grabbed her calf with his hand just as she pulled back her foot to no doubt give him a swift kick. She struggled. Clay lifted her leg to keep her from doing any serious damage and rolled, holding her leg with his arm. Now she lay on her side with him half over her.

He groaned. Could he have made things worse? Judging from Winona's squeak of surprise, he didn't think so. His arm had slid between her legs and was now clamped between her thighs, against her soft, moist mound.

"You . . . weasel!" She tried to bite his arm.

Clay quickly pulled both his arms away and straightened his body and hers. But he didn't get off her. Now they were flush against each other. There was no point in trying to hide his erection, so he didn't.

"Do not push too far, *pohkeso*." Perhaps *kitten* was not the right word to describe his captive. *Wildcat* again seemed more fitting. All fierce spitting and clawing. No tears. No begging. Just defiance. Even in a position in which he could take advantage of her, she refused to panic.

She opened her mouth. Knowing she was about to spit another name at him, Night Shadow narrowed his eyes. "Do not. I have heard enough from you this day." He glared down at her. Though the light was fading fast, he had no trouble seeing the furious glint in her eyes. He was thankful that both her feet were pinned.

"If you do not wish to hear my opinion of you and your actions, then release me. And Spotted Deer."

"No."

"You have no honor. You are a coward. A—"

Night Shadow closed his mouth over hers in a fast, furious, hard kiss.

Startled, Winona was forced to bring her tirade to a halt. His lips took hers, moved over hers, and demanded a response. Hesitantly her mouth parted, and her lips opened and closed over his lower lip while he kissed her upper. Then he took her mouth into his. Submissive to his demands he kissed, suckled, and licked. When she gasped for air he moved to the corner of her mouth and used his tongue to lap and entice her to open wider.

Winona complied. Night Shadow, satisfied that he'd had the last word, decided to end the kiss. Maybe now she'd do as he ordered and stop with the names. His lips pulled away, but only to slant over hers and continue a gentle exploration.

Stop, he ordered himself. *You've proved your point.*

To his dismay, he couldn't stop. Instead he sank down onto his elbows so he could get closer, taste more of her.

Winona wrapped her arms around his neck, holding him hard against her. She moaned. Night Shadow opened his mouth wider and swallowed the sound, breathed it deep into his lungs and savored the sweetness. Beneath him her body softened, cushioning his. He felt himself sinking as if she were absorbing all of him into her.

He shifted upward, searching for a soft, warm bed for the throbbing length of him. Winona's legs parted slightly, allowing him to fall into the cradle of her pelvis. He basked in the feel of her soft, bare thighs against his. The knowledge that only his breechclout separated their bodies ignited the smoldering embers licking through his veins. Liquid fire gathered between his legs. Need for this woman consumed him and threatened to burn him alive.

He needed this. Needed her and wanted her with a wildness that left Night Shadow shaking.

"Sweet," he murmured, nibbling on her lower lip.

His left fingers tangled in long, silky-soft hair. "Soft."

She was gentle. Tender.

His. Only his. No one else would know this pleasure. Especially not—

No! He lifted his head. This woman was not his. Would never be his. She was a pawn. A tool to end his torment and suffering. Nothing more, nothing less. He rolled off her, got to his feet, and rested his hands on his knees while attempting to calm his heart and ease the tightness in his lungs. He felt as though he'd been punched in the gut. Knocked in the head.

What had started out as retaliation for her defiance had released emotions he'd thought long buried. The soft, loving part of him had died the day Jenny had been taken and his family killed. He'd been left for dead, and dead he'd remained.

He clenched his jaw. Gentleness would not get his sister back. Only by remaining focused and strong could he win. What had he been thinking to allow himself to be carried away?

Night Shadow repressed a shudder. He'd meant to teach this woman a lesson, and instead he'd freed something within him that was better off dead. Over the years he'd mated with women, usually widowed women, but not once had he lost control in this manner. Mating was a way to ease the tension from his body. It had never controlled him.

Night Shadow straightened. He had a mission, a quest, and nothing would sway him from making good on a promise he'd made while his life's blood had seeped from his wounds into the ground. He should have died, but sheer determination, the need to avenge the wrongs done to his family and hold his sister in his arms once more, had given him the will to live.

But the kiss shared with his captive, the verbal sparring, her innocence and courage had called forth a deep, aching need for the loving touch of a woman.

Night Shadow jumped to his feet and strode back to the fire he'd started. Impossible. What he felt for his captive was simply lust. Nothing more.

The dream started out the same. She was a child, darting through the trees. She heard her own laughter, and the laughter of someone behind her. Breaking into a small clearing, she saw her mother sitting in front of a tipi.

"Ina! Ina!"

She ran into her mother's outstretched arms. Though her mother was sad most of the time, she hugged her tight.

Suddenly there was noise. Lots of shouting. And screams. Her mother stood and shoved her away.

"Run," her ina cried. "Run."

But she didn't. She couldn't. Too much noise. Too much blood. It was everywhere. It even sprayed over her.

Then she saw the bear. He was covered in blood. He'd killed and now he was after her. But this bear wasn't fun. He didn't make her laugh. He frightened her. And he'd hurt her.

She ran as fast as her small legs could, but the bear grabbed her from behind. She screamed.

The dream changed abruptly. She was a grown woman now, walking alone in the woods. The child, where was the child?

Always the dream was the same. First the child, then the woman seeking the child. She shifted onto her side, curled into a ball, and tried to end the dream.

But it continued, followed its course, and held her mind captive. She walked toward a stream. Thirsty, she needed water.

Suddenly she was floating above the woman in her dreams. "No," *she cried out. She tried to wake up. She knew what was coming.*

Get away!

But the woman didn't hear her warning. As she dipped her hand into the stream a body floated toward her. The water turned red. The woman jumped back. Another body joined the first, then another. A cloud of death rose from the bloody stream and threatened to swallow her.

The woman woke with her hands held out from her body. She shook. Her heart pounded and she felt chilled to the bone. Tears ran down her cheeks and she sat, drawing her knees to her chest as she rocked back and forth. Just a dream. It was just a dream. She repeated those words over and over. It had felt so real. Real enough that she could still hear the screams, taste the fear, and see the blood. The blood had been everywhere.

She rubbed her forehead to ease the ache that usually followed the dream. As always, the dream left her shaking, sick, scared. No one knew of this dream. Not even her mother had known. She'd always been ashamed of this dream of death. She'd been well loved, so to dream of death made her feel as though she were betraying her parents' affection.

Even in the beginning of her dream she'd felt loved. And cherished. So why did the dream always end with blood and death? And why did she always wake feeling afraid? Why did she end up feeling so lonely and sick?

The young woman called forth memories of happier times to replace the nightmarish images, but no matter how many fond memories came to mind, she could not forget the sight of blood, shut out the screams, or still the pounding fear when she heard her mother's voice telling her to run.

Chapter Seven

Twilight seeped across a land imbued with shades of gray. Clouds, pale pewter and charcoal, painted the sky. Some were gilded with silver light, but all stormed across the sky like buffalo racing through the prairie.

Shadows from powerful trees faded and merged with pale rock formations that jutted from the earth like so many twisted, skeletal hands. Carpets of low-growing shrubs fought for footholds among the granite crags.

Standing on a high, rocky ridge, Hoka Luta scanned the rough land below. The acrid scent of the impending storm mingled with his blood and sharpened his senses. Outwardly he appeared calm. In control. But fury hovered just below the surface of that facade.

He wanted to roar. He wanted to curse the

heavens and scream, but he didn't dare. He worked his jaw, gathered the bitter taste of fear, and rolled it around his tongue. Instead of spitting his defiance for all to see, he swallowed.

Life was about control, and control meant power, and power was . . . everything. With power you could be who or what you wanted, do what you wanted, have what you wanted. Hoka Luta sneered at the land below and flexed his arms. He craved power. He deserved power, and anyone who stood in his way would be cut down.

Like Clay Blue Hawk.

Red, like the blood of his enemy, crept around his vision. He'd killed Clay Blue Hawk. Sliced him, and watched tiny rivers of blood flow into the earth. He'd seen the life fade from his eyes.

Anger hammered relentlessly at his temples. Control.

He used his emotions to gain whatever he needed or wanted. But right now, just as he had fourteen years ago, hatred threatened all he desired—and who he'd become.

Closing his eyes, he willed his emotions away and turned his mind to the facts. Clay Blue Hawk lived. How was that possible? It had to be a trick.

Lifting one hand, he relaxed his fingers and

118

stared at the knife he gripped so hard it left an imprint on his palm. The knife had once belonged to his father, until the old man had foolishly lost it in a game of cards to Clay Blue Hawk's father. As much as Hoka Luta wanted—and needed—to believe that this was a trick, the knife he held wouldn't allow it. The proof of Clay Blue Hawk's survival lay in his palm. His hand closed back over the smooth, cool handle. Clay Blue Hawk had lived and now he sought revenge.

Hoka Luta narrowed his eyes. How had his old enemy found him? Henry Black Bear of the Cheyenne was no more. Over the years he had taken on many names, lived with many tribes, until becoming Hoka Luta, long-lost son of a powerful Sioux medicine man.

He'd made a new life for himself. He was respected. Feared. And powerful.

As he glared down from his lofty height, a tremor rumbled through him. Clay Blue Hawk would soon know of his power. Holding the knife high, Hoka Luta ran his finger over the sharp edge, drawing a bead of blood.

Clay Blue Hawk would regret taking his woman, and he'd regret living when he should have died. Hoka Luta flung the knife down into the rocky soil and threw his head back.

"I offer my blood to the spirits and ask that

they lead us to the enemy." The blood dripped from his finger. Slowly he drew his bleeding finger down his chest, anointing himself with his own blood.

"I will spill the blood of my enemy and wear it so that all will know of my power," he whispered.

Behind him, Hawk Eyes and his warriors paced, anxious to be off but not daring to interrupt him.

Power.

The knowledge that Winona's father was anxious, that he yearned to resume tracking the enemy, gave Hoka Luta even more power.

Power was being in control. No one dared to interrupt him. Not even the chief. Hoka Luta was in control. Pleased, he turned, satisfied to see everyone waiting and watching him.

Golden Eagle came forward. "The horses are rested and ready to go."

Hoka Luta heard the impatience in his voice. The man's frustration at the delay was another sign of his power. Only because Hoka Luta was a medicine man, and only because he said he needed to ask the spirits to guide them, had they stopped this long.

He wanted to let Clay Blue Hawk get a bit farther ahead. The one thing Hoka Luta could not allow was for Winona's family to find his old enemy. Clay Blue Hawk would reveal the past. And if Winona learned the truth?

No, he'd not think that far ahead. Instead he silently met Golden Eagle's anxious eyes. The man standing in front of him would one day become powerful. By marrying the man's sister, more power would be within Hoka Luta's reach.

It wasn't the position of chief he desired. No, that carried with it too much responsibility and risk. The real power came from being a medicine man. Everyone sought the wisdom of the medicine man. They listened and obeyed.

He allowed his gaze to sweep over the gathered warriors and restless pacing of their chief. Power. None would dare rush him, not Golden Eagle and not the chief. He turned back to the ridge and the long drop below.

Letting his hands fall to his sides, he shook his wrists. Bear claws and teeth rattled as he closed his eyes and tipped his chin to the stormy sky. "Our enemy toys with us. He leaves messages, but hides. He taunts us with blood on my bride's dress, and locks of her hair. He draws us farther from our people; he is a coward."

Those messages from Clay Blue Hawk worried Hoka Luta. The knife and drawings were something no one understood but him. What other items from the past did his enemy hold? Hoka Luta could not afford to let the others find evidence that might give away his secrets.

He paused. Silence hovered like a heavy shroud, but he felt the agreement of the warriors behind him. He knew people. He had studied them and knew how to manipulate them. Lifting his hands overhead with practiced grace, he swept them forward, bent down, and brushed his fingertips over the ground. He then stood abruptly, his arms shooting straight up, fingers stabbing the heavens.

"I see many lakes, streams, and caves in this land. There are dark forests, many places for the enemy to hide and watch. He leads us. We must not be drawn into his trap."

He paused, then turned slowly. Staring at the chief, he dropped his hands once again to his sides. "We must separate."

Hawk Eyes stepped forward. Hoka Luta stopped his protest with a single look.

Power.

"One can travel faster and unseen. A group as large as ours cannot move as the wind. I will go ahead and mark the trail. I will watch our enemy show himself and take him captive. He will not know I am there."

"If you are spotted he may kill my daughters."

He leveled a calm, knowing stare at the chief. "As one man, I can move unseen. I can steal back your daughters, and when I have them safe, you can attack. Do not forget, the others may be with him or riding to meet him." He slyly reminded the chief that the other three trails had disappeared, that his warriors had failed.

When they'd found the piece of bloodied dress, they'd also discovered that the group had separated. Two of the horses appeared to carry the weight of two. Each had gone in a separate direction. Hawk Eyes had noted toe scuffs in the dirt near that last message and had proclaimed that to be a sign from his daughter.

Golden Eagle nodded thoughtfully. "They will come back together, and for that reason I say we stay together." He looked to his father.

Hoka Luta let his head fall back. As expected, silence fell once again.

Power. It hummed through him.

He waited, holding himself completely still. Then he began to sway ever so slightly, chanting and thanking *Tate*, the spirit of the wind, for his counsel. Bending at the waist, he picked up a small, flat stone and threw it up into the treetops to his left. Three crows launched themselves skyward. Two flew downward, away from the ridge. One flew to the west.

"Behold," he said. He fell silent as they watched the birds fly out of sight. He kept the satisfaction from his features. He'd heard the birds earlier and had taken a chance. Had the birds each flown in a different direction he'd have simply used it to fit his needs. Had they all flown as one in one direction, he would have had to give in to the son.

Power. Manipulation. Knowing the world and how it worked and using it to his own advantage . . .

Hawk Eyes nodded. "The spirits speak. One crow goes alone. We will follow. Leave us signs so we may follow more swiftly."

Hoka Luta squared his shoulders. "I will go on foot so I can move unseen, and silent as the wind. Perhaps the horses could use a longer rest. That will allow me to get ahead."

This time he received no protests.

Keeping his stride even, he walked through the parting warriors, retrieved what he needed from his horse, and headed out.

But as soon as he was alone, fury threatened to overrule the tight control he'd maintained for the last few days. Every muscle strained with the need to run and find Clay Blue Hawk. Trees and shrubs surrounded him. All was quiet, but he was not fooled. His old enemy was out there somewhere.

124

Fighting the urge to scream and shout for his enemy to show himself, Hoka Luta examined the ground, moving slowly so as not to miss any sign.

By nightfall he'd found a lock of hair twisted into a bundle. Like the other two messages, this was meant to be found. The trail was just hard enough to follow to require slow going. Hoka Luta walked long into the night.

When he finally stopped he pulled his father's old knife from the leather sheath he'd tucked it into. He didn't think about the man who'd sired him. He was dead—killed by Clay Blue Hawk's father, but dead to him before that. He'd been weak, controlled by the whiskey he craved.

Power vibrated through him, cloaked him, lived within and around him. As he stared at the gleaming blade, the remaining anger drained. He would triumph in the end.

Embers scattered and popped when Winona poked at the fire with a twig. Across from her, Clay broke the stick he'd used to cook his fish, then tossed the pieces onto the fire. The flames quickly consumed the offering.

She didn't speak. Neither did Clay. Not a single word had passed between them since that kiss. Winona jabbed her stick's burning tip into the dirt. She refused to think about the kiss. And she absolutely would not think of the intimate feel of him against her. She stared into the fire. Where was her father? How was her mother doing?

Hoka Luta must be worried as well, and angry. He'd be searching for her along with her father and brother, ready to avenge the wrong done to her. Leaning back against the boulder, she wondered how Spotted Deer was handling all this. She was alone and had to be scared. Thanks to Clay.

But remembering his nightmare, she knew he'd suffered in his past. Who was Jenny? Was she the reason behind all this suffering?

Did it matter?

All that mattered was getting herself and Spotted Deer safely back home. She sighed. Home for her wasn't the same. She'd arrive back home just to leave it again to begin a new life with Hoka Luta.

Winona peered out into the night. Above them, a stone ledge provided cover. Clay had found an alcove, not deep enough to be considered a cave, but sheltered enough to protect them from the storm that was sure to break soon. Of course, Winona felt as though she'd fought a storm already. Her reaction to that kiss with Clay confused and angered her.

She'd enjoyed it! She sent Clay a dark look. Had he ensnared her with some sort of magic? Was she losing her mind? She only knew she should not have savored it and definitely should not have wanted him to continue after he'd stopped. What was wrong with her?

Her gaze settled on the fire's twisting flames. Yellows merged with reds and formed new shades. Each color rose and fell to the beat of its own rhythm, like a man and woman dancing to something special that only they shared.

No. No. No. Think of something else. She was not attracted to a man who was her enemy. A man who'd taken her from her family.

But what had been taken from him? Who had been taken from him?

Winona recalled his cries, the pain in his voice, and the wildness and grief in his eyes when he'd woken.

Give her back.

Don't touch her.

Bastard.

Yes, someone had hurt him. Badly. The wound on his face had healed. Not so the one in his heart and mind.

Disgusted with herself for caring, she tried to concentrate on Hoka Luta. But thoughts of him only served to remind her that Clay had ruined her wedding day. If not for him she'd have danced the mating dance and taken the first step toward forging a deep bond with her mate.

Clay had ruined it.

She broke her stick in half. Clay had taken something irreplaceable from her. Even if Hoka Luta rode in right now, rescued her, and married her, their first night together would forever be marred by Clay. Like a thorn embedded deep in the flesh, he'd intruded into all their lives.

Until now, Hoka Luta had been the only man to kiss her, to touch her in an intimate manner. She'd had no doubt that he wanted to mate with her—she'd felt his desire. Winona closed her eyes and remembered Hoka Luta's kiss, the feel of his mouth claiming and controlling hers.

He'd touched her breast, his hand hard and possessive, and when he'd pressed his manhood into her belly, he'd been hard. Like Clay. But unlike with Clay, she couldn't remember how she'd felt, whether his touch had heated her blood or left her weak with a bewildering need.

All she could recall was being thrilled that Hoka Luta wanted her. And nervous. He was so big and strong. In his arms she'd felt as though he could have smothered her. She'd figured it had to be due to the fact that a woman's first time with a man was said to hurt.

Guilt pounded in her head. She hadn't felt like that in Clay's embrace, and that upset her. She should have been frightened. Opening her eyes, she stared at Clay. His lips had been firm, but gentle. His body had been hard, but warm and comforting.

His size and strength had made her feel safe and secure, even though he'd been angry. And Clay's hard manhood against her, separated from her skin only by his breechclout, made her long to know the pleasure of mating. She hadn't feared pain.

Irritated that she couldn't stop thinking about Clay, she glared at him. He wasn't paying attention to her. It was as though she wasn't even there.

She picked up a small pebble and tossed it into the fire. He didn't blink. She didn't like being ignored, especially since he'd forced her to come to the fire. She wanted answers. He'd disrupted her life, and that of her entire tribe, and she had the right to know why.

Her mouth puckered with annoyance. All during the meal she'd tried to goad him into revealing what she wanted to know. He'd ignored her. No matter what she'd said, what names she'd used against him, he'd kept his silence, and that frightened her more than if he'd yelled and threatened her.

Watching the shadows play across his features, Winona tossed the sticks into the fire and helped the flames resume their dance.

Again Clay didn't flinch at the popping, or back away from the sudden flare of heat. He was still lost in the fire. What did he see? The past? Did he see that the flames seemed to be mating, see how they became one?

She closed her eyes. This was silly. She'd sat before countless fires and not once had she thought these sorts of thoughts. Not even when she had sat across the fire from Hoka Luta the night he'd arrived.

With the red paint Hoka Luta wore, the flames of the fire had made him seem darker. Larger. Fierce. He didn't give orders verbally. A look was all that was needed to send his warriors running to do his bidding. He'd even commanded her with his eyes, sending her a look of reproach when he'd caught her staring at him. Shamed, she'd immediately cast her gaze downward.

Drawing her knees to her chest, Winona rested her chin on her fists. She hadn't liked the way he'd made her feel that night. Her mother often watched her father, and White Wind seldom took her eyes off her husband. But Winona told herself that Hoka Luta was right. As the son of a medicine man, he deserved higher respect.

Besides, he was everything she wanted in a mate. He would take care of her, provide for her, give her children. He'd teach her how to be the perfect wife, and she'd make him proud of her as they walked together through life.

She frowned as she thought of something else. During their supervised walk the night he'd arrived, he'd spoken sharply to her when she'd walked at a slightly faster pace in her excitement.

At the time she'd dismissed his curtness. But now it bothered her. She shivered and rubbed her temple. What was wrong with her? When the tribe traveled, men always walked ahead of women. They had the weapons. Their job was to protect their family.

But there had been no reason for her to walk slightly behind him that night. Couples always strolled shoulder-to-shoulder. Frustrated, she tried to clear her mind. Captivity had to be responsible for the confusion circling in her head. She needed to subdue her inner voice—perhaps a verbal battle with Clay would do the trick.

She cleared her throat. He didn't respond. Didn't even seem aware of her presence. Dropping her arms to circle her shins, she leaned forward, trying to see his expression, but the shadows hid his thoughts from her.

What was he thinking? What was he feeling?

The questions raced through her mind, were on the tip of her tongue, but she bit them back. He was the enemy. She didn't care what he thought or felt.

Deep lines etched his face and spoke of suffering—in the past, as well as right now. He looked lost, alone, even hurt, and she wanted to know what had happened.

Seeing him like this made him seem human. Gone was the cold control. Sitting across from her was a man who felt deeply. Who'd been hurt deeply.

A cold breeze stirred the air and blew bits of debris into their shelter. She shivered. Since Clay's nightmare she'd spent a lot of time wondering what had happened to him in the past. If she knew why he sought revenge then perhaps there was something she could do to help resolve this situation and free herself and Spotted Deer.

Judging from his dream, it had to do with a woman named Jenny. Jenny had been taken from him. Had she been killed, and if so, by whom? Hoka Luta, or a member of his family?

She thought of her father. If someone hurt or killed his wife, he'd take whatever actions necessary against the enemy. So who was Jenny? Clay's wife? If so, what had happened to her? Winona knew the answer would not be good.

She drew the tip of her finger along the surface of the ground, making snake trails in the loose dirt. The fire began to die and the air grew colder as the wind picked up. She smelled rain. Shadows closed around them. She brushed off her finger and tugged her dress tightly over her legs for warmth.

Glancing to the side she saw the bedding. She should take it and get some rest. Clay wouldn't bother her. Each night he slept on the hard ground in just his shirt and leggings. But for some unknown reason Winona couldn't leave him lost and alone in the past.

So she sat. The night grew darker. Wind howled through the trees, and a flash of lightning lit the sky and illuminated their shelter. Clay lifted his eyes from the dying fire. Winona caught her breath. There was no life in his gaze. No soul mirrored there. Thunder boomed overhead.

He'd said he had no heart. She hadn't believed him. His demand earlier that she come to the fire proved that he was aware of her, her movements, and that he didn't wish any harm to her. And there was that kiss, and the life that had pulsed through him. No, he had a heart. He felt.

What he lacked was a soul.

The wind whipped around them. Still, Clay didn't move.

133

Standing, she retrieved the bedding. Taking one fur, she draped it around Clay's shoulders, then took her place across from him, wrapping the blanket around her shoulders.

He looked surprised. His eyes narrowed but he didn't speak.

Winona shrugged. "If you die, then we will not meet up with your warriors, and I will never see my sister again."

Clay stared at the stone wall behind her. "I have walked through death's door but escaped before it slammed shut." His voice sounded far away.

Surprised that he'd spoken, and of something so telling, Winona had no trouble believing him. Something had destroyed the man inside.

Earlier he'd smiled and laughed during their banter. She still didn't understand what she'd said to bring it out. She lifted her brows. She'd forgotten about that.

I have no heart.

I have walked through death's door but escaped before it slammed shut.

Could a man with no soul laugh and find amusement in something so simple as words? She frowned into the embers. Clay felt pain, and for a man to feel pain, he had to be alive.

There was life in him, somewhere deep in his soul.

Sneaking a look at him, she saw only emptiness. Something tugged at her. Pity? Yes, she felt sorry for him. That realization drew another frown. She didn't want to feel anything for him. He was using her to gain revenge. He'd denied her a maiden's greatest desire—a loving husband—and then had used the sister of her heart to gain her compliance.

He'd taken her away from everyone and everything that she knew and loved. Why should she care whether he truly lived or not? She sighed softly. There was no reason, no reason at all why she should care, but she did.

Rubbing her forehead, she tried to tell herself that she was just tired and confused. Clay was the enemy. Her father would kill him. Hoka Luta would kill him. He might not be dead as he claimed, but as soon as she was found, he would be.

Staring out into the night, she watched streaks of light explode across the heavens. If she had not left camp to go to Gray Rock none of this would have happened.

She slowly sat up straight. The rock. Her vision. In her mind's eye she saw again the vision of the *igmuwatogla*. Until now she'd forgotten about the vision. What did it mean? Had it been a warning?

She pulled from her memory every story

she'd heard about mountain lions. Some believed they were bad signs; others believed they were good. Signs of power.

She grimaced. Like the cat, she hadn't cowered, or given in to fear. Remembering her daring name calling, she admitted to herself that like *igmuwatogla*, she struck quickly and strongly, taking advantage of every opportunity to attack without showing weakness.

Her eyes glazed with exhaustion. She should rest, but her mind raced. The vision had meaning. Everything had meaning. What was it she needed to know? She closed her eyes and kept the image of the large cat firmly in mind.

The animal took advantage of a prey's weakness. Its favorite prey was deer. Winona's shoulders slumped. Spotted Deer was as gentle as the animal she was named after. And innocent. Well, mostly innocent, she thought, remembering their rather embarrassing encounter with Lone Shield.

Weakness. She opened her eyes and stared at Clay. His weakness lay in his torment. In the dead part of him. She could strike there. She dropped her head back onto her knees. No, she couldn't do it.

It wasn't in her to deliberately hurt someone, especially someone who'd suffered to the point where he felt dead inside. Winona lifted her head and sighed loudly. Clay glanced up at her. His features were shadowed but the soft glow of the embers softened his features and made his eyes seem warm.

In that moment Winona knew what she had to do. She had to teach him to live. To feel. To laugh. To feel the joy along with the pain. Life was a circle. Without pain there was no life. Without joy there was only sadness. Without love there could be only hate.

The spirits had given her the power of the cat to stand up against him and defend herself verbally, and even attack him to the point where he lost control.

They'd given her the power to make him laugh, which meant she had the power to make him feel. If he felt, he lived.

Igmuwatogla was power, being assertive but also knowing when to wield that power with a gentle hand. Clay needed to feel and to find his soul so that the circle of life would resume.

Could she do it? The past was the secret. Jenny was the key, but to use that weapon meant causing him more pain. Shifting, Winona prepared herself. Any woman or man knew that sometimes a wound had to be cut open to release the bad spirits.

Tucking her legs to the side she picked up another rock, this one the size of her fist. She braced herself mentally before she tossed the stone onto the fire. A shower of sparks flew up and outward, jerking Clay from his own world. He sent her an angry glare.

She ignored it and asked, "Who is Jenny? What happened to her, to you, that you no longer live?"

Chapter Eight

Night Shadow flinched. The sound of his sister's name was as painful and damaging as an arrow wound. Pain crashed through him. He tossed a handful of dirt onto the fire, then stood.

"I suggest you rest." He walked away. Around him the wind whipped into a frenzy.

"Coward."

He whirled around and stalked over to where Winona stood, arms crossed in front of her like a shield against his fury.

"You know not of what you speak. Do not interfere in matters that do not concern you."

Winona tipped her chin. With the dying fire behind him, he couldn't see her expression in the darkness.

"As I am here, and not wed to the man I love, it is my affair."

Sneering down at her, Night Shadow advanced. Above, another clap of thunder rolled across the heavens. The air seemed to grow thick, making it harder to breathe.

"The man you profess to love is my enemy." He fingered his scar. "Death was his gift to me."

A brief flash of light seared the heavens. "You did not die."

Inside him, Night Shadow fought a storm much more powerful than the one overhead.

"Wrong. I died here." He stabbed his finger at his chest. So many times he'd wished he'd died. The pain of losing his family and hearing his sister's screams had been too much to bear.

He'd wanted to die, but Jenny's screams had kept him in this world, a prisoner of his past. Even now the echo of that time drummed inside his head. It grew louder, insistent. He did not want to remember; didn't think he could survive if he had to relive it yet another time. But whenever he slept, he relived it. And died a bit more each day.

Winona's voice, firm with conviction, shot out of the dark—a thunderbolt of sizzling power that beat the shadows back. "You are not dead inside. You feel."

Night Shadow grabbed onto his fury like a drowning man. He took another step forward and towered over the woman who in such a short amount of time had managed to break through so many barriers.

He'd hated before, but had been able to bury the pain. She'd released it, and it was more than he could bear; the darkness of it threatened to swallow and destroy him.

That she affected him so violently made him hate her. Made him hate himself, and the entire world, even more. He grabbed Winona's hand and slapped her palm against his scared face.

"I *hate*. I seek revenge. If that is life, then I live." He released her hand, expecting her to flee in fear.

She didn't. Her palm slid down the side of his face slowly, stopping to cup his jaw. "And what about Jenny?" she asked.

Night Shadow jerked back as though struck.

She stepped forward, her voice soothing and compelling. "Clay, tell me. I want to know."

Another flash from above revealed the sadness in Winona's eyes. A cry rose from deep inside Night Shadow. Hate and anger he could handle. But he couldn't bear pity, didn't deserve the compassion he saw deep in her eyes.

"You would do better to fear me instead of angering me." He spun around and strode away. He could not admit to himself that she was right. He'd spent his life running from his past—from the knowledge that he'd dared to survive when everyone else but Jenny had died.

Winona ran after him. "Hoka Luta will come and bring with him many warriors. It is you who should feel fear."

At the sound of his enemy's name, white-hot pain shot down the side of his face. He grabbed his head with his hands. "Jenny was—is—my sister," he bit out. Bitterness choked his throat.

"Clay—"

The past exploded inside his head. Blood. Death. Screams.

"No!" he shouted. "No more. God, no more," he moaned.

He couldn't take much more, yet he couldn't let the past go. More than anything he feared forgetting. So he welcomed the darkness in his heart and soul. He used his memories to feed the hate. As long as he hated, he was driven to find his sister and kill his enemy.

But at that moment, for just a moment, he desperately needed to feel something—anything—else. Reaching out blindly, Night Shadow pulled Winona hard against him.

The wind whistled around them. It howled, calling to the thunder. Bolts of lightning cracked and shattered the dark sky—and Winona's last vestiges of guilt for her desire to help Clay. Hoka Luta was his enemy. What had he done to Clay? Or to Jenny, Clay's sister? She needed to know, but she couldn't fight or even protest when Clay's lips crashed down over hers with the same intensity of the mountain storm.

His chest heaved and his fingers bit into her upper arms as his breath came in ragged gulps that sounded more like sobs. Winona couldn't struggle. The agony in his voice stabbed her, held her immobile. She'd never seen or felt such emotion, such need.

Something inside her needed to help this man who was her enemy. He didn't care that he'd die for taking her. He thought himself dead already. She knew better.

The passion in his kiss, whether from hate or fear or need, spoke of life. And she responded by matching his movements, his intensity, his emotion. He needed; she gave. He hurt; she soothed. He moaned; she whispered softly.

The clouds burst open. Rain beat down on them, and her legs trembled. Winona slid her arms around Clay's neck, fearing she'd fall and be washed away on the tide of the storm.

"Oh, God," Clay whispered. He turned his head, scraping the side of his face against hers.

"Run," he ordered. "Go."

Winona turned his head back to hers and found his mouth. She should go. But she

couldn't. She was needed. Clay needed her and
she needed to learn the truth. Though the past
had nothing to do with her, her path had
crossed Hoka Luta's and now this man's. Her
belief in the circle of life, and that she was here
with Clay for a reason, kept her where she was.

"No." She pressed her mouth against the corner of his. She didn't understand what was happening. She only knew that she was bound to
him tighter than with any rope, tighter than any
threat.

She needed to see him smile, hear him laugh.
She had to find out what had happened to him
and try to put it right. She could do this. Surely
this was the message behind her vision. When
threatened by the enemy, mountain lions at-
tacked the most vulnerable place on their victim. Clay's was his past. Jenny. His sister.

She could drive him over the edge with her
newfound knowledge, but in her heart she
knew the spirits wanted her to use her power
over him to heal his pain, to end all this before
he died. Power ripped through her.

"I will not run," she whispered, gripping her
slick arms tightly around his neck to keep him
from wrenching free. "Do not run from me."
She licked the rain from the corner of his
mouth. It tasted salty.

"You are a fool." Night Shadow groaned, but

he didn't shove her away. He slanted his mouth back over hers, then forced her mouth open and thrust his tongue inside.

Sensation struck deep inside Winona's belly. With each thrust of his tongue, an inner ache rose from between her legs. It radiated outward, stretching even to her toes.

Clay's mouth commanded hers. His tongue taught hers what to do, his lips guided, showing, then waiting for her to follow his lead.

Withdrawing his tongue, he kissed her again. He had no need for words. Winona knew what he wanted and complied—eagerly. She needed to taste him, feel him, claim him as he'd claimed her. She plunged deep inside but his tongue evaded hers.

Frustrated, she sought and demanded that he allow her to do all to him that he'd done to her. She nibbled his lip, ran her tongue along the outside of his mouth.

Desire snaked up from her center. Her breasts ached. Her throat clogged with emotion. She moaned and leaned deeper into him. His hands roamed her back, slid down, and cupped her buttocks. He brought her hard against him.

She moaned and finally captured his tongue. She reveled in the feel of his mouth: the roughness of his tongue, the smoothness of his teeth.

Lost in a cloak of heat and aching need, Winona felt as though the cold and rain didn't matter. Clay was no longer the enemy. All that mattered was this: the heady feel and taste of him and the way her body responded to his roaming hands.

When he urged her closer and pulled her up onto her toes, she gladly rose up. His hands dropped to the backs of her thighs, and with little effort he lifted her and thrust hard against her.

Winona cried out and dropped her head back. Clay ran his lips down her throat. Winona wrapped her legs around his waist, but it wasn't enough. Something tightened inside and threatened to burst.

She'd never felt this strange need. She had to be closer to Clay's pulsing hardness. She felt his throbbing need, felt his heat through the cloth separating them. But it only teased and tormented. She needed to feel his flesh against hers.

"Clay," she begged.

Night Shadow froze. Clay was dead. He was Night Shadow. He lived in the dark shadows of life. He'd spent almost half of his lifetime searching for his enemy—a man who'd once been like a brother to him. Nothing could be allowed to come between him and revenge. Not even this woman.

But his hands moved up and gripped her tighter instead of pushing her away. His mouth held hers, fed off hers. He took from her all that she offered and more. Each time she pulled her hips away he pulled her back and stroked her hard with his erection.

And with each stroke and her moan in his ear, he felt a little more of the warrior fade and Clay, the man who needed light and love, take over. He'd denied himself all need, had punished himself for fourteen years by refusing to enjoy or take what life offered. Until he found Jenny and killed Hoka Luta he didn't dare walk in the light. Once he did, he might never face the past, the darkness, his enemy.

He tried to stop, but like the storm he was out of control. He stumbled to the closest tree, tore his breechclout to the side, and thrust hard against her. Winona shuddered and gripped him harder with her legs. Over and over he slid against her slick mound.

"Can't stop," he murmured. He didn't want to cause her pain. He tried to find his release outside, but her heat beckoned and tempted him more than he thought it possible to resist.

"Do not s-stop." Winona gasped as he moved her hips faster.

Her passion, her need, drove him deep inside her. Winona cried out, dropping her head to his shoulder and biting him through his shirt. He leaned his head back and tried to pull out, but her slick warmth held him captive.

Winona lifted her head. "Hurt," she whispered.

Clay, the man lost in the arms of a woman he'd taken violently, shuddered and pulled his hips from the cradle of hers. To his surprise— and his downfall—Winona refused to release him. Her legs tightened, her sheath convulsed, and he felt on the edge of going over.

"I ache. Make it go away." She sobbed as she rotated her hips against his pelvis.

The realization that the pain she spoke of came from desire nearly sent him over the edge. He pulled out, then drove back inside. Slowly. Carefully. He tasted her tears, felt her shudder, and felt guilt and shame war with selfish and desperate need.

Then they were rocking hard against each other, fast and demanding. He thrust hard and deep and felt her convulse around him. Her cry mingled with his, loud in the sudden silence as the storm left as fast as it had arrived.

Chapter Nine

Winona tucked her head into the hollow of Clay's neck. Each breath was a soft gasp, as if she'd just run wild across the prairie. Small spasms continued to rock her insides, and her heart thudded against her ribs. She'd had no idea mating was so wild and primitive. She'd feared when her time came that she wouldn't know what to do. She smiled softly. Her body had known exactly what to do.

In her ear she heard Clay's ragged breathing, felt the warm air leave his lips and slide down her neck. His hands still cupped her buttocks and held her tight against him. It felt so good. She wanted to say so but was afraid to move or speak. How did a woman act after mating with a man she barely knew—one who wasn't her husband? One who was the enemy?

Slowly, as her body calmed, she became aware of the stark silence—and the wary stillness radiating from Clay. Instinctively Winona knew things had changed between them. Neither spoke, but slowly she felt herself slipping from his grip until she stood on the ground.

Above his head, the bright lights of the stars and moon had reclaimed the night sky. Clay's eyes were clouded. "Damn you," he whispered. He stepped back from her. He looked vulnerable. Stricken.

Winona smoothed her dress back down and gripped the soft deerskin between her fingers to steel herself for whatever came next. Emotionally, she was spent. Physically, she felt alive as never before. The air, crisp and fresh from the storm, cleared her mind and cooled her body.

"Clay," she began.

"Clay is dead," he bit out harshly, then turned and strode away from her.

Winona shook her head as she followed him. "A dead man does not feel—the good or the bad. He is lifeless. You felt pleasure. You gave pleasure. Whatever you say, you cannot deny the truth."

Clay ignored her.

"A dead man does not run. Only a man who feels, or fears, runs." She spoke softly.

"A dead man uses people without regard." He turned his head. "As I used you."

Winona narrowed her eyes. They stopped at the edge of the small stream they'd been following. "You did not use me."

"You know nothing of the ways of men." He waded into the cold water.

"That is not true," she said. Her gaze lingered on the wide expanse of Clay's broad back. Moonlight bounced off the water, cascading over his shoulders and down his broad back.

"Not now. Not after... after that." She wasn't sure what to call it. *Mating* seemed cold and impersonal, and what she'd felt was definitely personal. Very personal and pleasurable. "You needed me."

Clay slid into the water. Unsure of what to do, or whether to join him in the water to clean herself, Winona waited. When he resurfaced, he lifted a brow when he saw her watching.

"I needed your body. Any woman would have done," he said, his voice dripping contempt. "You are a tool of revenge. The man you think to marry took something precious from me. I did the same, and if you are foolish enough to marry him if he somehow survives, then he will know I had you first." Clay strode from the stream.

Winona sucked in her breath. "You lie," she

whispered. She'd felt his passion, his need, his anguish. He could not have taken her so coldly, like an animal driven by primitive need—or a man consumed by hate.

Clay waded out of the water. "It does not matter. The end result is the same."

Winona stumbled back, reeling as though he'd punched her. Her lungs demanded air but she couldn't breathe. Tears blurred her vision. She'd given Clay something she'd given no other man. What she'd felt, shared with him, had been beautiful. How could he destroy it—her—like this?

"I was wrong," she choked. "You are dead inside." She whirled and ran. It didn't matter where, just so long as it was away from him—and a betrayal that left her feeling as though he'd crushed her very soul.

Night Shadow's gaze followed Winona's flight. Maybe now she'd leave him alone. How many times did he have to warn her off topics best left alone? He'd given her plenty of warning, so if she got hurt it was her own damn fault. He was dead inside. He lived for one purpose only.

Swiping his clothing from the shrub where he'd tossed it, he stormed away from the river.

He stopped inside the shelter. The fire had all but died. Bunching his buckskin shirt in his hands, he glared at the garment. He was cold. Tired. And ashamed of his actions.

"Hell," he ground out. It didn't surprise him that he'd cursed in his father's language, so he repeated the curse, adding several other colorful words he remembered.

Ever since he'd spoken his childhood name, a name he'd not breathed aloud in so many years, his past had begun to take over his thoughts. He was even thinking in English now—a habit that had taken many years to break.

His father, an American trapper, had insisted that all his children speak English around him. Only when he and his siblings were alone with their mother or visiting her people had they been allowed to speak *tsehese-nestsestotse*, the language of the Cheyenne.

Faint images of his childhood emerged from the shadows of his mind. Night Shadow always kept the past buried. It did no good to remember what he'd lost.

He even blocked that nightmarish day from his thoughts, focusing on his only reasons for living—revenge and finding Jenny.

But Night Shadow was losing the battle with Clay Coburn, a boy proudly named after his father. For the first time that he could remember, the boy he'd been threatened to step out of the past and bring with him memories of a happy time.

Laughter from the past echoed through his head. He closed his eyes and clenched his fists and jaw. It hurt to remember, but he was too tired and drained to fight the love and laughter that he'd grown up with. He'd been loved and happy until Henry Black Bear's father killed Clayton Coburn.

Pain exploded in Night Shadow's temple and traveled down along the path of his scar. "No!" he roared, smacking his fist on the shelter's granite wall. He'd lost so much. Damn it, he wanted it back.

"The past is dead and you died with it," he whispered hoarsely. "You are Night Shadow. Clay Blue Hawk is dead."

There was just enough left of the fire to cast a soft glow over the shelter's rugged walls. He moved over to a pile of twigs and tossed a handful onto the fire. A long shadow jumped from the fire onto the walls. Though he remained still, the dark figure danced and writhed.

Shadows existed not in the light nor in the dark, but somewhere between. There were no colors in that existence. No life. No sound. No emotions, just a flat, spiritless existence. He was a shadow, a man hollowed by grief. Clay's body lived, but his heart and soul had been destroyed. It was Night Shadow who walked and talked, and it would be Night Shadow who'd avenge the deaths of his family and find Jenny.

But who was he at that moment? Was he Night Shadow, fearless warrior, or Clay Blue Hawk, a tormented man who now feared himself more than he feared anything or anyone?

Night Shadow would never have lost control of the situation with his captive. Night Shadow had no trouble relegating Clay to the deepest, darkest recess inside his shriveled and dead heart.

Furious with the confusion and inner turmoil roiling through him, Night Shadow dressed and gathered his skin of water, pouch of food, and fur blankets. Though he'd planned to spend the night and give his horse a much-needed rest, he'd changed his mind. He reached for his weapons. He needed to keep moving.

Running away again?

He dropped everything and whirled around, thinking Winona had come back to taunt him. But he was alone with only his doubts to trouble him.

"Damn her," he spat. He was not running. He was pursuing an enemy and searching for a sister. He was Night Shadow: a survivor, not a coward. Stepping over his belongings, he stalked down to the riverbed and followed a narrow trail along the edge.

Like that of the deer, which made and followed the same route to the river each day, his path was set. All he had to do was stay on that narrow trail and not let anything—or anyone—cause him to stray.

And should he choose to remain on the edge where it was dark, lifeless, and lonely, that was his choice. A small sound penetrated his thoughts. He stopped, his sharp gaze locating the source. Down in the water just ahead he saw a dark shadow near the edge of the glittering bank.

His gut clenched against the sound of his captive's soft sobs. The sound held him frozen. He couldn't move. Not even to run. From deep inside his mind her cries released other cries. Screams begging for him to save them. Cries of pain and fear.

His legs wobbled, nearly sending him to his knees. His reaction made him afraid that he was losing his mind. He feared for his sanity should Clay rise and overpower the warrior.

As Clay, he'd nearly been driven mad by the dreams and memories. Night Shadow had saved him. Now, for the first time, Clay had risen. He was strong, and he wanted to live.

Clay desperately called back the harsh warrior who was fearless and willing to do whatever it took to find Jenny and kill Henry Black Bear. The tears of a woman would not stop him, or give life to a man who had no life to live.

And yet two long strides carried him down to where Winona sat in the cold, shallow water with her knees drawn up to her chest. He froze. Rays of silvery light washed over her, revealing curving bare skin. Though he'd touched her, been consumed by her, he had yet to see her without her clothing.

His gaze traveled down the line of her spine. Water lapped at her buttocks. Remembering the feel of those soft, rounded handfuls of flesh made him swallow hard.

His fingers had gripped her, urged her hard against him. He'd dug his fingers into that curved softness as he thrust hard into her, and had held her while spasms rocked them both out of control.

"He'kotoo'estse!" he ordered. *Be quiet. Please*, he begged himself, afraid of losing control.

Winona's sobs didn't stop, though they were now muffled, as though she'd covered her mouth with her hand. That made him feel worse. Guilt spread through him. Glaring down at the top of Winona's bent head, he reminded himself that this was war. Sometimes the innocent got hurt.

But he'd never intended for Winona to get hurt. That was why he'd separated her from her friend—he hadn't wanted to use force to keep her under control. And still he'd hurt her in a way he'd never envisioned. Night Shadow tried to blame her for pushing him beyond his limits, but he couldn't. He and he alone was responsible for his actions.

"Nehetaa'e." He softened his voice but was at a loss as to what else to say or do. How did one stop a crying woman? He saw her shivering and knew he had to get her back to the fire.

He repeated his order in English. "That's enough. Stop so we can talk." So he could find the words to tell her he hadn't meant to hurt or use her.

"G-go a-away," she mumbled.

Night Shadow frowned. "No. You are cold. Come out of the water. The fire will warm you."

"N-no."

Sighing, Night Shadow ran his hand through his hair. Why were women so stubborn? "Did we not have this conversation already today? Do I need to carry you to the fire?"

He tried hard to gentle his voice, but frustration, guilt, and worry made him sound harsher than he'd intended.

To his relief, Winona stood slowly. He swallowed hard. In his concern for her he'd forgotten that she wasn't wearing any clothes. "Where is your dress?"

Without answering, Winona walked over to a bush where her dress hung. Her hair, a sheet of silvery midnight blue in the moonlight, slid down her back when she shoved it over her shoulders. The long strands swept across her bottom. He forced his gaze back to the water.

"I washed it." She sounded embarrassed. Her voice dropped to a thready whisper. "It was stained."

Now he felt stupid. She'd lost—no, he'd taken—her innocence. Nothing he said or did could give her back that which she'd lost. But Clay, the man who'd been touched by this woman, would apologize for the hurtful and untrue words he'd flung at her.

"I'm . . ." He frowned when he saw her lift the dress off the bush and hold it over her head. "You cannot put that on. It is wet." He yanked his shirt over his head, walked over to her, and pulled the shirt over her head, sliding his hand beneath her heavy curtain of hair and pulling it free.

Needing no encouragement or orders, she slipped her hands into the arms, then tugged the hem down over her bare skin.

"P-pilamayaye."

Night Shadow opened his hand and watched

her damp strands of hair fall in a tangle from his fingers. When she shivered violently, he scooped her into his arms. "We will talk after you are warm."

Winona didn't struggle. She lay limp in his arms. *"Taku ehe kin ecel ecanu sni,"* she whispered brokenly in Lakota.

He glanced down at her closed eyes. "No, I did not keep my promise. I hurt you. That was not my intention." He entered the warm shelter and set Winona down. She backed away from him, her eyes wide in the firelight.

"You understand Lakota?"

Realizing he'd given himself away, Night Shadow shifted away from her. He tossed a few more twigs onto the fire and shrugged. "Some," he hedged, eyeing her warily.

"Sunka." She moved closer. "What does it mean?"

He tossed one of the furs to her. "We will talk in the morning."

Winona didn't catch the fur. It fell and landed in front of her. She stepped over it.

"Maka. Itunkala. Zuzeca." She moved around the fire, following him.

Night Shadow sidestepped her, crossing back to the other side of the fire. At his back the cold rolled over him. He sighed and sat.

"Dog. Skunk. Rat. Snake."

At her indrawn hiss of air, he added, "Do not forget *gnaska*." Her eyes widened.

"What?"

Night Shadow almost welcomed her fury. Anything was better than tears, so he made the same frog sound as she'd made at him when she'd called him a frog before.

"*Kukuse.*"

Night Shadow stretched out. "Yeah, pig too."

Chapter Ten

Clay understood Lakota! And yet he'd played dumb with her. Not once had he spoken to her in her own language, choosing to use the white man's tongue instead. Furious, she picked up the fur and stalked to the back wall. She sent him an angry glare, but he seemed unaware of her.

How dared he just lie down and ignore her? She longed to lash out at him, fling more names at him, but this time she wisely held her tongue. Drained physically and emotionally, cold to the bone and confused, she was not ready for another confrontation.

Sliding down the stone wall she sat with the fur over her legs. So much had happened. She felt as though she were being swept away by a spring flood caused by a sudden storm. She tried to wipe out the events that had changed her life forever.

She'd mated with a man who was not her husband; nor would he ever be. Winona had witnessed matings between many animals and gathered from other women that it was as natural as breathing or eating. Some seemed to enjoy it; others felt it was their duty.

But during those intense moments when she'd taken Clay into her she'd felt not just pleasure and a demanding need. She'd felt alive, full of power.

Frowning, she tried to make sense of her jumbled thoughts. She'd become a part of the world, not just part of the cycle of life but of the very essence of life. Coming together with Clay had set her free unlike anything she could have imagined. Not even sitting on her beloved Gray Rock had ever made her feel that way.

She'd become the wind, flowing in and around Clay. The heat of their bodies joining, hotter than the rays of the sun, had sparked off a storm that crashed over, around, and through them.

Leaning her head back, Winona bit her lower lip. She'd been part of Clay, and he her, and it had been wondrous. Beautiful. And hurtful. He'd taken the joy from it.

Staring into the fire, she shook with more

than cold. In her mind she knew Clay had deliberately hurt her. He'd been a wounded animal trying to bite anyone who tried to come near him.

Winona dropped her head to her knees. In her heart and mind she knew this meant that she'd sliced through some barrier he'd erected around his heart, but it didn't help the pain of his words go away. Sniffing, she tried to think of something else, but she felt so miserable inside. Her mind and heart felt bruised.

Watching Clay sleep, she thought it was obvious that what had happened between them meant nothing. He hadn't lied. He'd used her. Her eyes blurred. That hurt far worse than the brief stab of pain that came with losing her maidenhead.

"Don't you dare start crying again." Clay's voice sounded irritated.

Winona glared at him. He hadn't bothered to open his eyes. Exhaustion settled over her shoulders. "To cry would mean I hurt, and for you to hurt me I would have to care about what you do or say to me."

She laced her fingers together and held her knees tightly to her chest. "I do not care," she said defiantly.

A long silence followed her false declaration. Clay sat up and ran his hands through his hair.

His shadow moved over her with each brusque movement. "You care," he said softly. A thread of sadness crept into his voice.

"Hiya! Makeya!"

No. Ridiculous.

"I do not care about you. You are *taskakpa*."

Clay's blank expression pleased her. She opened her mouth to tell him he was like the tiny insect who buried its head into the skin of animals or humans and stole their blood.

She didn't. Instead she closed her eyes and drew the fur tighter around her shoulders. She'd given herself freely and, in return, had taken what he'd given her as a gift into her heart.

"I am sorry I hurt you," he said.

She shrugged. "It was no worse than skinning my knee as a child."

Clay sighed but Winona ignored him. She didn't want to talk. And she didn't dare look at him or else she'd start crying again.

"I am sorry for that too, but I was apologizing for what I said."

Winona's gaze flew open when she felt his warm fingers slide down her cheek. One tear escaped. He caught it with his finger and rubbed the tiny bit of moisture between his thumb and forefinger.

"I did not use you."

NAME: _____

ADDRESS: _____

_____

_____

TELEPHONE: _____

E-MAIL: _____

_____ I want to pay by credit card.

__ Visa   __ MasterCard   __ Discover

Account Number: _____

Expiration date: _____

SIGNATURE: _____

*Send this form, along with $2.00 shipping
and handling for your FREE books, to:*

Historical Romance Book Club
20 Academy Street
Norwalk, CT 06850-4032

*Or fax (must include credit card
information!) to:* **610.995.9274.**
*You can also sign up on the Web
at* <u>www.dorchesterpub.com</u>.

Offer open to residents of the U.S. and
Canada only. Canadian residents, please
call 1.800.481.9191 for pricing information.

If under 18, a parent or guardian must sign. Terms, prices and conditions
subject to change. Subscription subject to acceptance. Dorchester
Publishing reserves the right to reject any order or cancel any subscription.

"I know." The tears flowed freely. She heard Clay sigh.

"Come here." He scooped her into his arms and sat in the same spot where she'd been sitting.

Winona pushed against him but he tightened his hold. "Be still and I will try to explain."

"Jenny?" She held her breath.

"Jenny." He hesitated. "It is a sad story and the telling of it does not change who I am." He gently turned her head to face him. "Or what I must do."

Winona allowed him to arrange one fur beneath her and cover her legs with the other. She sat in the cradle of his legs. His leggings added to the warmth surrounding her.

Resting her head against his chest, she waited.

Night Shadow wasn't sure this was a good idea, but he was tired and worn from carrying his burden alone for so many years. Though many knew of his past, few knew just how deeply affected he was. He wasn't even sure he could speak of his past, but he needed to try to explain. Only then would Winona understand what drove him. Perhaps if she understood, she wouldn't hurt as much.

Nothing had changed within him. He couldn't

afford to let emotions cloud his vision, but he knew he was on the edge of allowing this woman to come between him and his past. He had to tell his story and get it over with. Put her from his mind and heart. Finding his sister and killing his enemy were the only things that mattered to Night Shadow, but Clay yearned to take his place in this world. He wanted to share his pain with someone who saw more than most.

So Night Shadow gave in to Clay and a woman who'd found a way into his heart. First he told her of his Cheyenne mother and his sister Catherine Youngbird, his two younger brothers and his baby sister, Jenny, painting a picture of a family who lived among the animals his father trapped for their fur.

His mother had loved his father, and had left her tribe to travel with him. She'd borne him children and created a tipi filled with love and laughter. There'd been other trappers who'd also taken Indian women as wives, including his father's partner, who had one child, a boy one year older than Clay.

Clay had grown up with Henry Black Bear. Henry's mother had died when he'd been young, so the boy had often lived with his family when the men left for days at a time to set their traps or take their hauls to the trading posts.

Grateful that Winona didn't speak or ask questions, Clay took a moment to gather his thoughts. When she gently stroked the back of his hand, he tightened his hold on her.

"I was fourteen when my father left to take our furs to the river. It was his partners' turn to take the canoes downriver to the trading post." Falling silent, Clay closed his eyes.

"Two trappers brought him home. Dead."

He felt Winona draw in a deep breath. He forged onward. "They weren't sure what had happened except that there had been a fight between my father and Henry Black Bear's father after a game of cards.

"I buried him and planned to take my mother, sisters, and brothers home to her family. But Henry's father showed up, drunk and in a rage."

Clay felt his throat tighten. "He went after my mother, said he had claim to her. She fought him and stabbed him to stop him from raping her. She didn't kill him—only wounded him, which made it worse. He would have killed her if I hadn't shot him in the leg." He fell silent.

"The man had been like a father to us. I didn't want to kill him—even though it was clear he had murdered my father. I just wanted him to leave and never bother us again."

His voice hardened. "I told Henry to take him away before I killed him. He did."

Clay's voice turned bitter. "Henry's father died a week later. I was away from the tipi playing with Jenny. She'd been pestering me, so I chased her, and when she ran back to our mother I stayed away. I needed to be alone."

He'd gotten his wish. His absence had left his family vulnerable. He'd been the man, the protector, and he'd failed. Clay wrapped his hand around Winona's hair and rubbed the soft strands between his fingers. His jaw trembled.

Winona shifted beneath him. "You blame yourself." It was a statement, not a question.

"I heard shots. But by the time I ran back, Henry had already shot my mother. Catherine had the shotgun. We all knew how to use it, as we were often left alone. She missed. Henry didn't." His voice broke.

"I'm not sure what happened to my two younger brothers. They'd gone out to check the traps and bring them in."

Images of Henry Black Bear standing over him with a knife dripping with his own blood blotted out everything. "He told me he killed them." His voice broke. "Taunted me with how easy it'd been."

Clay shuddered but held nothing back, left out no detail. "He gutted them as though they'd been animals."

Behind his closed eyes, Clay saw it all again.

Felt it. He and Henry had fought. Clay, distracted by Jenny's screaming and the blood of his mother and sister, had allowed emotions to surface that had nearly cost him his life. He'd struck out blindly, and Henry, with his taunts of his brothers' gruesome deaths, had the winning weapon.

He fell silent, sick after all this time.

"Jenny?"

"Sold."

Over and over Clay heard Jenny screaming for him as he lay helpless and dying. Rage quickened his breathing, but he called upon an inner strength to calm himself. He was no longer a weak boy named Clay who'd failed. He was Night Shadow, a warrior of merit. And he would avenge the destruction of his family. He'd known for years where to find Henry Black Bear, or Hoka Luta as he called himself, but he'd waited. Controlled his need for vengeance.

He planned. Waited. Watched. He could have killed Henry anytime. Not once had Henry been aware of his existence, or how close Night Shadow had come to him. His enemy continued to live only because Night Shadow had failed to learn the whereabouts of his sister.

Opening his eyes, he lifted his hand to smooth the hair from Winona's face. Once again the fire had died down. Embers glowed hotly, like the ball of hate burning in his belly. In his arms Winona stirred. The silence between them was broken only by the softly crackling fire.

"Clay, what if Hoka Luta does not know where Jenny is after all this time?"

"Pray that he does," Night Shadow answered coldly, resuming control. Clay was gone now, but for the first time since that fateful day he admitted to himself that the odds of Henry producing Jenny after all this time were slim to none.

"If he cannot return her?" she persisted. She turned in his arms and looked at him.

Night Shadow felt his gut tighten. The warrior knew what he would do. The man balked. He wanted a life without hate and pain and guilt. He yearned for the love and laughter he'd once known and taken for granted.

But the warrior who'd emerged from the broken boy needed to watch Henry die a slow, painful death—but not right away. Taking Winona was only the first step of his plan. Night Shadow planned to destroy Henry's new life and leave him a broken man. As he'd left him.

In his arms he felt Winona tense as she awaited his answer.

"I will sell you as he sold Jenny."

Winona slumped in his arms. "You would hurt my family? Me? What about Spotted Deer?

She has no connection to any of this. And you said you would not harm us."

"My family was innocent yet he destroyed them. All of them. This is war. Sometimes the innocent get hurt."

Regret brought exhaustion sweeping over him. Night Shadow would not have felt anything. His course had been set. If he somehow found a way to go on with his life he'd never have the strength or courage to return to the shadows. Until he found Jenny he had to brave those shadows.

Dropping his head to rest on Winona's, Night Shadow gave in to the needs of Clay and allowed himself to ask what-ifs for one night.

Hoka Luta could not be the cold-blooded murderer Clay accused him of being. Clay had to be wrong. Henry Black Bear and Hoka Luta were not one and the same.

Hoka Luta was honorable. He was the son of a powerful medicine man. He was respected and feared. Warriors spoke around the fire of his many brave deeds, and fathers sought him out on behalf of their daughters.

Winona chewed her lower lip. Doubt and denial whirled around her mind until she felt sick. It could not be. She couldn't have been so wrong about him. No one had anything bad to say about Hoka Luta. No doubts had ever been whispered about the man she'd chosen to marry.

Her father had been pleased with her choice; her brother spoke of the man's wealth and his generosity. Hoka Luta had given many gifts to her people. Clay had to be wrong. And yet deep inside, she knew he wasn't.

Clay's heartrending tale had been too real. Too painful. She hadn't asked how he'd survived or how he'd found Henry. Later. Right now it didn't make any difference to his past, or her future. Whatever happened, she wouldn't allow him to sell her or Spotted Deer.

Unsure of what to do or think, Winona tried to put everything from her mind. Behind her she felt Clay's slow and even breathing. The threat of being sold should have made her frantic to escape, but Winona didn't move.

Instead she thought of her family. Even though Golden Eagle was much older, the two of them were close. As a girl she'd followed her only brother around, pestered him and made him play with her.

Her favorite games had been having him chase her, or clinging to his back while he raced like the wind across the prairie. She smiled. The wind had rushed past her and made her eyes tear. Her laughter and excited shouts and giggles had always seemed to make her brother go faster or leap higher.

Remembering the fun times she'd had with Golden Eagle, Winona fully understood Clay's need to find his sister. From the little he'd said she knew he'd been as caring and loving a brother to Jenny as Golden Eagle was. To this day brother and sister shared a close relationship, even though he was now married with four young children.

But no matter how much Clay needed to find Jenny and avenge the deaths of his family, Winona couldn't allow him to do it at her expense. She and Spotted Deer were innocent, and creating wrongs to right wrongs would not bring his family back. Nor would it allow him to ever fully live. So where did she go from here? What should she do?

She had no answers. Just questions. What if Jenny was alive, still living as a slave? Winona couldn't imagine not being safe and loved.

She thought of Spotted Deer. The death of her friend's parents could have left Spotted Deer alone, but her family had taken the girl to their tipi and their hearts. What if Jenny had had no one? What if she waited and prayed each day for her brother to find her? There was also the chance that she now had a loving family and didn't remember Clay. Would the truth destroy her new life?

Winona closed her eyes. She didn't know what to do. Children taken captive from their enemies were usually adopted into their new families. If Jenny had been sold at a young age, she most likely had a new life. Trying to think back to when she'd been three winters old, Winona couldn't remember much. Her earliest memory seemed to be her fascination with her brother and his willingness to let her climb onto his back and sit on his shoulders so she could feel grown-up. Did Jenny remember Clay?

Tired, sore of heart, mind, and body, Winona put Jenny from her mind. Her concern lay with Clay and finding a way to convince him not to go through with his plan. She had to. Her father would not give up. Clay would die, and she had to do everything she could to prevent it.

Not an easy task. From a distance one of her father's arrows could kill Clay without her having a chance to tell him Clay's reasons for taking her and Spotted Deer. And then there was Hoka Luta. If he remembered Clay and understood the messages Clay left, then he would also be after Clay to finish what he'd started.

Despite Clay's warmth at her back she felt chilled. If Clay died it would be her word against Hoka Luta's. Winona hated feeling helpless.

Hugging Clay's arms tightly around her, she

vowed to keep him alive. If only she could escape and find her father first, then together they could confront Hoka Luta and learn the truth. But until she and Spotted Deer were reunited she had to keep Clay away from father. Not even for Clay would she sacrifice her best friend.

Chapter Eleven

The bear jumped into her dreams with an ear-shattering roar. Standing on hind feet, the massive animal lifted his paws high. Curved, sharp claws reached out and out and out with deadly intent. She ran. Always in the dream, she ran—and screamed for him to go away and leave her alone. His roar drowned out her screams and sounded like laughter. Mean laughter.

The faster she ran, the smaller she became ... until everything loomed large and frightening. Out of breath, she stopped and looked behind her. The bear was gone but she was still scared.

She eyed each tree as she backed away. He could be hiding. He did that sometimes. He liked to jump out and scare her.

"Kaa," she screamed. "Make him stop. Make him go away."

Something hard at her back stopped her retreat. She spun around and screamed. The bear had sneaked around the trees silently and now stood over her. He shook his bear head and roared. She ran. He laughed.

Over her shoulder she saw a man stalking her with his hands held high, fingers curved like a bear's claws. The bear head he wore sat askew. She knew he wasn't a real bear. But he still scared her. He was mean. He thought it funny to scare her. She tried not to be afraid because then her brothers would tease her.

With a fast lunge the bear grabbed her by the arm. His hand was so large, his grip so hard, her arm hurt.

"I got you. Now I'm going to eat you." He bent his head down. The nose of the dead animal stabbed her own nose as her tormentor lifted her arm to his mouth.

At the feel of his teeth scraping her flesh, she yelled, "Mama! Kaa!"

She squirmed and struggled free, then ran again. Hide. She had to hide from him. She hated him and wished he'd go away forever. She fell, hurt her knee, but ignored the pain and blood as she crawled beneath a bush. She heard shouting. Fighting and arguing. Then silence. That scared her even more until she heard a familiar and loving voice.

"Come out, Jenny. He's gone."

Jenny willed the tears to stop flowing down her cheeks. Kaa had come. He always came. He called her again but she waited until she saw him—and saw that he was alone.

Crying, she ran into his arms.

Her vision of Kaa faded. But instead of the nightmare ending, it began again. The same, yet different.

Because this time there was more blood.

This time Kaa did not come.

No one came.

She whimpered in her sleep; the sound, so soft as not to be heard by anyone else, was enough to wake her.

Sitting, she breathed a sigh of relief that she'd been able to escape the dream. But she could not forget the screaming. Lots of screaming. Resting her head on her knees, she let her calf-length dress slide down between her legs.

Breathing slowly and deeply as her mother had taught her to do when the night spirits came to visit, she closed her eyes and forced herself to relax. Keeping her eyes closed, she turned her sight inward, focusing on her center.

Darkness swirled. It took effort to keep the lids of her eyes closed while she rolled her eyes upward. When she had her focus, she willed the black away and called upon calming colors. Her mother had taught her to see colors and call upon the wisdom of the spirits to help her when she was troubled.

Black slowly gave way to blue, a deep, dark blue. Truth. Healing. Knowledge. Blue meant feeling safe, warm. Cool and comfortable. Yet she wasn't safe. Her spirit was troubled.

For many years the dreams had stayed away. Now they were back, worse than she could ever remember. They came every night now. She knew the spirits were speaking to her, trying to tell her something. Were they a warning? If so, the spirits had been trying to warn her of something terrible since she'd been a young child.

Keeping her focus on the color swirling behind her closed eyes, she wished there were someone who could tell her what they meant. Her tribe's shaman had said years ago that the dreams were memories of her past, yet she recalled only a happy childhood.

Frustrated that, like all the other times, she knew nothing new, she lay back down and opened her eyes, the black of the night chasing the blue color away.

Tonight the colors and their meanings did not soothe. For the first time they frightened her. The spirits wanted her to learn something, but she suddenly didn't want to know what the dreams meant.

Wait. There had been something new in tonight's nightmare. Tonight she'd called out a name. She tried to remember the name the child had called out—but it was gone. Her head ached and her skin prickled with tiny bumps. A chill slithered down her spine.

That name was important, but it eluded her. It frightened her, the grown woman, yet the child had called out to him. Who was he? What did this night's dreams mean?

The more she thought the more her head ached. Finally she put the terrifying dreams aside and concentrated on her heartbeat. She turned the pounding rhythm of her body into the beat of drums. Slowly she swayed in a slow circle, moving only her upper body. She chanted inside her head using her power chant, the words and song known only to her. She repeated it as many times as it took to chase the night spirits away. Fast at first, then slow. Very slow.

Finally she opened her eyes and placed her hand between her breasts and felt for the tiny pouch the size of her thumb that lay nestled there. She drew it out and stared at it.

Her fingers found the shape of the tiny stone inside. She slid her finger inside and pulled out a gleaming chain and held it up. In the darkness she couldn't see the shiny gem but she knew it was red. Bloodred. Quickly she dropped it back into the pouch.

The stone and its color both frightened and

calmed her. For as long as she could remember she'd worn the pouch around her neck. Her medicine bag, her mother had said.

In the quiet dark of the night she questioned whether it was good medicine or bad. Lying back down, she curled into a ball and hugged her knees to her chest beneath her furs. As she drifted off to sleep, her fingers ran unconsciously over a short, thick scar just below her knee.

For the next four days Winona and Clay traveled by foot. Rock gave way to thick forests, then large and small rock formations again as they climbed with the land. Under other circumstances Winona would have loved to take her time and learn this new and exciting land. She loved the contrasts, and she loved the heights, ridges, and peaks.

But Clay didn't stop more than was necessary. And he didn't talk. He walked ahead of her and not once did he glance back to see if she lagged behind. She shot his back an angry glare.

Ever since that night in the cave when he'd told her of his past he'd been distant. She knew he blamed her for his weak moment as well as for what had happened between them earlier. Maybe it *was* her fault. Then again, just maybe she'd proven to him that he was far from dead inside. A man of his strong reactions was not a dead man. A man who brought out strong reactions in others, namely her, was not a man who did not feel.

Yet knowing that she was right, knowing that she'd gotten under his skin, didn't make her feel better. Kicking a small stone out of her way, Winona scowled. Why did she care? This man didn't care about her, didn't care that he was causing her and her family pain. He cared only about himself.

No. She had to be fair. He cared not about himself. But only for Jenny. Should Clay learn that Jenny had not survived she had no doubt he'd face Hoka Luta, kill him, and not care whether he died as well.

So what was she supposed to do? Keep making him angry to the point where they mated? Winona blushed as she remembered the wild joining of their bodies and the incredible pleasure she'd achieved.

She eyed Clay's fine form. As much as she'd like to repeat that wild night, she knew that was not the answer. Besides, many times over the last few days she'd tried to goad him out of his cold silence, and nothing seemed to work anymore.

Wiping her brow, she quickened her steps to

keep up. Though it was still early spring, and they traveled in the high hills, it was warm.

Clay had discarded his leggings and buckskin shirt. His torso held a sheen of sweat, and muscles danced up and down his back with each swing of his arms. And with each long-legged stride, his breechclout swung from side to side, baring teasing glimpses of flesh.

She remembered the feel of his fingers digging into her backside. Her fingers itched to do the same to him. A tiny dribble of sweat rolled between her breasts. Not paying attention, she tripped over a rock and nearly went sprawling. She caught herself.

Up ahead, Clay kept going. He had to have heard her, yet he never looked back to see if she was all right. Mad, she stopped. She'd had enough of this. Spotting a nice flat-topped boulder sitting in the cool shade of a towering giant piece of granite, she marched over and sat.

"I am resting," she declared.

Up ahead Clay didn't stop. Winona folded her arms across her chest, then changed her mind and put them behind her on the rock. Leaning back, she gave the appearance of not caring.

"Leave me a trail to follow," she called out.

Clay didn't stop. Winona didn't budge.

She tipped her head back and shook out her

hair to allow the cooling breeze to brush against the back of her neck. She closed her eyes and counted.

Wanji.

Nunppa.

Yamni.

Topa.

Zaptan. And kept counting. When she reached *opawinge*—one hundred—she heard a soft scuff. It was hard to keep from smiling. She might be his captive, but at the same time he was hers. That realization fueled her own sense of power. She thought of her vision, of the symbol of power the great cat inspired and spoke of, and knew she was here for a reason. Clay was a lost soul, and she had the power to save him.

Though he said nothing, made no further noise, Winona knew he stood glaring at her with his arms crossed over his chest as he fought for control. He was not happy with her. She bit back a smile. Strangely, the knowledge that she could break through his barriers sent chills of awareness through her.

The tips of her breasts tightened as if from a blast of cold air—or the touch of a lover's caress. She put that thought from her mind. She needed her mind sharp and alert, not drugged by pleasures of the body.

"What game are you playing?" Clay asked. Irritation edged his voice.

Winona resisted the temptation to remind him that it was he who was playing games. She shrugged instead. "I am tired—"

"I will say when we rest."

Winona opened one eye. Clay stood a few feet from her with his arms folded across his chest. "—of being ignored."

Her statement startled him. But only for a moment. He lifted one brow. "You are my captive. You will do as I say," he warned softly.

Lifting one brow in imitation, Winona sat upright and tucked her right foot beneath her left thigh. "You may be strong, but not that strong," she said, deliberately eyeing him from his strong legs up past powerful thighs to his broad shoulders.

Clay rocked back on his heels and silently waited for her to explain herself. Winona stretched her arms overhead and slowly brought her arms down. "Strong enough to carry me wherever it is you are taking me."

"Make no mistake, woman. I will sling you over my shoulder and carry you if you do not get up now." He took a step forward.

Instead of being intimidated, Winona smiled, stood, and walked around him. When he turned, she again went behind. "Stand still," she ordered.

Clay whipped around. "For what?"

Once more she moved around him. "If I must flop over your shoulder, I wish to be sure the view is to my liking." She paused to swish aside his breechclout.

"Yes, it will do." *More than do*, she admitted to herself. Swallowing hard, Winona forced herself to saunter casually around the rest of the way. Clay stood speechless.

Her boldness shocked her as much as it obviously shocked him. But she'd meant what she said. Clay could yell, shout, or boss her about, but not ignore her. She refused to be treated as if she weren't there, especially not from a man who'd taken her innocence and shown her the primitive beauty and power that came from being one with the elements.

She'd never felt that wild abandon or the desperate need that had consumed her. No touch of Hoka Luta's had even come close to igniting her senses. Not even his bold caress. She'd been enamored only by the thought of what he was doing, and what he'd wanted to do. She was a woman and she'd yearned to have a man treat her as such.

It still amazed her that her body had responded so fully to Clay and his passion. That knowledge alone would have kept her from going through with marriage to Hoka Luta. What she felt for Clay she suspected was the same feeling her mother had for Hawk Eyes, and White Wind for Golden Eagle. How often had she seen those around her exchange secret smiles or hurry off to be alone?

Clay only had to look at her to make her aware of her body and her reaction to him, the man. She moved close to him until she stood with her breasts just a hairbreadth away from his bare chest. She held up her hands.

"Now what are you doing?" Clay whispered the words hoarsely and took a step back.

The power of becoming a woman surged through her. She felt alive. In love. The thought nearly buckled her knees. She put it away to examine later, though the thought of being in love with a man who'd taken her captive didn't seem to matter right then.

All that she cared about was breaking through the barriers Clay had placed between them. Only then would she be able to determine whether or not the emotions he evoked in her were love. So she stepped closer and wrapped her arms around his neck. "You said you would carry me. I am ready."

"Are you crazy?" He looked and sounded dumbfounded.

Winona slid her hands down his shoulders and grinned. The man was definitely out of his element. She leaned in close. "Not any crazier than a man with a death wish." Her fingers rose back up to his neck and linked together.

"You know why I must do this." Clay looked torn between anger and anguish.

Winona used her thumbs to trace small half circles behind his ears. "For Jenny. But what good will you be to her if you are dead?" *And what good to me?* she asked silently. With each passing minute, each beat of her heart, she grew more confident and sure of herself.

Power. Love. They went together. But with the gift of both power and love came responsibility. In a flash of insight Winona fully accepted the responsibility to save this man.

Not just for Jenny—though she was determined to help him find his sister.

And not just for herself, though when he'd claimed her body, he'd claimed her heart. When he'd opened his heart to her, he'd joined their souls.

Night Shadow stepped back and pulled himself from Winona's arms. "No more talk. We leave now." He strode off with an even, uncaring stride. He didn't stop. Didn't look over his shoulder, but somehow he knew she hadn't followed.

Why wasn't he surprised?

"*Nehnesevatamestse!* Have pity on me!" He muttered the words in both Cheyenne and English, unsure if his command was directed to the spirits, his white God, or the woman who was quickly becoming a pain in the—

He cut the thought. Having her eye his flesh so deliberately had thrown him off center. Knowing that if he carried out his threat she'd be staring at his backside had been more than he could handle.

He came to a skidding stop. The woman had cleverly manipulated him. He whipped around. Though he couldn't see Winona, he had no trouble imagining her smug satisfaction.

Narrowing his eyes, Night Shadow quickened his steps until he was standing in front of his captive. She wanted to be slung over his shoulders like a sack of flour, fine. She wanted to stare at his bare flesh, fine. Let her stare all she wanted. It mattered not.

Without a word he rearranged his quiver of arrows, his bow, and the other belongings he carried, then bent, caught her around the waist and put her over his shoulder.

Night Shadow wasn't sure what reaction he expected. Squeals of indignation would have been nice. A spate of furious curses he could live with, and even agree with. But what made him nearly dump Winona back onto the ground was her soft laughter.

His lips tightened. This was no game. He found no amusement in taking an innocent woman captive or being forced into playing rough. He didn't want to hurt her, dammit, but he'd spent more than half his life waiting for this moment in time. Jenny had counted on him and he'd failed her. He'd not fail her now—if she was still alive.

"Clay?"

Night Shadow felt her elbows dig into his shoulders as she held her head up. Ignoring her seemed the easiest thing to do, so he started off walking down the path.

"Clay, I like watching the way your back moves when you walk. Your flesh dances beneath your skin."

Night Shadow bit back a groan and forced himself to move faster.

Ignore her, he told himself. If he didn't need her in order to get Jenny back, he'd dump her here and now and walk away. And never look back. His gut tightened at the thought, but Night Shadow refused to believe otherwise. There was no place in his life for a woman—any woman except his sister.

Unfortunately, he couldn't ignore the vision of Winona's head thrown back, passion overtaking her. He heard her hoarse cries, felt her tightening around him as he lost all control. His palm burned where he held her by the back of her thigh. One glance at her soft flesh tempted him to scoot his fingers upward and beneath the hem of her skirt.

Breathing harshly, Night Shadow quickened his steps. She flopped back down and he let her slide a bit further over his shoulder until his arms held her behind the knees. He smiled grimly, then choked when he felt one of her fingers trace the curve of his spine downward.

Hiding his start of surprise by jumping over a root, Night Shadow forced himself to breathe slowly. Deeply.

It is only a touch. She is only a woman.

Ha. Only!

Her breath warmed the skin on his back. He focused on the path ahead of him. Rocky. Twisted and covered with low growth that he had to shove past. Good. It gave him something to focus on. Anything was better than the feel of her fingers trailing across his flesh.

Her finger slid lower. His grip on the back of her knees tightened, but it didn't stop her from grabbing his loincloth with one hand, lifting it, and using the other hand to pull aside the part of cloth that cupped his buttocks.

He felt the brush of air and sun on his bare flesh and stifled a groan.

"Hmm. Much nicer from up here." She

paused. "I want to touch you as you touched me."

Night Shadow felt his loins tighten.

Say nothing! Do not react. Ignore her. She seeks to torment you.

"Clay?" She sighed when he continued to ignore her.

"It felt good when you touched me. Did it feel good to touch me like that?"

Night Shadow's control snapped. He was a man, only a man, and could resist no more. Furious that a great warrior like him could not control a small young woman, he stopped, dropping his weapons and bundles. He'd teach her a lesson. He was a warrior. A very controlled warrior who'd lost that precious control during their first encounter.

"Yes, dammit. It felt good. Like this." Running one hand up the back of her leg he caressed the skin behind her knee, followed the soft flesh of her thigh beneath her dress, then boldly cupped one smooth, rounded cheek.

Winona went limp. "Ah." She sighed. "Yes, like that." Her fingers crept down over one of his bare cheeks. She squeezed. "Your *nistuste* feels nice. Does it feel good when I touch you?"

That was it. Night Shadow had enough. He wasn't sure if he should dump her onto the ground and walk away or lower her to her feet and show her just how good he could make her feel.

He was hard. He had to put distance between them or he'd take her right then and there.

Remember Jenny, he told himself. *Jenny is your reason for living. For breathing. Jenny is all that matters.*

He bent forward slightly to set her back down onto her feet, but she shocked him by sliding down his front and wrapping her feet back around his waist. Her hands cradled the sides of his neck. She didn't say anything, just gazed at him with those large, innocent golden-browns.

Night Shadow, the cold, controlled warrior, was at a complete loss. Again. What was he supposed to do? He couldn't yell at her or shout out his frustration. He couldn't speak words of anger, as he had the night he'd taken her innocence.

So he just stared at her. "What am I going to do with you?" He hadn't meant to speak aloud. He couldn't believe he'd actually voiced his frustration.

Winona didn't laugh. She didn't smile or act smug at her obvious victory. Instead her eyes filled with tears and her hands crept up to caress the sides of his face. "You are going to live. With me. For me."

With that bold declaration, Winona kissed him hard. As soon as his mouth opened under the demanding insistence of hers, she slid down and walked off, leaving Night Shadow staring after her with an ache in his loins, eyes filled with wonder and fear, and a slowly thawing heart.

Chapter Twelve

Hoka Luta stared at a small square of brown-checked cloth stained with blood. Old blood. The edges of the cloth were frayed and tattered, but he recognized the trade cloth that his father had given to Clay Blue Hawk's mother.

She'd taken that material and sewn dresses for Clay's sisters, shirts for all the boys and men to wear when they went with their father to the trading posts. Both of their fathers had forced their children to dress in white man's shirts and buckskin breeches when they were around other trappers.

Lifting his head, he stood still and listened. He heard nothing but the usual sounds of nature. With one last glance around, he used his knife to stab the cloth deep into the earth. Going ahead of Hawk Eyes and his men, he'd managed to find each piece of the past Clay had left. And like this latest taunt, he'd been able to get rid of it before anyone else saw it.

Standing, Hoka Luta studied the ground and slowly retraced his steps, carefully erasing all signs of his presence. Finished, he glared through the trees in the direction that he was being led. He clenched his hands. He had no doubt that Clay Blue Hawk was leading him by leaving items from his past for him to find. His old friend knew he could not risk having Winona's father learn of his past.

Fury built deep inside Hoka Luta. Clay Blue Hawk sought not just to kill him but to destroy him. He toyed with him, taunted him, and with each piece of the past threatened to expose him.

Gathering his weapons, water skin, and a small pouch of meat and berries, he once more picked up the trail of his enemy and followed. Each step burned his hatred deeper. Each deliberately torn leaf and broken twig twisted his fury into a tight coil. He no longer cared about the girl. All that mattered was the new life he'd created for himself—and the respect his position as the son of a medicine man brought him.

He was a great warrior. He had the ability to slide through the forest and overtake his enemy, but he could not risk allowing Hawk Eyes or Golden Eagle to come across the bits and pieces Clay Blue Hawk planted along a trail a young boy could follow. So he continued ahead.

The land he strode over appeared drab and lifeless, but he knew better. He'd spent a lot of time as a youth and young warrior roaming the secluded and sacred hills. He'd traveled far and wide, and if given a choice between lush green meadows, thickly wooded forests, or this wild landscape, he'd take this.

Most of the trees were tall, thin, and scraggly. They were survivors; they had firm footholds in the soil and took what they needed, as he did. He was a hard man, like this stretch of land. He was resolved. Unbudging. Once he chose a path to travel, he seldom wandered off course.

Until now. Until the appearance of a man who'd once been like a brother to him. *Brother!* Deep inside he felt the twist of a knife, the pain, and bitterness welled up with enough force that he nearly lost what little control he held over himself.

Hoka Luta glanced up at the gathering clouds, and his nostrils flared as he drew in a deep breath. Always he remained in control. Control meant power. But he was not in control. Clay Blue Hawk had set the rules of this game.

Hoka Luta stopped. His chest burned with the need to release his fury. There was little he could do to regain control at the moment, but he had the power to lock the rage tightly inside himself. The time would come when he'd unleash his anger. But now was not the time. First he had to find the enemy and ensure his future.

"This is beautiful," Winona exclaimed. Tiredness faded, as did hunger. Tucking away the long, thin slice of *wakapapi* Clay had given her earlier, she stared out at the deep blue lake.

All day they'd hiked downhill, sometimes over rock or between tall formations that were nearly impossible to pass. Even with her love of heights and rocky perches high above the world, she'd grown tired of the climbing and squeezing and crawling on her hands and knees. And then the scraggly, barren, granite-covered land had given way to thick forest.

The appearance of the lake surrounded by carpets of thick, green grass on three sides made it worth it. As she slid her gaze from one side to the other, she smiled in delight. Deer scattered back into the thick forest as she and Clay walked around the lake. Enchanted, Winona slowed her steps to take it all in. She'd never seen a pool of water so blue. And so large.

She was used to long ribbons of flowing water cutting swaths through the hilly prairie, or small, secluded pools at the end of small creeks that branched out from the streams.

Stopping, Winona took it all in. It was perfect. Dark green clumps of trees and brush encircled the water, following the line of the lake, which wove in and out like white men walking when they consumed too much of their "golden water."

Staring at that large body of water, she felt suddenly aware of the dust and stickiness of travel. Maybe Clay would stop here for the night. Could there be a better place to rest? Glancing up into the pale blue sky, she had no trouble imagining the perfection of the night: a soft bed of grass, a blanket of stars, and the lapping of water along the rocky bank.

"Now what?"

Winona grimaced at Clay's annoyance. "This is a beautiful spot." She obediently trudged on when he resumed walking. "It would make a good place to spend the night," she grumbled.

"Forget it. We aren't stopping here."

Feeling rebellion rising, Winona opened her mouth to protest. But when she rounded a curve along the lake Winona stopped.

"Ohhh!"

Across from her, on the other side of the lake,

the forest thinned, revealing nearly white rocks lining part of the water. Trees rose in the background, but to the left there were no trees. The white rocks were bare of greenery. No dirt. No plant life. Only water lapping at their base.

Her gaze followed the formation. Two of the strange rocks looked as though they were toads squatting in the water. The one between them was long, almost flat on top. In her mind's eye she saw herself running and jumping over the smooth surface.

But it was the slab of dark gray formation rising up beside them, to their left, that stole the speech from her throat. Rising sharply and slanting upward from right to left, it looked as though some unseen hand had tried to slice the granite into three pieces, but even the blade of nature had not been able to cleave the rocks apart.

"I have never seen anything so . . ." Words failed her as her gaze followed the middle section of rock. There was a strangely curved outcropping that looked as though there were a cradle board made of stone fastened to the center of the granite slab. She tipped her head to the side.

Or perhaps it could be a war bonnet, like her father's. She could easily imagine the top curve as a band of feathers, and the two longer pieces on the sides resembled twin tails of feathers. Several pointed but thin slices of rock below looked like steps with a few trees planted in and among the rocks. As with the white formation, there was no green or brown earth at the base. Just water lapping against rocky base.

And the water! Once more her gaze sought the blue that was so clear, it mirrored the image of the rocky formations. Winona ran past Clay, ran around the lake's curves, everything forgotten.

She was tired by the time she reached the craggy rocks, but she had to see if she could climb them. Scrambling over the white boulders, feeling as small as an ant, she didn't stop. But when she reached the imposing slabs of brownish rock she did stop, unsure how to get up to the top, or if there was a way. She felt very small staring up with her head tilted all the way back.

Clay passed her and found a foothold. "Thought you wanted to spend the night down by the lake."

In her haste to reach the formations, she'd forgotten all about Clay. Laughing, she followed, her earlier annoyances forgotten. "I want to climb to the top of the world and be one with the sky and heavens."

Clay glanced over his shoulder. She shrugged

but couldn't keep the smile off her face. "I love rocks," she said simply.

He smiled back, a genuine, amused grin. "I know. I watched you climb to the top of that tower of gray rock the day I took you captive. I saw you sitting on the edge and I . . ." He looked startled, as though caught off guard by her exuberance. ". . . figured you'd fall and kill yourself and leave me with no captive," he added.

Winona shook her head and laughed again. The sound as it echoed off the rocky walls made her feel wonderful. "Never." Elation filled her. She felt alive. Keeping up with Clay as he took the lead was easy. She even made climbing and squeezing between narrow slabs easier by grabbing the water and food pouch from him to tie them around her narrow waist. She would hear no excuse that he could go no farther.

Clay slid behind a tree. To Winona's disappointment, the trail ended. The granite wall in front of them was smooth and the trees too far from the fissures and cracks higher up. Frowning, she scanned the scene. There had to be a way.

Clay headed down, following the line of trees that were too far away to use in their quest for a path that led upward. Winona followed only after realizing that there was no way up from where she stood.

Rounding the trees, she stopped abruptly. Clay was gone! She turned in a circle. From where she stood she had a clear view of the lake. But she wasn't up high—just several feet from the water level.

"You coming or not?"

Winona whirled around and searched for Clay. To her astonishment she found him squatting in a tiny opening high above her. She hurried around the trees, down to where the water lapped against a very tiny bit of earthen bank, then climbed up and over the next rock that sat like a squatting warrior. Then she went around several small seedlings.

She searched the granite base, climbed over more rounded, smaller chunks of rock, and finally gave up.

"Clay!"

A tap on the shoulder startled her. Spinning around, she found Clay watching her. He looked smug. She narrowed her eyes. "Where are your weapons?" Her gaze widened. "And the bedding?" Her voice rose to a squeal. "You found the way up!"

He jerked his head. "You coming or not?" He took the water skin from her, turned around, and disappeared behind a tree. Winona ran, nearly slipping in her haste to stay close to him. She followed him around, up, then down again.

This time he ducked low and crawled on his hands and knees through a small, narrow opening that hadn't been apparent when she had tried to find the way up.

She followed, amazed at the tunnel made of many smaller rocks and a large one that had fallen on top and had created this natural, narrow tube. When Clay stood, she rose to her knees and gasped.

She now stood in an open area surrounded by towering sheets of granite that looked to run the width of the huge formation. Clay went back down on his hands and knees into the tunnel. Winona heard him moving the large rocks she'd had to squeeze by inside the hidden tube and realized he'd cleverly disguised the entrance to make it look like nothing more than a pile of boulders and rock.

"How did you find this?" Wonder filled her voice as she followed him. He stopped at another concealed opening and squeezed past. Excited that they were in the very heart of the mass of rock, and getting close to the top, Winona turned sideways as well.

When she came out, she stopped and could only stare. They now stood in a long cavern, except that the ceiling wasn't solid. Light spilled inside from several places where the cap of granite slabs had weathered and fallen between the slashes that from the ground made it look as though there were three separate towers standing shoulder-to-shoulder.

The next turn revealed a hole in the side. She stood on her tiptoes and peered out. The wall was so thick she could have sat on that tiny seat and gazed out at a world far beneath her.

"Forget it. You will not climb up there. Agreed?"

Winona rolled her eyes. "Fine. As long as there is somewhere up here that leads to the top."

Staring out the opening she could see the entire lake area. Laughing, she ran to catch up with Clay, who'd stopped in a totally enclosed area. His weapons lay against one wall. Supplies were piled up against another. Winona lifted her brow.

"I assume we are staying?"

"For a while." Clay started sorting through the supplies. At his back the enclosure narrowed, but she saw a tiny pinpoint of light from way back. Winona set her load down and followed that luring light and found the way to the top.

Once there, on top of the world, she knew she could have stayed there forever had it not been for Spotted Deer and her family.

* * *

Seeing Eyes prepared for battle. This battle required no weapons, no prayers to the spirits—though they couldn't have hurt. She needed no warriors at her side, for her battle was with her husband. And at that moment it was a silent battle of wills as he glared up at her and she calmly waited for him to speak first.

Without taking his eyes from her, Hawk Eyes addressed one of the warriors she'd ridden with—one of two who'd come back to camp with the news of Winona's capture.

"I gave orders for you to bring warriors, not women," he said. "Or children," he added after spotting his grandchildren. Displeasure darkened his features and made him even more formidable.

"The wife of my chief would not be left behind." The warrior offered no more. No more was needed.

Hawk Eyes folded his arms across his chest. "Explain yourself before I send you back. All of you." In turn he glared at each woman and child.

Seeing Eyes calmly dismounted and stopped before her husband and chief. "I am needed here."

"This is no place for women. Or children," Hawk Eyes lashed out. "You will return immediately and wait for our return." He softened his voice. "I will bring our daughters home."

Seeing Eyes moved past him and started unloading her horse. "*We* will bring our daughters home."

"Wife!"

Narrowing her eyes, Seeing Eyes placed her hands on her hips. "Husband, do you forget who has the gift of sight? Do you not think to ask if I had more visions or even what warnings I might have been given?"

Hawk Eyes sighed. Behind him, several warriors snickered. Turning his head, he speared each with a look that sent them running to carry out their assigned duties. When only Golden Eagle remained, he resumed his outraged stance.

"Speak now of these visions and warnings so that you may return home."

"I have nothing certain to impart to you yet. The visions come, but I do not understand their meanings." She held her hand out to stop her husband from speaking angry words.

"If I am far from you when they become clearer, it will take too long to find you and warn you of what I have seen."

She glanced around. She'd seen so much, yet could tell him so little. Mostly she saw colors, and a child who became a woman. But what worried her was the red—too much red staining the visions like bloodshed.

"You know what I say is true."

Though unhappy with her presence, her husband didn't argue further. He knew she spoke the truth.

Golden Eagle took up the battle. "My mother has explained her presence. What is yours?" He addressed his wife.

White Wind had dismounted and now stood at her mother-in-law's side. She wore a cradle board on her back. Baby Dove heard her father's voice and started fussing for him.

"We are family. My mother needs the help of her daughter. No doubt she will now have to cook many meals. I will help her." Her Lakota after many years as part of the tribe was fluent. In addition to becoming wholly Sioux, she'd also learned how to manage her husband every bit as skillfully as her mother-in-law managed her own.

Golden Eagle brought his brows together. "We have no need of women. We take care of our own meals when we go to war."

White Wind nodded. "That is good. Then your mother and I will not need to work while we are here. We brought our own food and can take care of ourselves." She tipped her chin ever so slightly.

Both men looked thunderstruck. "You will return home with our children," Golden Eagle ordered. "I will speak with you later about your foolishness in leaving home and bringing them along as though this were a . . . a *picnic*." He used the white man's word for days spent eating and doing nothing—one of his wife's favorite activities.

"Speak now, husband." A playful breeze flirted with her hair, which had come unbraided—helped by the small hands of her daughter. White-blond hair floated around her face, making her look more like a spirit than a flesh-and-blood woman.

Seeing Eyes ducked her head to hide her amusement. Her daughter-in-law was not easily intimidated. She walked around and relieved the younger woman of the cradle board.

Hawk Eyes stepped forward. "My wife has reason to be here. I can even allow you your reasons, but there is no excuse to bring the children."

Striking Thunder stalked over to his father and grandfather, his young face filled with indignation. "I am no child." He gripped his miniature bow in his hand—his new and bigger and stronger bow. "With my father gone I am a man, and a man protects his women."

"I am here to help as well." White Wolf came to stand beside his older brother. At seven he was nearly as tall as Striking Thunder.

Seeing Eyes lifted Dove out of the cradle board. She didn't dare look at the two grown men, for she was positive they felt as she did. At nine winters, Striking Thunder had insisted that he be allowed to travel with them.

"Your grandfather does not like to lose battles, little one, but this battle he has lost," she whispered to the baby. She then handed her granddaughter to her daughter-in-law.

Golden Eagle looked as exasperated as his father. He stared down at his young daughter, who came to stand between her mother and grandmother.

Star Dreamer, Wolf's twin sister, took her grandmother's hand. "I see visions." It was all she offered in her small and uncertain voice.

Shaking his head, knowing he'd lost, Golden Eagle lifted a brow to the infant. "And the baby? What reason does Dove have to be here?" he asked.

White Wind handed the baby to her father with a smile. "Her food supply is here."

With that, the two women, along with Star Dreamer, began unloading their supplies, while the two boys moved to flank their father and grandfather.

Behind them, the band of warriors scattered with grins on their faces.

Chapter Thirteen

Night Shadow woke in the early morn to a dark, cold, and damp room. Lighting a fire was now too risky, as the smoke could be spotted from far away. He was glad he'd had the foresight to bring lots of heavy fur robes.

From where he lay on his pallet, he watched sunlight shining down through the rocky ceiling in the back, revealing a world of floating dust particles. Rolling over, he glanced over at Winona's pallet. It was empty. His captive normally woke long before him.

He shook his head as he sat up. Good thing he didn't need to worry about her escaping or doing him harm. Instead she seemed determined to prevent him from bringing on his own death—something they argued over at least once a day. Frowning, he ran a hand through his hair, then stretched his arms over his head. "Not today," he whispered. Soon her father's warriors would pass through this area, but not today.

He sprang to his feet and headed for the back of his new hideout, then climbed up to the top. Today he wanted to see the sheer joy that he was beginning to understand as part of Winona herself.

Though she could be vexing, troublesome, and even maddening, she also fascinated him. And made him wish his life was different, that he had more to offer her.

Climbing to the top, he frowned. He'd been sure he'd find her up here sitting. She'd spent most of yesterday here, coming down to sleep only when he'd threatened to come and get her.

He walked around the top to be sure. He even glanced down to check that she hadn't fallen. Remembering the sight of her far above him the day he'd kidnapped her, Night Shadow shook his head. She'd given him more than a bit of a scare, but when he'd brought her here she'd come alive in a way that drew him like honey drew the bears.

Her excitement even that day when he'd watched and waited for her had drawn him. Her fearlessness, and her joy at standing on top of the world, had been obvious, and she had

charmed him. He shook his head. Her skill at
rock climbing still amazed him, but her calm
acceptance of her fate at his hands confused
him.

Far below, he spotted movement. He narrowed his eyes. Right at that moment he was
far from charmed or amazed. He was furious at
her for disobeying his order to stay within the
cavern. There she was, walking and twirling
along the edge of the lake as though she had
no care in the world.

Watching wisps of fog drift off the water, fingers of cotton that seemed to hold and caress
her, he felt his anger give way to something that
scared him even more. Desire. She was surreal
down there, yet he knew only too well how real
she was, how real and alive she'd made him
feel when he'd merged their bodies as one.

Refusing to think of that stormy night or the
fierce passion that had created a storm unlike
anything he'd ever known, Night Shadow spun
around and strode out of his temporary home.

She is not for you. She was not, yet his body
protested by remembering how she'd touched
him and teased him and spoken to him. His
loins longed to feel her soft mound pressed
against him, with her legs wrapped tightly
around his waist.

He tried to convince himself that Winona was

not special, but it didn't work. No one else had ever engaged his mind, his body, and his soul as she had done.

When he'd made love to her, she'd had all of him. The joining of their bodies had satisfied more than his manly needs. She'd satisfied some emotional need he even now refused to examine or admit to having.

Dropping to his hands and knees, he crawled through the short, narrow passage. Ignorance seemed the wisest course for the time being. As he stood, he fully admitted to himself that he was running away from something that could rock his world and bring it crashing down upon his head.

The lake enchanted Winona. As soon as she'd seen the misty fog floating across the water she hadn't been able to resist coming down to greet the new day. The grass beneath her bare feet was wet and cold. The fog enveloped her in a cloudy cloak, and she loved it. She felt alive, a part of this hidden world.

Drawing her dress over her head, she tossed it aside, then waded into the water. The cold made her squeal, but she plunged in and ducked her head beneath the water. Shoving her hair back when she surfaced, she glanced up at the towering rock. Clay would wake soon and he'd be furious with her for disobeying his orders not to leave her prison. She gave a mental shrug.

He would just have to get over it. She knew, as did he, that her family was not close to them yet. That would change soon, and she planned to take advantage of this moment.

Clay underestimated her father and his abilities to track them. Frowning, she felt some of the spell of the early morning fade. Long into the night she'd tried to think of some way to get Clay to change his mind and abandon his risky plan. She sighed. There didn't seem to be any way she could convince him otherwise.

Turning to wade back to the bank, she froze at the sight of a very angry Clay watching her. The mist swam around him, parting behind him like hands reaching out. In the gray morning, with his features partially hidden, he looked formidable—and desirable—with his legs spread in a stance that made her even more aware of him as a man.

Her gaze roamed upward from his knees, lingering on strong thighs that made her remember the feel of him, the strength of him when he'd mated with her. She blinked back the images but hungrily swept her eyes upward to his narrow waist. His angry stance didn't frighten her. Instead it made her want him desperately.

219

Clay wore just his breechclout—and a furious expression. She scowled. She'd rather he wore a look of intense need. Glancing down to be sure she was mostly hidden beneath the water, she grinned mischievously. "If you want to bathe, I'll turn my head while you undress." Winona knew full well that he hadn't come down to wash, but she wasn't going to let him intimidate her.

To her surprise he slowly untied the leather thong around his waist and dropped the cloth between his legs. She fell back into the water and nearly choked when she forgot to close her mouth and hold her breath.

Of all the reactions she'd expected from him, his baring himself to her had been the last. She'd figured he'd shout, threaten, and make her return. But not reveal himself.

Standing back up, she wiped the water from her eyes. Clay hadn't moved. She gulped. When they'd mated she hadn't seen him. Only felt him. All of him. She suddenly felt very warm.

"Did you change your mind?" Amusement edged his angry voice.

Winona lifted a brow. She'd issued the challenge. He'd accepted. Now what? She smiled. She'd play. Having him ignore her had infuriated her. He wasn't ignoring her now, so she couldn't complain.

Rising up onto her toes to reveal her shoulders and the tops of her breasts, she tilted her head back. "Um, no, not me. Have you?"

Clay splashed into the water. Winona gulped. She should turn her head. It was one thing to eye him with wisps of fog blurring his image. It was an entirely different matter watching him come closer. Lifting her eyes to his, she caught his silent challenge.

By the time he reached her she was more than uncomfortably aware of him—and desperate both for his touch and with the need to touch. She'd teased him on the trail by boldly kissing him to prove that he needed her. Her plan had served to remind her how much she'd needed him.

Clay ducked down into the water and brushed past her legs as he moved to deeper water. Winona released her breath. She hadn't even realized she'd been holding it. Deciding that she'd been a bit hasty in her challenge, she moved toward shore.

An arm grabbed her by the knees and yanked her underwater. Winona barely had time to grab a breath of air before water closed over her. Her hair floated in all directions. She turned to shrug off Clay's hands as he pulled her into deeper water.

Dawn's tiny finger of light pierced the water

through the mist. The dark, murky lake water turned blue-white. Clay's hair seemed liquid gold as his body shimmered in the light. Their feet tangled as they treaded water. Finally Clay propelled them up. She let out her breath and grabbed another just in case.

Clay had other things on his mind. "You are a fool to play this game." He pulled her close.

Winona sighed when the tips of her tightly budded breasts were crushed against his chest. "It is no game," she admitted, needing him to understand that what she felt for him was real.

"You are innocent and naive."

Winona stopped him from saying anything more by placing a finger over his lips. "There are some things a woman just knows." She put his hand to her heart. "What I feel here is real."

Clay released her and started swimming toward shore. Winona lunged after him, and this time she shoved him beneath the surface. When he came up spluttering, they were closer to the shore. Both stood. Winona poked her finger into his hard chest.

"We are meant to be together. Your soul calls to mine. You feel it. I know you do. The spirits brought you to me, and me to you."

"You think I lost my family and nearly died just so I could be here at this time for you?" He gave a bark of laughter.

Winona didn't back down. "Clay, I do not know why your family had to die. I do not know why you and Jenny were spared. But you were. You were meant to live."

Clay turned his back to her. "Maybe I would rather have died."

Placing her hands on his shoulders Winona leaned her check against his shoulder blade. "No, your spirit chose to live. From what you said, you should have died but you did not. You chose life over death. You can tell yourself that you lived only for your sister, but you lived for yourself. I know this because there is so much life in you." Winona paused but he said nothing.

"Clay, once again you are being given that choice. To live or die."

Turning, Clay grabbed her upper arms and pulled her close. "I should live for you, is that what you believe?"

Winona placed her arms around his neck. "No. You must live for yourself—for that boy buried deep inside you and for the man shaped by a tragic past."

"That man has nothing to offer." Clay sounded desperate, as if he wanted to live but didn't know how.

"You are wrong. He has much to offer," Winona whispered.

Clay wrapped her tightly in his arms and kissed her—hard, deeply, full of desperate need.

Winona opened her mouth and used her tongue to gentle him. Clay's mouth softened. His kiss turned tender. Finally he lifted his head and scooped her up. He carried her out of the lake to a patch of grass near a stand of trees. The mist hung low and patchy. In the east, pale blue sky was just showing morning color.

Winona rested her head on his shoulder. "I want to stay down here, with you. I want to share with you the beginning of this new day." Her hand curved against his jaw. After today he probably wouldn't allow her come down into the open, and she, in her need to protect him, would do her best to keep him hidden away as well.

She shivered, but it wasn't from the cold. Fear that she'd discovered love only to lose it made her skin crawl, and her arms tightened.

"In case you are unaware, you have no clothing on, and it is cold." He stopped to stare down into her eyes.

Winona ran her fingers along his jaw. "Neither do you," she said.

Clay carried her to a spot near the lake and sat down, pulling her into his lap with her back to his chest. He bent his knees. Hers followed

224

the line of his. Her buttocks rested against his manhood and her arms were wrapped beneath her breasts. His hands crossed over her arms and slid up and down her upper arms to warm her.

Winona leaned her head back into the hollow of his shoulder and neck. "I love mornings."

"You are crazy," he muttered.

Winona laughed softly. Yes, she was crazy. She was suddenly sure of her love for this man who made her do things she'd never have thought she'd do—like let her arms drop so his hands slid down to cover her breasts completely. Her hands rose again to hold his arms to her. Content—for the moment—she waited for the sun to rise.

Night Shadow watched Winona, no longer surprised by anything she did or asked. She had to be crazy, yet it was her unpredictable nature that he lov— liked. She fascinated him. Attracted him. Amazed him.

He wanted to be the man to put stars in her eyes and create the warmth of the sun in her laughter. He needed her smile to nourish him and set him free. Realizing his thoughts were taking him down a path he had no business traveling, he turned his attention to the sunrise—and the woman sitting naked in his lap as though she'd done this forever. Yet this was the first time she'd purposely revealed her body to him, and it had seemed as natural as breathing.

Night Shadow rubbed his chin over the top of her head. She had scared him, telling him they were fated, that this was meant to be. How could he even think for a moment that his family had died so he could find happiness with this woman? Impossible! He'd never be able to live with that.

But he couldn't deny that he was alive. He'd been spared. Did he have the right to throw his life away? Was there a reason he'd been spared? Night Shadow closed his eyes.

No, he refused to believe he'd been spared. He'd just been stubborn enough to live and not give his enemy the satisfaction of killing him. He'd lived only to find Jenny and prove to Henry Black Bear that he'd failed.

But could there be more, as the woman in his arms kept insisting?

The question raised doubts that he'd not known were there. But they were, and at that moment he admitted that they had always been there—he'd just buried them, refusing to acknowledge or find the answer to those questions.

Burying his head in Winona's neck, Clay, the man, sought distraction. He was still a coward.

He still feared the answer, for it could very well change all that he'd become. And all that he'd based his life upon.

Winona tipped her head to the side, inviting him to nuzzle the side of her neck. He could not refuse either of them. Not at that moment when, in their own sheltered world, life seemed perfect.

He kissed her soft, dewy skin, ran his tongue along her jaw until she shifted her head back further to offer her mouth to his. Holding her tight, Night Shadow felt Clay the man take over and merge with the hardened warrior. He became one man with only one need: this woman.

Winona felt alive as never before. The air, cool and moist, sharpened each of her senses as she watched ribbons of pink and yellow unfurl across the sky, spreading, twisting, and weaving soft, dreamy pastel shades into a morning blanket.

Behind her, warm puffs of air warmed her cheek, her jaw, and the back of her neck. Turning her head slightly so she could breathe in his scent, she sighed. "I think the sun has risen."

"So has something else," Clay murmured in her ear. His tongue swirled around the inside of her ear.

"Hmm, is it as pretty as the sun rising in the east?"

227

Clay chuckled. "Better, Golden Eyes. Much nicer." His hands, cupping her breasts, closed tight. He squeezed her gently.

"That feels nice," she said. She loved the sound of his endearment. It meant he had feelings for her. She ran her palms up and down Clay's thighs.

"Yes." He lightly ran his palms over the tips of her breasts, then took each one between his thumb and forefinger and rolled the firm flesh.

Winona arched her back. Inside she felt as though there were a connection between what he was doing and the ache spreading deep inside her. With each squeeze she felt the throbbing grow between her legs. And sitting on top of him she felt his hardness. "I want to see you."

"You saw me." His hands went back to caressing and palming her breasts. He couldn't take his eyes off them. They were a perfect fit for his hands—molding nicely to his cupped palms as though his hands had been made just for her.

Fated.

Clay shoved the word from his mind. He did not believe in gods or spirits or fate. Life happened, the good, the bad. The beauty and the ugliness of life just happened.

So why could he not accept the bad in his life?

"Clay?" Her soft voice drew him out of his thoughts.

"I'm here, Golden Eyes."

"No, you were elsewhere." She turned slightly to stare up at him.

Clay buried his lips in the hollow of her neck. "Keep me here with you, Golden Eyes, if only for a little while."

"For as long as you want," Winona promised, strangely teary-eyed at his request. To herself she vowed to keep him forever. She already had his soul; they were two hearts, one soul. Now she just had to convince him to take her heart and give his in return.

Clay's arms tightened around her. "I want. See how much I want." He shifted, pulled her harder against him, then ran his palms along the outside of her thighs. When he reached her knees, he nudged them apart.

Winona closed her eyes when she felt her legs fall open like the wings of a butterfly. She felt open. Exposed. And embarrassed because she knew Clay was staring down at her.

Before, she'd been mostly concealed by the way she sat, his arms across her chest to block his view. And in the water he couldn't have seen her clearly.

"Open your eyes." Clay blew a breath of warm air into her ear.

"Why?" Her voice broke when she felt his hands moving along the inside of her thigh. His hands stopped just below the heart of her, as though framing that part of her.

"So you can watch." He slid his hands around and lifted her up slightly.

Winona felt his hardness spring up between her thighs and move gently against her throbbing center. She drew in a shaky breath and gripped his outer thighs with her hands. "I do not think I can do that," she whispered.

"Coward."

Her eyes flew open at the soft taunt. "I am no coward."

The sight of him proudly against her, with her soft, black hair spread out in front of him, brought forth waves of heat. He pulsed against her, and Winona could not have torn her gaze from him for any reason.

Lifting one hand, she hesitated. Was he hard or soft? She stared at a small bead of moisture forming at his very tip.

"Do it," he said softly in her ear. "Touch me. See what you do to me. Know that I want you."

Winona needed no further encouragement. She stroked one finger up the side of him. His skin felt hard and hot. Using two fingers, one on either side of him, she repeated her stroke. The skin moved with her fingers, up, then down. Against her back she felt Clay shudder.

She smiled and closed her hand over him and stroked, holding him firmly. Hard and soft. The feel of him thrilled her. She ran her thumb over his tip and sighed with pleasure. "So soft," she said. "So hard."

Another shudder came from Clay, followed by a moan. Winona didn't have to ask if she was hurting him. She knew he hurt in the same way she hurt: deep inside where only they could ease each other's pain with the same pleasure as before.

"I think you have learned the feel of me well." Clay tried to get her to turn around.

Winona wasn't finished. "Not all of you." This time she stroked all the way up and over the tip of him, smoothing his moisture across him with her thumb. "I like the feel of you," she said.

Clay stopped her. "Yes, I like it too, and if you do not stop you will see how much I love your touch."

Winona wasn't sure what he meant.

"Should I show you what happens when you don't stop?" he added.

Winona's eyes widened. "Yes," she said hoarsely.

To her surprise Clay slid his fingers into her soft curls. She jerked. "You said you'd show me." Not that she minded whatever his fingers were doing—but she felt as though she should glance away and not watch his fingers part her and reveal a part of her she never looked at.

Clay nibbled the flesh along her neck. "What better way to show you than with your own body?" Slowly his middle finger moved over her. "Watch. See how much I love to touch you."

Enthralled, Winona watched his finger move in a slow circle. Her fingers dug into his thighs and her own legs trembled. "Clay," she moaned. She tried to rotate with him but their positions made it hard for her to move.

"Remember how I felt?" He pushed his finger down deeper into her folds, then returned to his stroking. This time she saw moisture on his finger—her moisture. Wonder kept her eyes glued to his slow, knowing strokes, and the breath of cold air against her throbbing heat heightened the sensations he was arousing deep inside her.

"I remember." She gasped. "I will show you how much I like this if you do not stop," she said, panting.

Clay chuckled. "Don't stop. Show me how much you like this. Let me hear how much you like it." Without warning he increased the pressure and moved his finger in a fast, tight circle.

Winona pressed the backs of her thighs hard

against the front of his, seeking, needing, wanting. Desperately needing what his fingers were giving, she tried to lift herself to increase the hard feel of him as he stroked her.

Clay shifted his finger slightly, sliding down just a bit. Winona cried out as her hips jerked. She hadn't thought he could increase the pleasure, but he had, and now something inside of her tightened. His left hand fondled her breasts, rubbing and squeezing and palming.

Faster Clay went. Harder and faster and tighter, drawing the throbbing need from deep inside her out to the center he controlled with one finger. She rolled her head back and forth, panted, bit her lip.

"Don't hold back." He groaned. "I want to hear you."

Winona opened her mouth and cried out as her head went back, her hips jerked up, and she felt herself shatter skyward, leaving her body convulsing far beneath her.

Chapter Fourteen

Clay slid his hands beneath Winona and re-arranged her, turning her over, lifting her hips up, bringing her throbbing, wet heat hard against the part of him that burned for release. He moaned, his breathing ragged, his pulse pounding.

She surrounded him with heat and softness. His sensitive head found her swollen heart. Moisture leaked as he jerked with an uncontrollable urge to rub himself over her. He slid between her slick folds and shuddered at the incredible feel of her softness cupping his hardness.

He pulsed, and slid up and down over her slick heat. He wanted to pull back and drive himself deep inside her. He desperately needed to feel her around him, have her body grasp him, but he fought his need, tried to slow his heart, his pulse. His fingers convulsed, biting into her soft buttocks. She whimpered and moved against his sensitive tip.

"Ah . . ." He gasped for breath. The swollen heart of her desire brushed against him, making him tremble uncontrollably. "Don't move." He released his hold on her, pulling his body away from hers as he lowered her back the ground.

"No!" In one quick movement she grabbed him and brought him hard against her. "More," she said in a gasp. "Like before."

Clay glanced down at their nearly joined bodies. Watching, he pushed himself down her moist folds until the very tip of him rested in the hollow of her moist core. One push. One hard thrust and he'd find heaven. Paradise. He'd find the very essence of his soul.

"Clay!"

The soft whimper had him drawing in a deep, shaky breath. His gaze traveled up and over the soft mounds of her breasts to the wild desire in her eyes. "I need to feel your heat, and the way your body clings to mine. I want to feel you tighten around me, and pull from me all I have to give." He pulled back slightly, lowered her hips, and spread her knees.

Winona shifted her hips and held out her hands. "Now, Clay."

Clay leaned forward and took her lips in a hard, drugging kiss that left them both breathless. "I need all that and more," he whispered against the corner of her mouth. Trailing his lips across her flesh, he felt her shudder with each nip, each lick, as he followed the line of her jaw, the curve of her throat, and the gentle rise of her breast until he found her nipple with the tip of his tongue.

He closed his lips over the hard bud and suckled, nipped, and soothed with his tongue and lips. Beneath him Winona grew frantic. Her hands dug into his shoulders and pulled at his hair in an effort to bring him hard against her. Her hips lifted; her legs sought his hips. She pulled, begged, but Clay refused to stop until he'd paid the same tribute to her other straining breast.

Then he stared down at her with wonder as he moved until he was poised to enter her soft, moist sheath. The tip of his manhood pulsed with hunger and need, and his heart nearly burst with emotions he'd long thought dead. For so long he'd needed no one. But all that had changed—all because of a spirited, courageous woman.

Winona wrapped her hands into his hair and pulled hard. "You are taking too long," she said in a gasp: "Let me feel you inside me. I want to join with you, be one with you—"

Clay needed no further invitation, couldn't wait any longer, but still he retained control. He needed to feel, to remember each moment of this joining. He entered slowly, one inch at a time, feeling her tight sheath close around him. Once fully inside, he held himself still, enthralled.

Lowering his head, he found her mouth and kissed her slowly, deeply. Winona moaned beneath him and bucked her hips to bring him into her deeper, harder. She pulled back, trying to start the rhythm that would bring them both release. But Clay stopped her frantic movements by pressing his pelvis down harder onto hers, pinning her to the soft mat of grass beneath them.

The slower he went, the more she squirmed and rocked against him. She nipped at his lips, pulled her nails down his back, and bucked hard against him until finally he could not stop himself from pulling out in one long movement and thrusting back inside in one long, powerful stroke.

Winona cried out and lifted her legs, wrapping them around Clay's waist to hold him to her. "No more games," she said, pulling his mouth back to hers.

"No more games," he said in a gasp, merging his mouth with hers. Tongues dueled and vied for dominance. Hips rose and fell and came together with soft sounds that drove Winona higher and higher.

"C-Clay," she moaned, digging her fingers hard into his buttocks.

"Now, Golden Eyes."

Winona arched her hips at the same time as Clay, felt his shuddering release all the way into her soul as she burst into tiny sparkles—a rainbow of color that greeted the dawn.

Winona should have been exhausted after their last bout of lovemaking. She sighed. Then smiled. After two days and three nights in Clay's arms learning the difference between mating and loving, it was a wonder she could move, let alone remain awake while the rest of the world slept.

Rolling out of Clay's arms onto her stomach, she stretched her arms and legs out. There wasn't much room in the small space to stretch sideways. If she tried, she'd end up jamming her elbow into Clay's nose. In this tiny tipi above the world there was barely enough room for two to sleep—and only if one person slept on his or her side.

She turned her head. Clay slept soundly on his side, his back to the slanted wall, which was actually a rock that was wide at the bottom and tapered at the top with a hollowed-out bottom. It sat on top of the center tower. Beneath her the rock sloped gently, forming a natural bed.

There were other groupings of boulders, but none formed a miniature home so far above the world below.

Winona didn't think there would ever be such a magnificent place on earth. She could lie here all night and never feel as though she'd absorbed all the beauty spread out below her.

The large lake rippled gently in the silvery moonlight, and stars blinked brilliantly across a sky of velvet that stretched as far as she could see. She sighed with contentment.

Turning onto her back, she gave another stretch. The fur beneath her cushioned her from the hard, cold surface of the stone and warmed her with her own body heat. Between her and the wall, the fur that she'd used as a blanket lay discarded. Her head fell to the side. Clay had proven himself to be a very nice, very warm blanket.

Lifting one hand Winona ran her finger across the ceiling, then giggled. The amount of room between floor and ceiling was not much, and their first time making love in this cozy nest, Clay, lost in the throes of passion, had raised himself up and thrown his head back— and nearly banged himself unconscious.

Winona turned back over and laughed into the pile of furs beneath her. She'd laughed so hard—until Clay recovered and renewed his thrusting with vigor.

Her shoulders slumped. Just the memory of his sending her from a fit of laughter to a writhing mass of screaming need made her go weak.

"Go to sleep or I will force you back below," Clay grumbled beside her. He sounded cranky, amused, exasperated.

Raising herself up on one elbow Winona trailed her fingers down the light dusting of hair covering his chest. "How can you sleep?" She leaned forward and followed her fingers with her mouth.

Growling, Clay rolled on top of her and bit her playfully on the back of her neck. "You have the eyes of a cat, claws like a cat, and you stay awake all night. You, I fear, have been misnamed."

Winona rested her forehead on the fur, arching her neck up to allow Clay easier access. She shivered. The contrast of his soft mouth, moist tongue, and rough skin moving over her extra-sensitive flesh made her groan and shift her hips.

Her breathing sped up. "Clay . . ." She tried to turn over so she could touch him, see him, and feel him hard against her and, ultimately, deep inside her.

241

"Not this time, my wildcat."

Winona moaned. "You are teasing me. I will never sleep if you stop."

Clay bit down on one earlobe, then suckled the pink flesh. "Who said anything about stopping?" He slid one hand beneath her.

Feeling two of his fingers sliding into the moist folds that concealed her tiny bud, Winona gripped the furs with her hands and lifted her head in anticipation.

Clay dropped his head so that they were cheek-to-cheek. His fingers squeezed, then stopped, over and over. "See all those stars in the sky, my golden-eyed wildcat?"

Panting, trying to move her hips and set the pace, Winona groaned. "Yes. No more talk." She desperately needed him, so she tried to turn over. "I want you. Inside. Hard and fast. Like last time."

Warm breath slid over her mouth. "Not yet. Not this time. First you are going to soar alone and I'm going to watch." One finger began a slow, leisurely circuit around the swollen heart of her.

Winona contracted her buttocks tightly together, then released the muscles. Over and over she tried to get him to move faster. But the more she demanded, the slower he went.

"Clay . . ."

"Slow, Golden Eyes. Slow. Make it last. Feel each pulse of your heart. Feel the need rushing through you. Feel me touching you." The rough pad of his finger slid across her swollen bud.

Winona bucked and bit down on her fist to keep from screaming.

"Do you feel me?"

"Yes," she whimpered. She felt. She needed. She hurt, and only he could provide the release she needed.

"Inside," she begged. "Let me feel you too. I need to feel you," she moaned.

Clay slid his hard length over her.

"Do you feel that?"

"Y-yes." She gasped. She felt him—all of him—sliding in and out between her twin cheeks. She lifted her bottom, trying to entice him into entering her from behind like a male cat mated with a female. "You feel good." She gasped. "Very good."

"Good. Know what I feel?" His fingers stopped their dance.

"N-no."

He slid one finger lower, deeper, until he sat poised at her entrance. "Hot. Soft. Slick. Ready for me."

"Yes. Yes. Yes." She wanted to scream that she was ready. Past ready. She was desperate. She needed him to release the flood of passion pounding deep inside her.

Clay dragged his finger back and pressed up and down, following the rhythm of her frantic movements. She felt herself tightening, building. But the soaring release stayed just out of reach.

"Lift your head. Let me see you."

Winona did as he instructed. She stretched her hands out, searching for something to hold on to. Clay rose up slightly to allow her more freedom of movement and slipped his other arm beneath her chest, just above her breasts.

Then his finger spread her slick moisture over and around her. "Move. Hard and fast. Let me see you fly. Let me hear your pleasure."

Winona took all that he offered and more. She moved herself over him, controlled the pressure. Clay's tongue trailed down her body, tracing the curved line of her spine.

Pulling back his other arm, he slipped his other hand between her legs. Two fingers entered her deeply.

It was all Winona needed. She tightened. Another hard stoke across her sensitive flesh followed by the sinking of his fingers deep inside her sent her shattering across the night sky like a star traveling from one side of the heavens to the other.

*   *   *

Clay had never seen or felt anything as beautiful as this woman coming apart in his arms. Winona responded to his every touch with a wild abandon that enticed him. Ensnared him.

Each shudder, each muffled cry of pleasure, each gasp and plea and each tremor that rocked through her increased his own joy. The greater her response, the more he gave. And the more he gave, the more she returned.

Their loving was a circle. A flexible, ever-widening circle. Whether they took it slow and tender or hard, fast, and wild, their circle matched their needs. Watching and feeling her respond not only to his hands, but his voice, had brought him to a stronger, harder, and more desperate need for her.

His need for this woman threatened to consume him. Rolling over onto his back, he pulled her on top of him. Her back lay against his chest; the back of her head rested on his shoulder.

Bringing up his knees, and hers with his, he allowed his legs to fall open. His knees almost touched each side of their private little haven. Hers rested along the inside of his, leaving her wide-open to the soft, cool breeze that swept over them.

Using both hands to separate her, he gave one hard upward thrust. Her heat surrounded him. Tiny convulsions gripped him and urged him to move and find his own release.

She arched her back and tightened her sheath. Silently she urged him to stroke and find his release, but he held himself still. While he wanted nothing more than to thrust mind-lessly, he also wanted to savor the slick heat, the throbbing in and around him.

He reached up to cup her breasts. Pulling in a deep breath, he drew her closer. She moved with each breath. Her hips ground into his pelvis. He suckled at her neck and slid his hands down to hold her still. He throbbed and pulsed. Without even moving he was close to release.

"Clay, you are not being nice," she moaned.

He laughed softly in her ear. Pulling out until only the tip of him remained inside, he thrust slowly back into her.

"Slow, remember?" He repeated his leisurely stroke.

"Have I told you that you are a *heya*?"

Unable to help himself, Clay laughed. "A louse, am I?" He pushed himself in as far as he could, satisfied with her gasp of pleasure. Then he pulled all the way out.

Winona protested. "I meant *pejiwabluska*."

A walking stick! Clay thrust hard back inside, cutting off her amused giggle. "Save it for morning, my little *kimimila*. My sweet little but-

246

terfly." With that he stroked until, once again, they soared across the heavens, flying high and slowly sinking back to earth.

Clay woke past dawn and grinned. For the first time since he'd known Winona, he'd woken first. Normally she woke before the sun.

Her arms were draped over his body, her legs tangled with his. He shifted. She rolled onto her back but did not wake. Though they'd spent much of the night making love, he couldn't think of a better way to start the new day.

Winona stretched. "Is it morning?"

"Yes, Golden Eyes, it is morning." Glancing out across the lake to judge the time, he spotted a flock of birds taking to the sky. He went still and scanned the area. Minutes later his eyes followed the flight of three deer who leaped across the green grass until they disappeared back into the thick undergrowth.

Frowning, he rolled Winona off him and lifted himself up as far as he could without banging his head.

Winona turned over and peered out at the tranquil lake. "What is it, Clay?"

Clay backed out. "Come on, Golden Eyes. Get moving. I think we have company."

Keeping low so he wouldn't be spotted, Night Shadow watched Winona slip back into the hidden cavern through a narrow opening behind one of the wide rocks. He followed with the furs. Their clothing had been shed below.

Once below, he dropped his armload of furs and used a piece of hide to wash himself while Winona did the same. The silence grew heavy between them. Their idyllic time together had just come to an end. Even after her father moved on, nothing would be quite the same.

When he went to the small, naturally formed window, Winona followed. Anyone who was out there was still too far to see him from this distance. Winona got down and peered out through a tiny fissure. "I do not see anyone."

"They are there." Of that Night Shadow was certain. Moving, he knelt down beside her. They stared at each other. "You are amazing."

He still couldn't believe that Winona wanted to help him. It didn't matter that there was nothing she could do to change his mind. The very fact that she wanted to save him from her father did something strange to his insides.

"You could be free with one shout," he said, the backs of his fingers sliding down her check and along one side of her jaw.

"I will never be free again," she whispered.

Night Shadow knew her words had nothing to do with her sister. What she did now she did for him, and with him. She truly amazed him.

The last few days were the happiest, most peaceful days he'd had since losing his family.

Drawing in a deep breath, Night Shadow resumed watching. The waiting should have been easy. The hard part was done. His prey was within reach. But would all this bring him Jenny or just more heartache?

He glanced out of the corner of his eye and watched Winona. Somewhere hidden by the trees her family searched. For the first time since embarking on this mission he wished he could have achieved revenge without causing more pain and suffering. Was it right for him to put his need to find his sister over the good of others?

He was no better than his enemy. He grimaced. That wasn't true. And had there been another way he'd have chosen it. But Henry Black Bear would never have told Night Shadow the truth, and once Henry knew Clay Blue Hawk lived, he'd never stop trying to kill him in order to keep the past buried.

Night Shadow rubbed the back of his neck. He'd had no choice but to strike at Henry in a more public way. With Winona's father involved, Henry would have pressure on him to return Jenny, if for no other reason than to keep Clay silent until Henry found and killed him or was killed.

Nor would Henry reveal the truth or meaning behind the messages that Night Shadow had given to Sharp Nose to leave along the trail once they'd separated. The other two warriors had been instructed to ride off separately for a day, then backtrack. Crazy Fox was to follow Winona's father and his warriors and keep an eye on Hoka Luta while Dream Walker kept Spotted Deer safely hidden.

Night Shadow could only hope that Henry wanted the chief's daughter badly enough to produce Jenny. Reaching down to take a strand of Winona's dark hair between his fingers, he brought the silky strands to his nose and inhaled sunshine.

She met his gaze and smiled at him. Night Shadow drew in a deep breath and leaned down to plant a kiss near the corner of her mouth. "I will never let you go." He had no intention of letting Winona go back to Henry Black Bear.

"I do not want you to let me go."

Her words warmed him. And made him feel guilty. What kind of life could he give her? Her father would never stop searching for her, and if he kept her with him they'd have to live alone, for he wouldn't risk innocent people being killed if her father found them.

"I want to help you." Her fingers slid along his jaw.

"I know. But what you ask is impossible."

Winona sighed. "You are thickheaded."

"So you tell me—often." He returned his attention to the lake.

Shadows from the trees lining the lake emerged. Warriors on foot with bows drawn crept into view.

"Shhh," he said, grateful for an excuse not to discuss the matter. He'd never agree to meet with her father and present his story.

Tense minutes crawled by. Finally a group on horseback left the concealing woods. He heard Winona draw in a deep breath as she saw members from her tribe below. "What are they doing here?" She whispered the question.

Night Shadow frowned when he saw two women and several children in the group. "Who are they?"

"My mother, my brother's wife, and their children." Winona's voice caught.

"I'm sorry, Golden Eyes." And he was, for if she stayed with him—if he could not release her—she'd never see them again.

"It is not too late to stop this," Winona whispered, looking at him.

He clenched his fist and ignored her.

"Clay, if I go to my father with your story he can help."

Throwing her an angry and frustrated look,

he held up his hand. "No. If your father didn't kill me, Henry Black Bear, the man you are to wed, would. Even if it meant being killed himself, he would not let me live long enough to tell my tale."

Winona stood. "First, I am not going to marry Hoka Luta, or Henry or whoever he is. And I am smart enough to talk to my father alone. Once he knows the truth, he can take Ho— Henry prisoner and make him tell us where Jenny is."

She sent him a pleading look. "It is a better plan than dying if he does catch you."

The man in him needed her more than anything. But the warrior, far too used to being in control, could not take what she offered. It wasn't just pride or his distaste for failure. It went deeper. This was something he *had* to do. Henry wasn't just his problem; he was Clay's redemption, and until he'd met Winona, he hadn't realized now important it was for him to come face-to-face with his past.

Since his Golden Eyes had come into his life, the man inside had broken through the walls of the self-imposed prison he'd erected and was slowly merging with the emotionless warrior.

Night Shadow had planned and waited for this moment. Night Shadow, the trained warrior, would not hesitate to kill Henry, a man who'd cold-bloodedly wiped out a family of women and children. But he had to know that the part of him that was also Clay Coburn could go through with it. Clay had to face his past and end the hatred and torment in order to claim his future.

Staring down at Winona he knew it would be so easy just to take her away and disappear. There were many places they could go where no one would find them. But it wasn't the life he wanted for her, their children, or himself, and this wasn't something he could ask others to do for him.

He didn't tell her what he only now understood. Finding Jenny and learning of her fate wasn't his salvation. It was only part. He had to face Henry and face his past with all the horror, betrayal, and his own feelings of guilt before he could release the bitterness and hatred that held him chained to the darkness.

With this woman, he'd seen light—walked in it and wanted it totally. And because of the gift of life she'd given him, he was determined to come to her a whole man. Not two men. He had to blend Clay and Night Shadow into one.

Chapter Fifteen

Standing near the stone window fashioned by Mother Earth's loving hands, Winona stared out into the foggy morning. A pale sea of moist, thick cotton floated far below her, concealing the dark blue lake and bright banks of green grass.

She rubbed her arms. Moisture dampened her skin and collected on the brownish-gray walls of granite. Breathing in the chilling air cleared her mind, but her soul felt frozen. Shifting slightly, she rested her shoulder against the clammy wall and watched Clay gather his weapons and strap on his knife.

Dread crept through her heart. Neither begging, pleading, nor anger could sway him from leaving their safe haven to scout the area to be sure her family had left. Rubbing her hands up and down her arms, she sought the words to keep him from leaving. Moving close to Clay she rested her palms on his shoulder and stared down at his head. Her fingers trailed through the golden-brown strands of his hair. It was soft and silky. Her fingers tightened.

"Stay with me, Clay. You have warriors following my father. Wait for them to come to you. You do not know where Henry is. It is not safe to go out."

Clay stilled. "I am a warrior. I will not hide like—"

Winona dug her fingers into the cool flesh of his shoulder. "Like a woman or child? At least you would be safe. Henry could be out there, watching. What if Sharp Nose or Crazy Fox cannot come to you without fear of Henry seeing them?"

Clay pulled away to sling his quiver of arrows to his back.

Shaking her head, Winona fought the urge to throw one of many large stones at his hard head. "You are a fool if you leave." She paused. "If you die, you fail me. And you fail your sister."

The tensing of Clay's shoulders was her only indication that her words struck him.

Tears welled in her eyes. Frustration made her want to scream, but she didn't dare. "Clay—"

Clay whipped around. His eyes were dark, hard as the stone walls surrounding them. "No more, Golden Eyes."

Winona clamped her mouth shut to hold back words of love. Her need for him was so great that she wasn't sure she could even put it into words without falling apart.

She whirled around and returned to the window. If he was determined to get himself killed there was little she could do. A single tear escaped. She loved Clay with all her heart and wasn't sure she could live without him. How could he do this to her?

Gentle pressure on her shoulders brought her around. Clay's fingers tipped her chin up, then spread along her jaw as he cupped her face tenderly in his hands. He leaned down and kissed her on the lips, licking the salty tears as they fell.

"I will be back before the sun is directly overhead, Golden Eyes." His thumbs smoothed over her face.

Winona closed her eyes, ashamed of her weakness. She shuddered when he planted a kiss, light as a wisp of fog, near her eye.

"I love you," he whispered.

Then he was gone.

Winona kept her eyes tightly shut. He loved her. The tears flowed faster. In her mind she

called him every name she could think of. If he
loved her, how could he leave? How could he
love her and yet not do all in his power to spare
her this hurt and worry? If he loved her, he'd
do everything in his power to live.

For her.

With her.

Filled with fear and despair, Winona opened
her eyes and stared around at the place that had
become a cozy home in so short a time. How
could she have fallen in love a man who was
stubborn, foolish, and so much a part of her that
if anything happened to him, she wasn't sure
she'd survive?

Tipping her head back, she sighed. Love was
not as pleasant as it seemed to an outsider, she
realized. Love hurt. It was not supposed to
hurt, but it did.

Closing her eyes, Winona thought of Clay, of
all the things she loved—and hated. She
frowned. She loved his loyalty, his devotion, his
strength.

Where most young men in Clay's position
might have given up and not survived Henry's
attack, Clay had lived—not for himself, but for
a young sister he so clearly adored.

Winona sighed. Clay's devotion and the
depth of his feelings for those he loved made
him who and what he was. Did she have a right

to try to hold on to him for herself? Slowly she moved away from the window. No, she did not. Clay's path had been set long before she'd met him, and had she been his younger sister, she'd have wanted to know that she'd never been forgotten.

Love was selfless, yet all-encompassing. And it was that selfless love on his part that kept Clay from hiding from his enemy and relying on his friends to do all the work. Especially now that he had her. She knew he had to resolve his past in order to have a future—with her.

Though she knew all this deep in her heart, it didn't ease the ache. And that, she knew, was part of loving. Stooping to pick up a thick fur, she carried it over to the largest crack beneath the window and sank down. It was going to be a long day.

Night Shadow moved slowly through the trees to a place he'd arranged to meet Crazy Fox, who, according to their plan, was to stay behind after Winona's family continued on. Sharp Nose would also be near and would return to the cavern as soon as he led Winona's family and the rest of the warriors, including Hoka Luta, to a place not far from the lake.

The false trail would dead end with one last message: a place and deadline for Jenny to be returned. Then, as soon as Dream Walker returned with Winona's younger sister, the six of them would head for the next place of hiding Clay had chosen—a place they'd be able to remain for the summer until it was time to see if Henry Black Bear produced Jenny. The Sun Dance, held at the end of summer, seemed a long way off.

He drew in a deep, cleansing breath of air, felt the wetness burn his lungs and dampen his skin. He'd done all he could, and if Henry didn't return Jenny by the time the Sun Dance was held, Night Shadow wasn't sure what he'd do. He only knew he could not sell either Winona or Spotted Deer, as he'd threatened. If this plan to get his sister back failed, then he'd have no choice but to go after Henry Black Bear.

Then what? Return Winona to her family? His gut clenched. *No!* He needed her. She was the air he breathed, the warmth that glowed deep inside him, and the nourishment his soul needed to thrive. She was the light that chased away the darkness of his past—she was his future and he would not part with her.

Yet could he take her away from all she knew and loved? Could he take her from her family, knowing that she might never see them again? Unfortunately, that was their only choice. Her father would not accept him—not after taking her from her family, no matter what Winona claimed.

And what of Winona? Could she live with him, live with always looking over their shoulders, fearing that her father's warriors had found them? He tightened one hand into a fist. Had Winona been his daughter he'd never stop searching for her—just as he'd never stopped looking for Jenny and never would. Until he learned of her fate he could not rest, and so he could not expect different from Winona's father or brother.

That stopped him in his tracks. His entire adult life had been spent in a world of pain and uncertainty. Worrying, wondering, and feeling so damn guilty. Yet he'd justified doing the same to others. Winona's entire family: mother, sister-in-law, nieces and nephews—women and children—had all joined in the search.

Darkness stole into his heart, blotting out the ray of sunshine Winona had brought into his life. He knew he could not put another through that pain and uncertainty.

Night Shadow tipped his head back and stared at the clearing blue sky high above the towering trees. As much as it hurt, he knew he'd return Winona to her family at the end of the summer. If he had Jenny back at his side, he'd have proof of Henry's black past, and then perhaps her family would forgive him. If not, he'd be dead before he had a chance to explain.

The wall of trees closed around him; the large granite formation where the woman he loved waited was out of sight, yet Winona's will pulled at him. He kept going, didn't glance back. This was what he'd lived for. He would not hide and let others take all the risk. At least, that was what he tried to tell himself.

But deep down inside there was another reason he refused to consider Winona's plan to go to her father. He was Night Shadow, a man unafraid to go into battle against his toughest enemies, yet he feared that Winona's father would be so furious with him that he'd keep him and Winona apart. Or worse, that once back with her family, Winona would choose them over him, leaving him more lost and alone than ever before. So even though he planned to return her, he selfishly yearned for whatever short time he had with her—even if he had to steal it.

Night Shadow hated the doubts chasing through his mind. He tried to still the tumble of thoughts. He stopped, took several deep breaths, and sought control. Around him the sun had cleared the fog, but his heart still felt cold and dark.

The sudden hush that fell over the land

drowned out his inner voices and had him silently cursing. He'd been so lost in his own thoughts and fears of the past and future that he hadn't been paying attention to the present.

He glanced around, moving his head slowly, his gaze piercing through dark shadows and thick shrubbery. Not a single bird fluttered or sang. The branches of the bushes no long rustled as wildlife scurried from him.

Damn. He wasn't alone. Someone was out here with him. Who? And were they aware of his presence?

The zing of an arrow flying over his head was his answer.

From the top of the granite formation Winona found a narrow crack that separated the towers. Perfect. Not too big and, she hoped as she stared down, not too small. She needed a place where she could see everything without fear of being seen. Turning onto her belly, she lowered her feet down and found a foothold.

Slowly and carefully Winona climbed down the rough walls, remembering her path, each hand- and foothold. In one spot she had to rest her back on one side of the rocky slab and inch down with her feet opposite her.

Finally she stood on solid rock. With barely enough room to maneuver she made her way to the edge and dropped to her stomach. Though not as high as the very top, this deeply shadowed cleft afforded her a full view. She eyed the area below.

If anyone managed to climb the smaller, yet sheer-looking rock just below her, they still couldn't get to where she lay. The space was too far to jump across, yet if anyone came this close, she'd have plenty of time to leave before she was spotted.

Winona settled down to search the rocks and trees for movement. Anger rose with each passing moment. Clay should have returned already. The sun was directly overhead.

She thought of Hoka Luta. He worried her. He hadn't been among her father's warriors earlier that morning. What if he was out there, watching, waiting? What if Clay's plans failed? What would she do if anything happened to him? And Jenny? Was she still alive?

Winona knew that should anything happen to Clay she'd take up the search for Jenny, for she couldn't imagine losing her entire family, just as she could not imagine waking up without Clay at her side.

In so short a time she had fallen in love totally. Forever. She remembered the hard, cold man she'd first met—a man living in the painful shadows of his past. This morning he'd worn that same hard, cold expression, yet she knew he was anything but unfeeling. He felt—deeply and completely. He was a devoted brother who'd never forgotten his baby sister, nor had he ever given up in his determination to find her.

He'd also been kind. Not once had he taken his anger or his need for vengeance out on her. Instead he'd done his best to keep his distance. Again, she thought, he'd been seeking to stay in the shadows.

She smiled softly. But she'd drawn him out into the light. He smiled, laughed, and teased. He'd shown her the man he'd once been, and could become once more—unless her father or Hoka Luta killed him and took him from her forever.

Her smile faded. Her fingers scraped the rocky ledge as she drew them into fists. What would she do if something happened to Clay? She couldn't bear the thought of losing the man she loved.

She got up on her knees, ready to go in search of Clay. She had to convince him that together they stood the best chance of convincing her father of his innocence.

Her shoulders drooped as she glanced around the lake. She had no idea where Clay was. Or her father. Or Hoka Luta. Settling back down, she shifted to remove a sharp stone from beneath her ribs and sighed. There was little to do but wait. And watch.

The sudden flurry of ducks landing in the water startled Winona awake. Disoriented, she realized she'd fallen asleep. Her gaze sought the sun's position and, with horror, she realized it had already began its descent. Though there remained many hours of daylight left, the passage of time had Winona jumping to her feet. What if Clay had returned and hadn't been able to find her?

Hurrying, she made her way back up the nearly sheer rock wall, fretting over the painstakingly slow going. Finally she emerged and ran back to the enclosed cavern.

As soon as she entered, she knew Clay had not returned. But to be sure she went to the back and climbed up. He wasn't up on top either. She scooted into their stone tipi and searched the lake area below.

Dropping her forehead to the hard surface, she closed her eyes. Something was wrong. Rubbing her eyes, she went back to searching the lake area. A reddish blur down below on the white rocks made her jerk her head up. She slumped back down when she saw that it was just a red fox.

Red fox. She sprang to her knees—and cracked her head on the low ceiling. Rubbing her bruised scalp, she stared down at the fox. Foxes were usually seen only in the dawn or dusk. They were masters of blending in with their surroundings. Many people who walked the land believed they were even able to shapeshift.

Winona sucked in her breath when the fox turned and darted across the white mound of rock and slid back into the concealing line of trees. It was an omen. The fox bore a message for her.

He'd come out of hiding to tell her something was wrong. Backing up, she ran through the cozy cave, then out. By the time she crawled through the tunnel and pulled aside the large boulders, she was breathing hard and frantically.

Once outside she wasn't sure where to start her search. Normally Clay left the towers for the lake by going over and around the white rocks. It was in the open in a few spots, but the grass on the other side of the towers made it hard to hide footprints, as the grass was soft from the damp banks.

Drawing in a deep breath, she made her way to the tree line where the fox had gone. Fear clamored inside her. Once in the shadows of the trees she stopped to listen. Nothing. How was she, one person, going to find the man she loved?

A strange noise had her lifting her head up and tilting her chin to the side so she could listen better. Was that a shuffle? Moving silently, she hid herself among the trees and waited. A twig snapped somewhere to her left. Who was there? Her father? Hoka Luta? Or one of Clay's warriors? *Please let it be Clay*, she begged the spirit of the fox.

She held her breath as the sounds came closer. There weren't any thick shrubs for her to use to conceal her presence, so she hunched down into the shadows. There was no time to flee back to the white rocks without being seen and heard.

Keeping her breathing slow and even, she prayed to the spirit of the fox to help her. The fox blended in with his surroundings, so she imagined that she was part of the trunk. She was brown with bits of green moss on her. Her figure was shadowed as were the trunks of the trees. In her mind she became one with her surroundings.

A shadowy figure emerged from a clump of trees. By the time Winona realized it was Clay, he'd passed by without seeing her! In that brief moment her heart had stopped. Not from relief that it was Clay and not someone from her tribe, but from the blur of red as Clay ran past.

Red fox.

Red blood.

Red Badger. Hoka Luta.

Fear deafened her ears as her heart pounded. Without thought as to who might be chasing Clay, she ran after him. "Clay," she called out as softly as she could.

Ahead of her Clay whirled around, whipping his knife from its sheath. He sagged a bit when he saw her. "What the hell are you doing out here?"

Spotting the arrow lodged in his upper arm, Winona ignored his question and grabbed him by the other arm. Her fingers shook. "You are bleeding."

"You noticed." Clay's breathing sounded labored, and his lips were tight with pain. "Your family is sure to be following. Now is your chance to gain your freedom."

Startled, Winona met his gaze, then stared at his bleeding wound. "We need to wrap this so the blood does not leave a trail."

Clay pulled away, then hissed in pain at the sharp movement. "Go. It's too late. There is already a trail."

Winona swallowed her fear, then used that very emotion to pull herself together. No one would harm the man she loved. Not as long as she was alive. If her father or anyone else caught up with them, they'd deal with her.

She met Clay's eyes with her own resolved gaze. "Now is not the time for you to be foolish or stubborn." She paused. "You have already been foolish this day."

Clay staggered back and leaned against a tree. "If you are worried about your sister, I'll release her. You are free to go—both of you. I will find Jenny some other way."

"No, we will find Jenny together." Winona reached out and took the knife from him.

Clay pushed away from her. "Go. Leave me. I do not need any help. This was doomed to fail from the start. It's been so long. She's not alive. And if she is, she'd never remember me." His words were slurred with pain.

"We can discuss that later. Right now we need to take care of you." She followed and pulled on his good arm, forcing him to stop. "Do you really want to die?" She softened her tone. "And abandon Jenny?"

Clay opened his mouth but Winona shook her head. "No more. Save your strength. You have waited this long. I will not let you give up now."

"Not your choice, Golden Eyes." He paused and swayed as blood continued to trail down his arm and fall to the ground to splatter over pine needles and tall green grass.

Winona pushed him back until he once more rested against the trunk of a tree. She grabbed hold of the front of his breechclout. "You need me; she needs you. No more. I will not listen to such talk." Lifting his knife, she whacked off a long length of cloth.

"Ahhh," Clay exclaimed hoarsely. He sucked in his belly and pulled away from Winona and the knife. "Careful!"

Rolling her eyes, Winona shook her head. "As if I'd hurt that part of you!" She bit down on the blade of the knife to hold it so she could use both hands to grab the feathered end of the arrow. She glanced at him. He held her gaze, his own softening with love. Finally he nodded.

Taking a deep breath, she broke the shaft so she could wrap his wound. With the long shaft he'd never be able to get through the narrow tunnel. As it was, she wasn't sure he'd be able to make it through on his own. She firmed her lips. He would make it back to their place of hiding even if she had to drag him herself!

Clay shuddered but didn't make a sound. Working quickly, Winona bound his upper arm as best as she could. Then she washed her hands in the lake, cut off the back of his loin-cloth, and washed the blood from him.

"Ready?"

He eyed her. Pain and wonder filled his eyes. "Now you are the foolish one."

Winona shrugged. "And you are a *waglula* to worry me so."

Clay yanked hard on her long hair. "We need to work on your name calling or find you more flattering names to use."

Reassured by a small chuckle from Clay, she made him go first so she could make sure he didn't leave a trail. When they reached the white rocks he was bleeding through the bandage. She used the damp cloth to wipe the blood before it fell onto the rocks.

By the time she got Clay back into their safe cavern they were both covered with sweat and blood, and Clay's face was as pale as the rocks below.

Chapter Sixteen

How could he have been so careless? Night Shadow had earned his name by moving silently, unseen and unheard. Night Shadow would never have been caught unaware. But once again Clay had let his guard down. This time, as the last time, he'd nearly paid with his life.

Echoes of the past crowded into his mind. Screams of pain and fear. Taunting laughter. Jeering hatred. All his fault for not being more careful. After his father's death he'd been responsible for his siblings and mother. He should have been on alert. Instead he'd allowed his own need for normalcy to distract him.

He'd tried to be his father. Clayton Coburn would have stopped to play with his children, but he would also have been alert to danger. Unlike Clay Blue Hawk.

In a foul mood, due to his own stupidity and the throbbing pain in his arm, Night Shadow watched Winona pace nervously.

"Come back and sit," he grumbled, hating the sight of his knife in her hands. He was the warrior. It was his duty to guard her. But every time he tried to stand, he nearly passed out— and got reprimanded as well.

"Go to sleep," Winona ordered. Her fingers flexed open, then gripped the handle of the knife firmly.

A whisper of air carrying her scent wafted over him as his fierce warrior woman strode past, careful to keep out of his reach—not that he could grab her with his injured arm.

Night Shadow sighed but fought the drowsiness beating at him. A faint whistle drifted through the window. He tensed but relaxed after a few moments when the second part of the signal did not follow.

Either Crazy Fox or Sharp Nose was in the area, and Night Shadow expected whoever had distracted Henry to show soon. Had one of them not been near to provide cover to allow Night Shadow to escape, he'd have been killed, and Winona would have been left unprotected. His drooping gaze followed Winona's every movement. Had she not disobeyed him and come for him, he'd have died. He knew he'd never have made it back into the rocky hideout on his own.

Night Shadow sighed and shifted. Stabbing white-hot pain traveled up and down his arm, driving the fatigue from him.

"Stop moving around." Winona came back to him, set his knife out of his reach, and leaned down to check his arm. She frowned at the signs of fresh bleeding.

"I'll live," he muttered, trying to pull away from her. Shame at his failure to detect the enemy made his voice harsh.

Sitting back on her heels, Winona rubbed her eyes with the heel of her hand. "Yes, you will." She lowered her arms and sent him a hard stare. "You have no choice in the matter."

Night Shadow picked up the broken pieces of the arrow and stared at them to keep his emotions hidden. He was touched by her fierce need to protect him as much as he was humiliated.

"I do not understand why Henry did not kill you. You said he surprised you." Winona shifted so her legs were folded to one side.

Night Shadow scowled as he stared at two lines of red paint that ran from the feathered shaft down to the pointed tip. Leaning his head back against the cool wall, he tossed the broken arrow away from them.

"A boy with a training bow could have surprised me," he admitted. With his teeth clenched tightly, Night Shadow closed his eyes, ready to endure her scorn. To his surprise he felt the tips of her fingers slide down the side of his face, tracing the rough edges of his scar.

"It was my fault," Winona said softly.

His eyes flew open at that. The last thing he'd expected or wanted to hear was her taking the blame for something of his own making. "No, Golden Eyes. You were right. I should have waited for night."

He shifted again, more to keep awake than to get comfortable. "Have to stay awake. Sharp Nose or Crazy Fox will come soon."

"It is a good thing one of them was around!" She jumped up and kicked a rock aside, shuffled his bags of supplies around, picked up the knife, and strode around the cavern.

Her movements were jerky, her steps firm, her shoulders and lips set. She was furious. Not *at* him—for him. Slowly his own anger melted away. How could he resist the fire in this woman? Something shifted deep inside. His Golden Eyes had turned into a force to be reckoned with.

Her anger as she tossed things around instead of carefully setting the items down as she usually did warned that there was more to come. He fully expected her to rip him to shreds for his foolishness. In truth, he welcomed it. Deserved it.

"Why did they not help you when you were injured?" Her voice was sharp, yet she kept the volume down in case anyone was near, though with the solid rock surrounding them it would be hard for anyone to hear.

Night Shadow lifted a brow. "They are not to blame. They had their duties."

Winona moved close and stood over him with hands on hips. "Do not make excuses where there are none to be accepted. Their first duty is to you."

Wincing, Night Shadow shrugged. "One of them saved my life." And he'd never live his carelessness down.

A hand slashing the air silenced him. "Do not defend them. You were injured and left to return alone." She paused and glared down at him. "I will make my feelings on this matter very clear to whoever was responsible."

"Calm yourself, Golden Eyes. You were there." Night Shadow basked in the warmth of her fury. He owed this woman his life. A thread of humor twisted its way through the pride rushing through him.

He lifted one brow. "What names will you call them?"

Winona whirled around. "You laugh at me!" She tossed her hair over her shoulder. "I will have my say."

Holding out his hand to her, Night Shadow smiled again. "I have no doubt, Golden Eyes. Now come sit down."

"There is much for me to do. I have other chores now." Her voice trembled.

"I am a chore?" He knew she referred to caring for him.

Winona sighed and walked back to him. She took his hand and allowed him to pull her down. "You are a chore." She gave him a half smile. "A very nice chore."

He saw tears gathering. "Don't cry, Golden Eyes. I will be fine." He'd rather have her yell and call him names. Anything but tears and sadness.

Winona leaned into his good arm. "You promised to be back early."

Holding her tight, Night Shadow rested his chin on top of her head. "I know. I worried you, and for that I am sorry."

Relaxing, Winona threaded their fingers together. "So you should be." She paused. "Who has Spotted Deer?" she asked.

Relieved to be discussing something—anything—else, Night Shadow replied, "Dream Walker."

"Is he trustworthy?"

Clay fingered a long strand of her hair. "He is like a brother to me. I'd trust him with my life. . . ." His voice faded with drowsiness. "He will come soon, with your sister."

Winona rose up onto her knees and urged him to shift and lean back against a pile of furs and belongings so that he could sleep partially sitting. Then she rejoined him, resting her head on his shoulder.

"I miss Spotted Deer."

"I know. I am sorry for that too. It was never my intention to take your sister. But . . ."

"You couldn't resist," she finished.

Night Shadow fought to keep awake, but the herb drink she'd prepared for him was making him drowsy. "I will have Dream Walker return her safely to your father. He will leave her in a place where she will be found."

"And me?" Winona asked hesitantly. "Are you going to send me away?"

He should. He planned to send her away. But not yet. He couldn't; he needed her too much, and he couldn't blame that on the part of him that was Clay. Night Shadow, the warrior, needed her every bit as much as Clay, the man. Slowly the two men he'd kept in separate compartments of his mind were merging, becoming one.

Tightening his good arm around her, he shook his head. "You are mine, Golden Eyes, but if you want to return, I will not stop you. I owe you for saving my life." He closed his eyes against the pain of losing her. He wasn't sure he could bear to lose another loved one.

Winona snuggled closer and pulled a fur around them. "That is good, for I am not leaving. Ever. I have chosen you and will stick to you like mud. Now sleep. I will protect you."

Night Shadow made an attempt to sound outraged. "You have your duties confused, woman. Protecting is warriors' work."

"Then you had best get well quickly. If you do not, I will think of more names to call you."

"Call me anything you want as long as you do not leave," he whispered, running the fingers of his injured arm through the soft strands of her hair.

Her hand stopped him. "Sleep." Winona twined her fingers with his and Clay gave himself over to sleep. But he did not let go of the woman he loved.

The next day Winona was back up in her high vantage point with her chin resting on her fisted hands. Brilliant blue water mirrored the rocks where she hid, and a warm breeze drifted around her while cold from the granite seeped upward through her body. The cry of an eagle pierced the air, as if tempting her to focus her attention on his majestic beauty.

But Winona kept her gaze focused on the warriors far below her. Her father and his warriors were scouting the banks, looking for tracks. Knowing that he would come and explore the rock formation once again, she slipped back down to where Clay slept.

He moved restlessly. She frowned and touched her fingertips to his forehead. No fever, but his sleep was not restful. She carefully checked his wound. Luckily for him, the arrow had torn through the lower part of his upper arm. It would mend with no permanent damage, but it would take time for the muscle to completely heal. In the meantime he wouldn't be able to use his bow or knife to hunt or protect anyone. That left the job to her.

Leaving his side, she hurried to the cracks in the rock where she could watch. Her father's warriors were closer now—so close that all she had to do was go to the window and wave her hands and her father would see her. Or she could just leave and go to meet her father.

But she did neither. Guilt brought tears to her eyes. She desperately wanted her father to know she was all right. Better than all right. She was in love and happy with Clay.

Well, almost. True happiness could not be had until Spotted Deer was returned, Hoka Luta was taken care of, and Clay was out of danger from both Hoka Luta and her father. And if they found Clay's sister, then their happiness would be complete.

She searched among the warriors for Hoka Luta. The more she thought of what he'd done, the ease with which he'd deceived them all, the angrier she became. He was clever. Cunning. He'd hidden his past so completely that if Clay hadn't survived no one would ever know of his true nature.

Winona didn't see him. With his red paint, he always stood out. She wasn't sure whether that was good or bad. Had Sharp Nose or Crazy Fox killed him?

No, they wouldn't kill him. Hoka Luta was the only one who could tell them what he'd done with Jenny. She followed the line of warriors as they moved closer. Some were now below, at the base of the three towers. She listened but couldn't hear much, just low tones.

Another noise reached her: a soft moan. Jumping to her feet, keeping her head down so she wasn't revealed in the window, Winona hurried to Clay's side. He thrashed and moaned. Fearing another nightmare, Winona stroked his jaw.

"Clay, wake up. You dream."

He muttered and swatted at her hand. "No," he began.

"Clay!" This time she pulled at his good arm. "Wake," she ordered in a harsh whisper.

Lost in his own world, Clay did not respond. Glancing over her shoulder, fearing that if Clay shouted out he'd be heard, she tried to reach him the only other way she knew.

She kissed him, keeping her mouth over his until he responded. His eyes flew open and he reached out.

"Golden—"

"Shush, my father is below. You must remain awake so you do not dream."

The pain of the past cleared from his eyes. He nodded.

"I need to go check on them, see if they are gone." She hated to leave him, but he lifted his hand to her cheek.

"Go," he whispered. "Go, but come back."

"Always," she promised.

Winona went back to where she'd been sitting. She didn't dare go up on top, so once again she peered through the cracks. Warriors swarmed everywhere below, some jumping across the white rocks, others directly below. Those she couldn't see were reflected on the mirrored surface of the lake.

She heard her name called. Had she missed a drop of blood? Did her father know they were here, hidden? She kept silent, and after what seemed like forever she saw them retreating back to the other side of the lake.

Winona couldn't stop the tears from flowing when she saw her father's slumped shoulders. He'd never forgive her for choosing Clay over him.

The child returned. This time the blue surrounding her was stronger. And a red light seemed to glow within. Calming her breathing, Seeing Eyes relaxed into the vision. She welcomed it, gave thanks for it.

The child stared at her solemnly. Seeing Eyes studied her. She knew this child, this quiet girl who screamed in the night. The child blurred and distorted until she became a young woman. The young woman raised her hands and the blue aura lifted and floated before her, forming a large lake.

Seeing Eyes breathed in through her nose. She knew the lake. *Yes, child. The lake. My daughters are there.* She was about to jump to her feet to go after her husband, but Winona stepped into the vision with a handsome man at her side.

His features were blurred, but Winona smiled

and hugged the rugged warrior. She was safe. Both girls were safe.

Seeing Eyes relaxed. But with a suddenness that left her sick, all three fell to their knees. Blood spluttered out of cuts and slashes and flowed into the lake, turning it from a place of peace to a place of death.

"No!" She shoved aside the vision and the leftover drowsiness and jumped to her feet.

White Wind rushed over. "What is it, mother of my husband?"

Star Dreamer joined them. "She had a vision." Her eyes still had a faraway look.

Seeing Eyes took a minute to kneel. "As did you, my sweet one."

The little girl tried to look grown-up, but her lower lip trembled. "I don't like visions. I want them to go away."

Hugging her granddaughter, Seeing Eyes smoothed her hair. "We have to accept the gifts the spirits give us. What did you see?"

"A rock, but bigger than Gray Rock."

"And did you see your aunts?"

She nodded. "They were inside the rock."

Seeing Eyes took her granddaughter by the hand. "Let us go tell your grandfather what we have learned."

Hoka Luta moved cautiously through the trees. He'd been so close he had nearly killed Clay

Blue Hawk, but his first shot had missed. He sneered. Not his second. A third would have found its mark, but someone had been close enough to allow Clay to escape.

Angry at his own impatience, he stared at the arrows lodged in the trunk of the tree. He should have waited, followed Clay Blue Hawk to be sure he was alone. But he'd allowed his elation to cloud his judgment. He'd lost control, and now he had no choice but to report to Winona's father.

If he did not show up as planned tonight, Hawk Eyes would wonder. Staring up at the arrows too high for him to retrieve, Hoka Luta didn't dare give the chief any reason to doubt his loyalty.

Tired from nearly constant travel with little sleep, he made his way around the lake, keeping to the deep shadows among the pines until he reached the white mounds of stone.

It was too risky to go any farther, so he went deeper into the foliage. He'd been hiding in the bushes high on a hill when Hawk Eyes had unexpectedly returned to the area and spotted Clay Blue Hawk's trail, then the blood on the ground.

He scowled. The old man was supposed to be camped a short distance away. Hoka Luta had waited for them to leave so he could look around on his own. Lifting his head, he stared at the towering rocks.

His old friend was there somewhere. He felt it. Knew it. But he didn't dare explore on his own. There were far too many places for an enemy to hide. So he decided to wait. And as he waited, memories from his past circulated. But instead of bringing regret or sadness, they fed his feelings of betrayal.

Clay Blue Hawk's father had betrayed them all, and destroyed Henry Black Bear. His battle had never been with the man who'd once been his best friend—not until Clay Blue Hawk had shot his father and brought about his death.

With nothing but bitterness inside him, Henry had avenged his father's humiliation and, ultimately, his father's death. But he'd failed all those years ago. Soon, though, he'd take care of Clay Blue Hawk. Then he'd be able to live the life he'd spent so much time cultivating.

And with Jenny far out of reach, there would be no other witnesses to his murderous past. He frowned. He should have killed the little girl instead of selling her. He hadn't given her a thought until the reemergence of Clay Blue Hawk.

Hoka Luta grinned. Even if Clay lived, even if he lost Winona and had to move on with his life or make a new life for himself, Hoka Luta had the satisfaction of knowing that Clay would never find Jenny.

Chapter Seventeen

Restless and edgy after two days of inactivity, Night Shadow dressed and reclaimed his knife. He was not going to stay in bed any longer— no matter what his bossy Golden Eyes said or threatened.

"You are not strong enough to be up." Winona refused to move out of his way.

A few minutes ago she'd tried a different tack. He eyed her curves. Not even the lure of having her lie with him could keep him inactive any longer. His arm ached, but at least it was healing, and he would not suffer permanent damage.

Night Shadow refused to look at her, afraid she'd talk him right back down onto the pallet. Truthfully, his knees were wobbly, and his arm ached fiercely, but he was a man, a warrior, and there were things that needed doing.

He'd enjoyed Winona's tender ministrations over the last few days. For the first time in many long years he'd felt cherished. But it was time to take charge.

"You question my abilities?" He grabbed the water skin, then strode around Winona to where his weapons rested against the wall.

"How can you even think of going out? My father may not have left. Henry might still be out there. Wait for the others to come. It is not safe." Winona followed him. Her arms were crossed across her chest, her eyes shadowed from fatigue and worry.

"We need water."

"Then I will go." She moved fast. She yanked the water container from him and stepped away. "You were nearly killed last time."

Night Shadow whirled around. "No! You will not." He held out his hand.

Winona battled silently with her eyes. He glared. She stared and held the pouch behind her back. "If you leave, I will follow."

Night Shadow narrowed his eyes. "You will stay here." He paused. "I need you to keep watch from above. Warn me if you see movement." He thought that idea ingenious. He'd never admit it to her, but already he was tiring, and the last thing he wanted was to argue with her or upset her. But he was a warrior, and it was his duty to provide.

Since losing his parents he'd denied himself any relationships but a few close friends. He'd spent all his energies on surviving, then planning. Glancing around him, he saw the makings of a home. A few days ago that would have sent him running.

Life had taken a new twist for him, a meeting and merging of paths. He was still getting used to the idea of those two paths, the past and the future, the man and the warrior, becoming one.

Winona lifted her brows. "And what signal would I give? Shall I stand up and wave my hands and shout for you to come back or hide?" Sarcasm edged her voice.

"Your word, Golden Eyes."

Winona refused to meet his eyes. Instead she walked around him and busied herself sorting through the supplies.

"I am waiting."

"You will have to wait a long time," she said, annoyed. "Do you forget that had I not disobeyed last time you would be dead?" She cleared the huskiness from her voice. "I will not give a promise I do not intend to keep."

"Yet you did just that, my sister," a soft voice accused.

Winona jumped up and whirled around.

Spotted Deer stood at the entrance to the main cavern with a warrior.

The young woman walked forward. "You promised to escape if you had the chance, yet apparently you did not."

"Spotted Deer!" Winona ran to her friend. The two girls hugged and cried. Winona pulled away. "Are you all right?"

"I am fine."

Narrowing her eyes at the two men who were talking in low tones, Winona pulled Spotted Deer toward the back of the cavern where sunlight spilled over them. "He did not hurt or mistreat you?" If he had . . .

Spotted Deer shook her head. "No. I was treated well. Like a younger sister," she added, her gaze going to the warrior.

Thinking of her own changed relationship with Clay, Winona frowned. "Do you care for him?"

"He was kind. I do not think badly of him." She took Winona by the hand. "And you?" Worry clouded her eyes.

"I too am . . . well." She cleared her throat. She didn't want to go into just how well, or the fact that this might be the last time she and Spotted Deer were together. If Clay sent her back with Dream Walker, she'd never have this chance to be alone with him again.

"Come." She pulled Spotted Deer back to where the two men were talking. Clay still had his weapons in his hands. She picked up the water skin.

"Now that your friend is here, he can get water and do whatever else needs to be done."

"I am no invalid," Clay ground out.

Winona reached out and grabbed his injured arm by the wrist. Clay jerked and bit back a moan.

"I see how well you are. How do you think to climb down the rocks and back up again? If you cannot free yourself from my grasp without pain, then you cannot use your arm. You will either fall, open the wound, or get caught." She paused. "Or get yourself killed."

She turned to Dream Walker. "If you are his friend, you will not let him go."

Dream Walker chuckled. "This captive of yours has a point. I will go for water and check to see who is around. Crazy Fox is following her tribe. Sharp Nose was following Henry Black Bear, who had separated himself from the others. He is the one who stopped Henry from killing you."

Just remembering how close she'd come to losing Clay made Winona's heart sink. And to think she'd nearly married Hoka Luta. She had Clay to thank for preventing the wedding.

"Where is Henry now?" she asked. She pointed to the bed of furs and silently commanded Clay to sit before he fell. Then she turned to Dream Walker. "You may sit as well. That way Clay will not feel intimidated that you stand over him."

Dream Walker shook his head. "I will meet Sharp Nose tonight in a place not far from here." He bent to pick up his weapons. "I will return shortly." He walked out, still chuckling.

Winona made Clay lie back down. Pain etched his mouth. She knelt beside him. "I am sorry, Clay. I could not let you go out there. You are not ready."

Clay opened his eyes. "I am not sure whether to thank you or—"

"I will take the thanks." Winona covered him. "Sleep to get your strength back."

Clay growled. "Do not push it, Golden Eyes."

She smiled and turned to Spotted Deer. Noting her friend's pale face and wide eyes, she pushed her down to another fur pallet across the cavern. "What is wrong, Spotted Deer?"

Spotted Deer shook her head. "I do not know. My head hurts." She glanced over at Clay, her eyes wide yet searching.

"He will not harm you," Winona reassured her. "He is going to have Dream Walker return you to my father."

"And you?" she whispered.

Taking a deep breath, Winona took her friend's hands into her own. "I will stay—my choice—with Clay." Worried about Spotted Deer, fearing her friend wouldn't understand or might feel betrayed, she lowered her voice. "I love him."

"What about Hoka Luta?" Spotted Deer's eyes were wide.

Winona glanced over at Clay, who was already sleeping. "He is the enemy. He is not who he claims to be. His name is Henry Black Bear, and he killed Clay's family and sold his baby sister. He took us to try to get Henry Black Bear to tell him where to find Jenny."

Spotted Deer swayed slightly. "The bear," she whispered, her eyes blurring. "The black bear." She shuddered.

"Your dreams have returned?" Winona rubbed Spotted Deer's cold fingers.

Spotted Deer nodded. Her lips trembled. "Every night. They are the same. Yet different. The girl, she calls out a name now."

Spotted Deer pulled out her medicine pouch and held it tightly in her fist.

"What name?" Winona asked. For as long as she could remember, Spotted Deer had been plagued by bad dreams.

"I-I am not sure." She tried to recall the

dreams. The black bear. The child. The older boy. And someone she loved and trusted. Then came the images of her mother and the sounds of screaming and the sight of blood. Then the bear came again. She rubbed at the scar on her knee.

"The bear," she said, her eyes closed as she recalled hiding from the bear who wasn't a bear but a boy with a bear head. She hid. Waited for someone . . .

"Kaa."

Winona's eyes were wide. "You've always been afraid of bears. You dream of bears." Winona remembered the time when she was six winters old and a black bear had wandered near their camp with two cubs. She and Spotted Deer had been playing in a shallow pool away from the swift current. All the women and children had fallen silent. Winona had loved the sight of the cavorting cubs splashing in the shallows and the warning stance of the mother rearing up on hind legs.

But Spotted Deer had started screaming and hadn't stopped until her voice gave out. Winona had never understood.

Spotted Deer shook her head. "Not a bear. A person. A game," she said, rubbing her temples, then her arms. She visibly shook herself. "I do not want to talk about my dreams," she whispered.

Winona held her breath as she stared hard at her best friend. Bad dreams. A fear of bears. And Clay, searching for his sister, his family killed by Henry *Black Bear*. No, it couldn't be. Could it?

Spotted Deer had parents who'd loved her, and she herself had known the girl for her entire life—most of her life. Spotted Deer and her parents had joined their tribe when the two girls had been small.

Frowning, she recalled everything Clay had said. Then the name Spotted Deer had said. "This name you hear in your dreams, say it again."

"Winona—"

"Say it!"

Spotted Deer closed her eyes, as if trying to hear the name in her head. "Kaa. I see a little girl running. In my dreams I am that little girl.

"Kaa," she repeated over and over, her breathing coming harder and faster as the screams in her head grew louder.

She dropped her medicine bag. She'd been gripping it so hard the knot in the leather thong had come undone. It fell to the ground.

Winona bit her lower lip. "Kaa," she said, drawing out the *aaa* sound. "Clay." This time she dropped the L sound and accented the *aaa* sound. She felt goose bumps break out along her arms.

"Jenny. Does that name sound familiar?" She watched Spotted Deer carefully.

Spotted Deer trembled and held her hands to her head. "Jenny. Jenny. Jenny." Her eyes flew open. "I have heard that name. Many times." Over and over she whispered the name.

Behind her, Winona heard a soft moan.

"Jenny." Clay was restless, as if trying to wake.

Winona leaned forward and whispered in her friend's ear, "We have to leave. Now."

"I don't understand—"

Winona didn't have time to explain; then it was too late. Clay had woken fully and was staring at them. "I heard her. I heard her calling me. Kaa. Only Jenny called me by that name." His gaze shifted to Spotted Deer, who was pale and hugging herself.

"Your name," he insisted harshly. He scooted close slowly, as though what he'd heard were nothing more than another taunting dream.

Spotted Deer backed away. "Spotted Deer . . ." Her voice trailed off.

Reaching out, Clay grabbed her ankle and gently shoved her skirt above her knees. The girl froze when he traced the most beautiful scar he'd ever seen. He stared at her in wonder. He'd heard her talking of dreams. Bears. And she'd said "Kaa."

"How did you get this scar?" His voice broke. "Tell me," he begged.

"A bear." Tears ran down her cheeks. "A bear chased me and I fell." Spotted Deer tried to pull away from Night Shadow.

Night Shadow gentled his hold on her as he took in her dark hair and eyes and studied her features. And he saw it: the wide mouth of his mother, the dimple of his sister Catherine, and a small dent in her chin—a gift from his father.

His voice turned husky. "Who came after you? Who saved you from the bear?" He tried to keep his voice soft, gentle and patient.

Spotted Deer shook her head. "I-I don't know."

Winona bit her lower lip and reached out to take her friend by the hand. "You do. You said the name. I heard you." She glanced at Clay.

Spotted Deer shook her head but she couldn't take her eyes from Clay's.

Clay fingered her long brownish-black hair. Only now did he see it wasn't the black of the night like Winona's.

"Who, Jenny? Who always saved you from the bear? Say the name. Say it again. Please," he begged.

"Kaa," she whispered, just now putting it together. "Kaa."

"Yes," Clay said, tears running down his face.

"Kaa. Clay. Your brother always saved you from the bears." He held out his arms and grabbed his sister when she threw herself into his arms.

"I cannot believe that you were so close all this time." He restrained himself from firing questions at her. She needed time to adjust. To trust. And that was okay. But right then he needed to hold her for just a moment.

He was Clay. Clay the brother. Clay the man, in love, and ready to take a chance on love and family. Night Shadow was still there, would always be there, but Clay didn't need Night Shadow to shield his heart anymore.

"Clay."

He turned to Winona. "We found her," he said.

She was crying. "Yes, we found her." She leaned forward. "We have proof," she said, her voice shaking, her gaze determined. "We have proof. We can go to my father now."

"No!" Not until Henry Black Bear was dead. He tried to sit, but Winona held him down. "You are a fool. Let me go and find my father. Let Dream Walker take us back. Let me stop this. All of it."

"No. Henry is my problem."

Jenny was watching them, confusion in her eyes. Winona quickly explained. "You are the key, Spotted Deer—Jenny. If Clay goes after Henry, our father will kill him." Her voice broke. "You are the proof that we need to convince my father that Clay was justified in taking us captive."

Jenny could only nod in wonder. "I have a brother." She reached out and touched Clay's face with her hand. "My sister is right: I cannot lose you. If my father . . ." She stumbled over the word.

Clay smiled. "You have had many fathers and they have all loved you. For that I thank the spirits, for you look well."

"Then listen to Winona. If our father does not kill you before you can even speak, our brother will."

"Or Henry," Winona added. "He can kill you and no one will question his actions. And if you die, it is our word against his."

"When Dream Walker returns, we will leave and meet the others. Then we will end this."

Winona stood. She wanted to cry in frustration. Clay refused to believe her. Even if he killed Hoka Luta, he was still in danger from her father.

Clay needed her to act first. Her father knew of Spotted Deer's dreams, for they'd started again right after her parents—her adoptive parents—had died. She could not let him leave. She had to reach her father first.

When Clay dismissed her concerns by putting Jenny aside so he could stand, she had no choice in what she had to do. Gripping the fist-sized stone in her hand that she'd palmed, she banged Clay on the back of his head.

For a moment he looked stunned; then he slumped over onto Jenny's lap. Jenny choked on her scream and looked up at Winona in horror.

"He will be all right. His head is harder than the stone. Now come on," Winona said in a hiss, grabbing Jenny by the hand. She had to get them out of there.

Jenny glanced back at Clay's unconscious form but didn't protest. She knew Winona spoke the truth. They had to reach Hawk Eyes first.

"What about Dream Walker?"

Winona didn't dare look back. If she did she'd never have the courage or the will to leave Clay. "Pray we do not see him or he us. Now hurry. We have to find Father. He is somewhere close by." She led the way out of the cavern.

Chapter Eighteen

Clay woke to a pounding between his ears. Holding his aching head, he struggled to sit. The room spun, threatening to make him pass out again, so he dropped his head between his knees and groaned softly.

What had happened? His searching fingers found a large swelling at the back of his head. Had he been so weak that he'd passed out when he'd tried to stand?

With eyes closed, Clay sought to remember. Dream Walker had returned. And he'd brought Spotted Deer. He remembered hearing the two women talking—he'd been resting, dozing lightly, secure in the knowledge that the woman he loved was close—her voice had soothed him.

Then the dream of Jenny. He must have

fallen asleep, for he always remembered his dreams of his sister. But this one had been different. It had seemed so real. And for the first time she'd called him Kaa. He'd heard it. He'd held her; he'd breathed in her scent.

His nostrils flared. The scent was still there. Was he out of his mind with fever? No. He slowly lifted his head. He'd been ready to go outside—to get water. Had he gone out and hurt himself? Turning his head to look around, he moaned as waves of pain shot through his head.

He closed his eyes again and waited for the pain and the sick feeling in his stomach to pass. This time he opened his eyes and kept them focused on the fur he sat on.

Still, his vision refused to focus. It blurred, and all he could see was a blob of red. He blinked but the redness didn't go away. Slowly he reached out, and to his surprise his fingers closed around a small, hard object. He picked it up and stared at the ruby necklace in the palm of his hand. He felt suddenly light-headed. This time he fought the weakness, shoved it from him. Slowly his eyes focused on the object in his hand.

Using two hands he pulled the tangled, blackened silver chain apart, finding the broken link. With shaking fingers he brought the warm stone to his lips.

His mother's necklace. How? He glanced around and spotted a tiny leather pouch on the ground. Picking it up, he brought it to his nose. It carried the same scent as the Jenny he'd dreamed of holding tightly to his chest.

Sucking in a breath, Clay struggled to his feet. It had been no dream. She'd been here. He'd really held her, spoken to her. He remembered all of it. Spotted Deer and Jenny were one and the same.

His sister had been so close all this time. He'd even sat with her family—Winona's family. But he'd never really noticed her. All his attention had been on Winona and his plan to take her captive.

Turning, he searched for the women. Then spotted the large stone lying where he'd come to. He picked it up and stared at it with disbelief. His arm hurt, his head hurt, but worse, his heart hurt.

Winona had done this to him, and Jenny had allowed it. The two women he loved and needed most were gone. He nearly doubled over from the gut-punch their betrayal caused.

He rushed out of the cavern. He had to find Winona and Jenny. Henry was out there. If Henry Black Bear learned who Spotted Deer was, both women would be dead. Rounding a bend, he ran smack into Dream Walker.

"Night Shadow. My brother. What is wrong?"

"No time. We have to find Winona. And Jenny."

"You do not look so well." Dream Walker followed Clay.

"You would not either if you had been bashed on the head with a rock," he muttered.

Hoka Luta knew how to wait, how to blend and not be seen. They were here somewhere. He'd seen a Cheyenne warrior arrive with Spotted Deer and he'd watched from his high vantage point not far from the towers of granite. They went into the rocky area, but he could not see where they hid. But they were there. He smiled grimly and ran his finger up and down his bow. He would be here when they came out.

So he waited. And watched. He controlled the rage festering in his mind. He kept the past distant. The future was more important. When he spotted movement on the rocks, he smiled. His smile grew wider when he realized that Winona and Spotted Deer had left the safety of their rocky hiding place.

As soon as the two women reached the white rocks, he moved to meet them. He'd learn soon enough what, if anything, they'd been told. The fact that they were alone was a good sign. Had they escaped? Could Winona lead him to Clay Blue Hawk?

He watched them jump down from the rocks onto the soft mat of grass near the edge of the lake. They turned and headed into the trees, toward him.

"Hurry, Spotted Deer." Winona stopped. "Or should I call you Jenny? I do not know what to call you!"

Spotted Deer wrinkled her nose. "I do not either," she said.

Hearing them speak, Hoka Luta felt his rage build. Jenny? The key to the past, the proof of his past deeds, had been so close all this time? And both women knew the truth. This was all wrong.

He clenched his jaw and tightened his hands into fists. Nothing had gone right. He'd been led by Clay Blue Hawk, had found the last message—the demands that Jenny be returned—and when he'd first seen the girls, had thought it was over. All he'd had to do was return the women and accept the gratitude of their family.

But things had once again gone wrong. Now he would have to kill both women to keep his past secret. Furious, he forced himself to remain hidden as they walked past. Control. Power. They were still his. He just had to keep a clear head. He followed silently. How easy it would be to just take his bow and two arrows and end their lives.

But he did not dare. Using his own arrows was too risky. Ahead, the women were talking in low, hushed voices.

"We will figure that out later. Come on. Clay will come after us and he will be very angry."

"How will we find your father?"

Hoka Luta cut through the trees and stepped into their path. "I will take you to him." He paused. "The spirits led me here, led me to you both. This will be a day to celebrate."

Winona and Spotted Deer looked startled, even a bit afraid. Then Winona smiled. "We are indeed fortunate."

Hoka Luta knew she planned to take her tale to her father. What she did not know was that she would not live to speak of Clay Blue Hawk or his family or his sister, Jenny. Both women were about to die.

Winona stepped in front of Jenny. The appearance of Henry had startled her, but only for a moment. He knew where her father was and could take them right to him. She sent him a relieved smile. "The enemy is behind us. We escaped. Where is my father?"

Hoka Luta pointed to the ridge behind the trees. "He is close. Come, let us go."

Feeling Jenny's fingers biting into her arm, Winona knew she didn't dare go with Henry. It was too risky. She needed her father. "Spotted Deer is ill. She cannot go far. We will hide here and wait for him. You can travel faster, and bring him before the enemy awakes and finds we have escaped."

Hoka Luta appeared concerned. "If your sister is ill, I will carry her." He reached out toward Jenny.

"N-no, I will walk," she said in a croak.

Winona felt Jenny's trembling and feared she'd break down. "She is afraid. Much has happened to her."

"Surely she is not afraid of the man you will soon be married to?" Hoka Luta lunged and grabbed Jenny's arm. He laughed when she screamed but quickly held out his knife to silence her.

"She is afraid. Why is that?"

Winona tried to free Jenny but Hoka Luta held her tighter. "Do not be foolish. You cannot hide the truth from me. You know more than you should."

"What is it I know?" Winona challenged.

Hoka Luta laughed harshly. "You know who I am, what I did. Just as you know I cannot allow either of you to live now."

He stared down at Jenny. "You have been so

close all this time. Too bad. Clay Blue Hawk went to all this trouble to find you, yet you were so close and he did not recognize his own sister." He laughed when Jenny whimpered.

"Let her go," Winona demanded. She tried to charge Henry, but he just shoved her away.

"You never were very brave, Jenny."

Jenny turned to Winona with tears streaming down her face. "Run, Winona. Get Clay—"

Hoka Luta's harsh voice stopped her. "I do not think so. If Winona runs, you will die," he said, bringing his knife to her throat.

Winona swallowed hard and stood still. Jenny's eyes begged her to go, to save herself. She shook her head. "I will not leave you."

Another satisfied laugh came from Hoka Luta. "Ah, that is better. Now move. Stay in front where I can see you."

Knowing she had no choice, Winona did as told. She led the way, following Henry's instructions. As they continued to climb, Winona grew more worried. "You will not get away with this. Clay will come."

Henry laughed. "He will not arrive in time. You two will die, and if Clay Blue Hawk comes, he too will die. Your father will believe that he killed you, or that the two of you jumped to your deaths. Either by my hand or your father's, he will die."

Winona continued to climb. When they reached the narrow ridge she stared down at the steep rocky slope on the other side. She swallowed her fear.

"Why do you hate Clay? It was your father who killed his father. He was only defending his mother. You know the truth."

Hoka Luta stopped. "Yes, I know the truth," he bit out.

She had to stall him. "Then tell me. Convince me that you were justified in your actions." She saw movement down below. To her shock, Clay stepped out of the trees directly below them.

"Henry Black Bear!"

Henry whipped around and used Jenny as a shield. "Clay Blue Hawk. At last. Come join us."

"No, Clay," Winona cried out.

Clay held his ground. "Let the women go. This fight is between us."

"Ah, Clay Blue Hawk, you are wrong. There is no fight. You will all die." He took a couple of steps back, dragging Jenny with him.

"Come join your sister. Prepare to die." He held Jenny tightly before him.

Winona knew Jenny was paralyzed with fear. That left her—she had to do something. But what? Seeing Clay starting to climb up to join them, she shook her head. "No, Clay, stay away."

He ignored her. Sweat shone on his chest and back and dripped down the sides of his face. He looked pale. He had to have been in pain yet when he met her gaze she only saw black anger there. Winona swallowed. If they got out of this alive, she'd have some explaining to do. She just hoped he'd forgive her.

"Move to the edge," Hoka Luta instructed Winona.

She moved closer to Clay.

Hoka Luta reached out with one hand and yanked hard on a strand of hair. "Not that way. Here. Over here." He pointed to the opposite side with the tip of his knife.

Winona moved slowly and stared down at the long, rocky slope. "You think I will jump?"

Laughing, Henry nodded toward the lake on the same side of the ridge as Clay. "You will jump—and before your father arrives."

Seeing her father moving along the lake, Winona felt nothing but fear. All Henry had to do was get rid of them, and if Clay was still alive it would be his word against Henry's. Clay didn't stand a chance.

"You will not get away with this," she said, hoping to stall. *Please*, she begged the spirits. Let her father spot her alive and know the truth.

Henry held the knife tip to Jenny's throat. "Now move. We do not have much time."

312

Winona saw Jenny's eyes widen, then narrow. "No," she said to Winona. "If you jump I will never forgive you. If I must die, so be it. But not you—" Her protest died when Henry yanked her head back and drew a bead of blood.

"I can cut her throat and still shove you over. I have nothing to lose."

Sick to her stomach, Winona knew Jenny was right. No matter what she did, they would both die, and so would Clay. She glanced at Clay. What were they going to do? She tried to get him to meet her gaze but he kept his eyes trained on Henry.

Where was Dream Walker? Where were his other friends?

Where was her father? Beneath her feet she felt the rocky ground crumble.

Seeing Eyes, White Wind, and the two boys were hidden down in the trees, watching the drama unfold. Afraid, Seeing Eyes didn't know what to do. Her husband was not here.

He'd left the women behind to go search the lake area one more time. Seeing Eyes's visions meant that their daughters were there, somewhere. Seeing Eyes had wanted to go with him, but he'd refused to take her. And no sooner had he been gone than another vision had come to her.

She knew there was no time to wait for her husband to return, so she and White Wind had drugged the two warriors left to guard them. After several long hours of searching, she finally spotted the rocky ridge she'd seen in several visions.

Beside her, Striking Thunder whispered, "I will go save them."

Her heart nearly stopped. "No, child. You must stay here."

"I can sneak close. I am small."

"Then what would you do, my grandson?"

He held up his small bow. "I will shoot him."

"You have not shot at a man before." She didn't dare allow him to go. She glanced over at her daughter-in-law, who was biting her lower lip.

The boy squared his narrow shoulders. "My aim is true. Those are my aunts. My father and grandfather are not here. It is my duty." With that he stepped away, dodging his mother and grandmother as they tried to grab him.

"Oh, heavens," White Wind said. "We are going to hear of this." She reached down to hold back her younger son. "You have no bow and arrow."

White Wolf looked grim. "I will go find my father and grandfather and bring them quickly." Then he too slipped away.

White Wind let him go. "Big trouble, my mother."

Seeing Eyes held her gaze. "You are right, daughter. But I am proud of my grandsons."

White Wind started forward. Seeing Eyes followed. "Where are you going?"

"You do not think I am going to just sit here, do you?"

Seeing Eyes groaned. She'd have some explaining to do, but she'd come this far. She could not just sit here and hope that her husband arrived in time to save their daughters.

Chapter Nineteen

Watching Henry carefully, Clay felt helpless. If he moved any closer he'd lose his sister. If he did nothing he'd lose the woman he loved— then his sister, for he had no doubt that Henry would kill them both.

"Let them go, Henry." He had to stall his enemy.

Henry laughed. "Not a chance, old friend. They know too much." Henry pulled Jenny toward the edge, where Winona stood. "If you try anything, Clay Blue Hawk, I will kill them both. If I die, so be it. But you will know that you caused the death of your sister."

Frustrated and afraid as never before, Clay let his gaze dart around, seeking anything that might help him. Somewhere behind him Dream Walker waited to help. But until Henry released

317

Jenny, there was nothing anyone could do. Any abrupt move from him would force Henry to kill one if not both of the girls.

Clay's gaze snapped back to the ridge below Henry. He blinked once. Twice. Then a third time. Hidden in the rocks a short distance down from Henry, Clay saw a child. He quickly realized it was one of Winona's nephews.

He stifled a groan. Could this get any worse? He saw the small bow in the boy's hands.

Now he had to worry about a child trying to be a warrior.

What kind of family did Winona have? Women and children in a war party, and small boys creeping up hills with bows and arrows? Where was Winona's father and his warriors? Hell, where were his own warriors?

As the boy got closer, Clay saw the look of steely determination on the boy's face and readied himself. There was no doubt that a small arrow was going to be let loose. He caught the boy's gaze. *Wait*, Clay tried to communicate.

Clay shifted to the side. Henry shifted as well.

"Not another move, Clay Blue Hawk, or I kill your bratty sister."

Clay froze. Satisfied, Henry took the knife from Jenny's throat long enough to motion to Winona to jump.

"Now!" Clay shouted at the same time that a miniature arrow flew from the bow.

Startled, Henry jerked back, then screamed when the arrow flew into his backside. Clay moved fast. First he grabbed Jenny as she threw herself forward; then he whipped his knife from behind his back where he'd hidden it.

"Now it is just you and me." He noted the blood running down Henry's leg.

Breathing hard, Henry crouched. "You should have died."

Clay shrugged. "You failed."

Without glancing away from Henry, Clay spoke to Winona, who had scrambled away from the edge. "Take Jenny and go."

"I am not going anywhere," Winona said from behind him.

"This is not the time to argue," Clay ground out. "Take my sister to safety."

"No, Clay. I am not leaving you."

He heard a scrambling noise behind him but dared not take his eyes off Henry.

"Your woman and sister are stubborn," Dream Walker said from behind him.

Clay breathed out a sigh of relief. "It is about time you showed up," he said.

"I saw the boy and didn't want to disappoint him by shooting first." He paused. "He did well."

Clay grunted. "Take the women and get them to safety."

"He will not take us anywhere," Jenny argued. She stepped to her brother's side. "He took away our family. He took me from you. Let him die a slow death—like our family."

Henry licked his lips and dropped his knife. He held out his hands. "Go ahead. Kill me," he said with a sneer.

Clay shook his head. "Pick up your knife. We fight."

"No. You want to kill me, then do it."

"Fight me, coward."

Henry smiled and took a step back. "If I die, you will never know the truth. You will never know why my father killed yours."

Clay stalked his prey. "Your father was a coward. He killed his best friend over a damn game of cards."

Shifting his eyes to the side, Henry shook his head. He gave a half bark of nervous laughter. "You fool. My father killed yours because he learned that Clayton Coburn had raped my mother." His lips twisted with hate.

"You lie." Clay jumped forward, grabbed Henry's knife, and tossed it. The weapon landed buried in the ground between Henry's legs. "Pick it up."

"No. We are brothers. Your father is my father." Henry held out his arms. "Can you kill your own brother?"

Clay felt sick at the cruel joke. "You are no brother of mine."

Henry nodded toward Dream Walker. "Ask your good friend. He knows the truth. He will say I speak true."

Without taking his eyes off Henry Black Bear, Clay shook his head. "You go too far, Henry." Henry Black Bear would soon die, and the murders of his family would be avenged.

Dream Walker walked over and joined him, standing to one side but not between the two men. "He speaks the truth."

Startled, Clay glanced from Henry to Dream Walker. "You expect me to believe that this man is my brother? How is that possible? I cannot believe it."

"In this, your enemy speaks the truth." Sadness tinged Dream Walker's voice.

Clay felt ill. Was he still sick? Weak, ready to pass out again? "If this is true, why have you never spoken of it to me?"

"It is the truth. Just as he is your brother, sharing the same father, I am your brother."

"We have always been brothers, you and I. Your family adopted me. My family did not adopt *him*." Frustration rose in Clay. He wanted to fight, not talk.

Dream Walker shifted so he could see both men. "You do not understand. You are my blood brother. We share the same mother, while you and Henry share the same father."

"Impossible." Clay's mouth went dry.

"My mother was caught in the sleeping mat of a trapper. Clayton Coburn. She made it clear that she wanted to go with this white man. My father let her go to him, but he refused to allow her to take me, his son, with her. I stayed behind to be raised by my father's family. He took another wife, who then became my mother as well."

Dream Walker paused. "I have known the truth for many years, but you loved your father and I could not destroy your image of the man who sired you."

Clay was speechless. "My father loved my mother, and she him."

Regret filled Dream Walker's voice. "Your father loved many women."

Henry's voice turned bitter. "My father would never have learned the truth had your father kept his mouth shut. But he got drunk, and taunted my father with the knowledge that he had no son while he, Clayton Coburn, had sired seven."

"No. This cannot be true." Chills ran up and down Clay's back. His father had been devoted to his mother—to all of them.

"Oh, it is the truth. I heard it all. Your father bragged about you, your two brothers, me, and two others—twins. That is why my father killed yours, then came to take your mother. He was after revenge. He was going to take her and use her the same way your father used my mother. He wanted a son. A true son."

Clay remembered Henry's anger, and the crazy words that hadn't made sense back then. He saw Henry take another step back and narrowed his eyes. "Do not move," he warned.

Henry waved his hands. "You were so smug. You had a father who loved you, gave you all he had. But my father refused to have anything to do with me once he learned the truth. Even after you shot my father, I nursed him back to health, but still he refused to accept me as his son. He talked about leaving. Alone. Said he had no son."

Henry paused. "I killed him. He had no son. I had no father." His voice rose with fury.

Shocked, Clay stared at the man who'd once been his best friend—an older brother. "So you killed my mother, brothers, and sister, and tried to kill me."

Smirking, Henry took another step back. "Yes! I hated you. All of you. Even though my father killed yours, you still had each other, and I had no one." His voice rose as he slid one foot back so his heels were over the edge.

His mind numb, Clay lowered his arm. After all that had happened, all that had been said, what was he to do? This man was his brother, yet he'd killed Clay's family out of bitterness and hatred—and Clay could not find it in his heart to forgive. A brother in blood Henry might be, but not in spirit or in his heart.

Yet even as fury demanded that he avenge the deaths of his family, Clay spoke, his voice low. "You should have told me. We would have welcomed you into our *family*." The word burned his throat.

"And would you accept me now, my brother?" Scorn laced Henry's words, even as sadness slid over his eyes.

"No. You killed your brothers and sister, and the woman who cared for you." Clay stepped forward. "You took your young sister and sold her and left me, friend and brother, for dead. Do not speak of family. You wanted no family then, you have no family now."

"Then we speak of this no more." Henry's eyes glittered with malice as he shifted slightly. Rock crumbled beneath his heels. "I took from you all who mattered. As your father destroyed my family, I destroyed his. Just as I take from you the right to avenge their deaths."

Realizing that Henry was about to end his

own life and deprive him of seeking revenge, Clay lunged forward. Henry smirked and stepped out of reach.

Winona ran to Clay and tackled him so he did not follow Henry. Jenny joined them, and together the three of them stared down at Henry's twisted body lying among the rocks. Moments later, warriors burst through the trees and ran up the slope to stand with arrows poised at Clay and Dream Walker.

Winona whipped around, keeping her body between her father and the man she loved. Jenny joined her. "No, do not harm him," she shouted to her father. Behind her, Clay tried to push past.

"Golden Eyes, I can take care of myself." Clay put his hands on her shoulders to move her.

"Not if you are dead," she muttered. She watched as her father and brother came forward.

"Do not harm them," she called out, staying in front of Clay. When the men in her family were several feet away, she held out her hands. "It is not as it appears," she told her father. "Listen to what he has to say."

"Move aside, daughter." Fury radiated from Hawk Eyes.

"No—" She broke off when Clay once more

tried to move her. Reaching back, she grabbed for his breechclout to hold him behind her.

She froze when she realized she'd grabbed too low.

"Golden Eyes, this is not the time." Clay sounded amused. Beside him Dream Walker chuckled, and Jenny turned red.

Winona didn't budge or release him. If it took holding him there to keep him behind her . . .

A flurry to her left drew everyone's attention. To her surprise her mother and White Wind, along with her two nephews, ran to join them. They stood shoulder-to-shoulder with her and Jenny.

"Wife!" The bellow came from both her father and her brother. Seeing Eyes patted Winona on the arm. "Release your man, daughter." Her lips twitched. "He will not go anywhere."

Clay cursed loudly. "I need no women and children for shields," he bellowed.

Seeing Eyes glanced at him. "Young man, you are to marry my daughter, and you cannot do that if my husband acts rashly."

Hawk Eyes held up his hand. All arrows lowered. He folded his arms over his chest and glared at each woman and child and the two warriors. "Explain. Someone explain what is ~oing on!"

Winona felt Clay's palms on her shoulders. "Allow me to explain, Golden Eyes." He turned her to face him. "Trust me and your father."

Frowning, Winona glared up at him. "You are stubborn." She eyed her father and brother. "And they are as well."

"You know me well." Clay brushed his fingers across the back of her neck as he stepped around her and walked with Dream Walker toward her father and brother.

Winona went to follow. Her mother stopped her. "Let him speak for himself."

Torn, Winona sent a worried look at her father. "Father—"

"Your father will listen. He may not like what he hears, but he will listen."

"You are wise, Mother. I just hope you are right," she muttered.

Seeing Eyes smiled and put an arm around both her and Jenny. "He will not think so, and will not for some time, I fear."

The women hugged and laughed, bringing dark looks from each of the men.

Clay told his story. Jenny and Dream Walker and Winona spoke only when called upon. Sharp Nose and Crazy Fox had also arrived. Sharp Nose produced the messages Hoka Luta had left along the trail. Following Hoka Luta, he'd found each one buried.

But before Hawk Eyes had a chance to do more than learn the facts, one of Henry's warriors who'd been traveling with Hawk Eyes stepped forward. "None in our tribe knew of his past. He lied to us, spoke falsely."

Clay stared for a long moment into the eyes of the warrior who'd spoken. "I knew him well, yet knew him not at all." Later Clay knew he'd go over and over his younger years spent with a boy named Henry Black Bear with mixed feelings, for Henry was a part of his past and together they'd shared many happy days.

In those days, Henry had been a brother in his heart. Now the man was truly dead to him. Forever. No longer would this man cause him pain.

The warriors from Henry's tribe nodded, and without another word they turned away.

Clay glanced over at Winona and felt as though the sun had risen deep inside him. When Henry had ended his own life he'd been furious. He'd needed to avenge the deaths of his family and the pain caused to him and Jenny. But, to his surprise, he no longer cared. The hate that had once been his shadow was gone, and all he could think of was the woman he loved.

He glanced over at her. She was pale, trembling from her ordeal. The day had been a hard one for her. Winona had her arms around her. Jenny looked shaken and on the verge of collapse.

Clay held out his arms to the two women who meant everything to him. Winona ran to him. He looked at Jenny. "Jenny," he whispered. "I never gave up hope that you would still be alive."

With a sob, Jenny ran to him, too.

"Welcome home, little one," he told her, holding her tightly. Winona stepped back. "It seems we have a new family to get to know." He stared at Dream Walker.

Star Dreamer walked up to him. She glanced back at her grandmother, then motioned him down. "There are two more brothers," she whispered.

"Yes, little one. I have two more brothers to someday find." He wasn't sure when, but when the time was right he'd also try to find the twins.

The little girl opened her mouth, then shut it and walked back to her grandmother.

"Come on, let's go." With an arm around his love and one around his sister, Clay headed down the hillside.

Epilogue

Summer ruled. Her breath swept across the land, turning the grass brown and brittle. Colors faded, and many streams were either dry or offered just a trickle of water for both man and beast. But high in the hills, in the shadow of a tower of granite near a large sapphire-blue lake, the grass had remained soft and green, the water glass-smooth.

Winona leaned back against Clay and stared up at the fingers of color streaking across the sky from the east. "I cannot believe we are truly wedded." She sighed.

Clay grunted. "We have been wedded for weeks."

Giggling, Winona gave a gentle tug to the fine strands of hair covering his knee. "Am I not worth two weddings?" Not only had her father insisted they return to be properly wedded, but then Clay's family had also insisted upon another wedding and celebration.

Clay's arms tightened. "You know you are. It was the separation until the second ceremony that I objected to. Dream Walker's doing, no doubt."

Threading her fingers through his, Winona snuggled close. "He is a medicine man."

"He is a pain—"

"He is your brother." Winona turned in her husband's arms and met his gaze.

"Yes, my brother," Clay agreed, wonder filling his eyes.

The shock of leaning that Dream Walker was not just a friend or brother in spirit, as he'd believed, but a half brother, had stunned Clay.

He and Dream Walker shared the same mother. Yet as wonderful as that was, learning the truth about his father was a betrayal almost too painful to comprehend.

"Stop fretting, Golden Eyes. I am fine."

"You are sad."

"Yes. I feel guilty. I wish I'd known the truth. Things would have been different."

"You cannot change the past, my husband." Winona smoothed her fingers down the side of his face.

Clay sighed and leaned into her caress. "The

332

truth does not lessen the pain or guilt." He rubbed his face in her hair.

Pulling back, Winona focused her gaze on his. "No. The past is gone. But you have the future. You have brothers, family."

Clay sighed. "Leave it be, my love."

Shaking her head, Winona slid her hands down his arms, massaging the tenseness from him. "I cannot. You have two brothers who are also your family, and they may need you and Dream Walker." Winona watched him wince in pain. He'd lost so much, yet he'd been given a wonderful gift. Not only did he have his younger sister back, he'd gained not one, but four brothers. Where there had been no family, Clay was now surrounded by family—hers included.

She turned back to watch the ducks float across the lake. "You will find them," she said. No matter what he said, she knew he would eventually seek them out. His first wave of excitement had waned, and when his father's betrayal had sunk in, he'd changed his mind about locating them, not wanting to bring more pain to others, or to deepen his own.

She knew it was fear—fear that they didn't need or want him, fear that his presence would stir up new pain for his brothers or their families—after all, he knew not their circumstances—

but most of all, he feared that if he found a new family he'd forget the family that had been ripped from his heart.

"Perhaps," he finally agreed. "Someday." He bent his head to the side of her neck.

Staring at the smooth, glassy surface of the lake, Winona didn't see the reflections of the lake but of the man behind her. The new, free-of-the-past man. She saw life, color, and rebirth in that crystal-clear surface.

Winona tipped her head to one side. "Clay?" She felt his forehead drop to her shoulder, heard his soft moan of frustration. She smiled.

"We are finally alone and you want to talk?"

Breathing deeply, Winona let the beauty of the lake setting wash over her. "We have time. Lots of time," she said. And it was true. Not only did they have the rest of the summer to explore this beautiful world where it all began, but they had the rest of their lives. But there was one last issue to address.

Clay straightened and sighed deeply. "I love you, Golden Eyes. Talk and I will listen. But not for long. There are other things on my mind." His hands moved upward to cup her breasts. "Many things."

Winona laughed softly and turned so that she faced him. Her fingers traced his jaw as she cupped his face and stared deeply into his eyes.

"You no longer live in the shadows."

Clay smiled. "Thanks to you. You fill my heart and soul with light."

"Your name speaks of shadows."

Clay understood. His tribe and family still called him by the name of Night Shadow, yet his wife called him Clay. It was the name she knew, the name of the man she'd fallen in love with, and a name he loved hearing from her lips.

"If you wish, I will inform all that I will be known as Clay." He reached out and just as gently ran his fingers through her hair and over her scalp.

To his surprise, she shook her head.

"You are no longer Clay." Winona rose to her knees. "It would please me to give my husband a new name."

Incredibly touched, Clay remained still for a moment. To hide the deep emotion that threatened to break free, he forced a grin. It wasn't uncommon for a wife to give her husband a new name. But in this case . . . ?

He tugged gently at a long strand of silky-soft hair. "I seem to remember that you have given me many names in the past. Dare I trust you?"

Winona's eyes watered. "As much as I trust my life to you."

Clay turned serious. He trusted her with his life. With his heart and soul. "Then speak, my wife, my breath, my life."

Taking his face between her soft palms, Winona moved close. "You walk in the light, not the shadows, and are brother to Dream Walker." She paused. "I give you the name Sun Walker."

The name brought tears to his eyes. It was true. He walked in the sun; he had light and laughter in his life. And love—more than he'd ever thought possible.

"It is a good name for this warrior, for it is because of you that I no longer walk in the shadows, Golden Eyes."

Winona held out her hands and stood. "Walk with me, my husband. Let us greet this day together."

Sun Walker pulled his wife into his arms. "Walking is still not what I have in mind, *pohkeso*." His hand cupped her buttocks and pulled her dress upward until his palms cupped her soft, rounded flesh.

Laughing softly, Winona wrapped her arms around his neck and stood on tiptoe. "*Mastinca.*" Giggling at his furrowed brows, Winona buried her head in his shoulder. Truthfully, he was her *igmuwatogla*, her lion, to his kitten, but as often as he tried—and succeeded in—mating with her, calling him a rabbit seemed fitting.

"Be warned, Golden Eyes: I will never get enough of you. I need you, your touch, your love, much more than I need food or even the air I breathe. You are everything to me."

This time when her husband lowered her to the damp grass, Winona didn't protest. Her need for her husband was just as great. With Sun Walker poised over her, Winona shifted her hips and invited her husband to enter. He bent his head to the hollow of her shoulder.

Overhead, the dawn colors swirled as if rearranging to paint a picture. She held her breath, transfixed by her husband's slow entrance deep inside her and by the sudden shape of a mountain lion peering down at her from the sky.

Igmuwatogla snarled once. *Use your power wisely to protect those you love,* he seemed to order. Then he was gone.

"Forever," she whispered, holding Sun Walker tightly to her.

"Yes, love, forever." Sun Walker lifted his head. "You are mine. Forever."

Winona shifted beneath him. She wanted him. All of him. Now.

"As you are mine. Now move. Take me to the stars."

Sun Walker pulled out, then slid slowly back

in until they were joined fully. "In time, Golden Eyes. In time. There is no rush." He breathed against her ear. "I love you, my wife."

Squirming beneath her husband's pinning weight, Winona groaned. "As I love you." When he refused to begin the rhythm she so desperately needed, she shifted beneath him. *"Witapima."*

Sun Walker slid out and laughed softly as Winona struggled to pull him back inside. "A toad, am I?"

"Clay—Sun Walker—please." She opened one eye. "A very handsome toad, then. A very big toad, if it pleases you, but if you do not stop teasing me, you will be a very flat toad!"

"Well, I cannot have that. So I will take care of my golden-eyed kitten lest she show her claws."

WHITE DUSK
ℐSUSAN EDWARDS

A winter of discontent sent Swift Foot on a vision quest, and he returned ready to be chief. Where his father brought shame upon their family by choosing love over duty, Swift Foot will act more wisely. He will lead his people through the troubles ahead—and, to do so, he will marry for *all* the right reasons.

Small Bird is the perfect choice. But for their people to survive the coming darkness, the two will have to win each other's hearts. On the sleeping mat or wrapped in furs, on riverbank or dusty plain, passion must blaze to life between the half-breed chieftain and his new wife . . . and they have to start the fire soon, for dusk has already fallen.

WHITE DREAMS
SUSAN EDWARDS

Why has the Great Spirit given Star Dreamer the sight, an ability to see things that can't be changed? She has no answer. Then one night she is filled with visions of a different sort: pale hands caressing her flesh, soft lips touching her soul. She sees the flash of a uniform, and the handsome soldier who wears it. The man makes her ache in a way that she has forgotten, in a way that she has repressed. And when Colonel Grady O'Brien at last rides into her camp, she learns that the virile officer is everything she's dreamed of and more. Suddenly, Star Dreamer sees the reason for her gift. In her visions lie the key to this man's happiness—and in this man's arms lie the key to her own.

Also includes the twelfth installment of Lair of the Wolf, a serialized romance set in medieval Wales. Be sure to look for other chapters of this exciting story featured in Leisure books and written by the industry's top authors.
